ABOUT THE AUTHOR

Scarlet Blackwell likes cats and hats and firmly believes that the only thing better than one attractive man is two attractive men.

Email:
scarlet.blackwell@hotmail.com

Webpage:

http://scarletblackwell.com/default.aspx

Blog:
http://scarlet-fiction.livejournal.com/

Facebook:
http://www.facebook.com/pages/Scarlet-Blackwell#!/profile.php?id=100001135500060

TABLE OF CONTENTS

In My Darkness, I Found A Light	13
A Tale of Two Halves	36
Guilt	53
RoMANce	70
This Wave Always Breaks	95
Happy Birthday	120
The Long Road Home	132
The Rent Collector	154
Homeless	180
Rematch	210
Charlie	224
My Love is Me, And I Am Him	269

VOLUME 1

SCARLET BLACKWELL

Published by Silver Publishing
Publisher of Erotic Romance

If you purchased this book without a cover you should be aware that this book is stolen property. It was reported as "unsold and destroyed" to the publisher, and neither the author nor the publisher has received any payment for this "stripped book."

SILVER PUBLISHING

ISBN 978-1-61495-291-6

Anthology Volume One
Includes stories:

In My Darkness, I Found a Light	A Tale of Two Halves
Guilt	RoMANCe
This Wave Always Breaks	Happy Birthday
The Long Road Home	The Rent Collector
Homeless	Rematch
My Love is Me, and I am Him	Charlie

Copyright © 2011 by Scarlet Blackwell
Editor: Jennifer Colgan
Cover Artist: Reese Dante
Photo credit: Dan Skinner, Cerberus Inc.

All rights reserved. Except for use in any review, the reproduction or utilization of this work in whole or in part in any form by any electronic, mechanical or other means, now known or hereafter invented, including xerography, photocopying and recording, or in any information storage or retrieval system, is forbidden without the written permission of the editorial office, Silver Publishing, 18530 Mack Avenue, Box 253, Grosse Pointe Farms, MI 48236, USA.

All characters in this book have no existence outside the imagination of the author and have no relation whatsoever to anyone bearing the same name or names. They are not even distantly inspired by any individual known or unknown to the author, and all incidents are pure invention.

Visit Silver Publishing at https://spsilverpublishing.com

NOTE FROM THE PUBLISHER

Dear Reader,

Thank you for your purchase of this title. The authors and staff of Silver Publishing hope you enjoy this read and that we will have a long and happy association together.

Please remember that the only money authors make from writing comes from the sales of their books. If you like their work, spread the word and tell others about the books, but please refrain from sharing this book in any unauthorized form. Authors depend on sales and sales only to support their families.

If you see "free shares" offered or cut-rate sales on pirate sites of this title, you can report the offending entry to copyright@silverpublishing.info

Thank you for not pirating our titles.

Lodewyk Deysel
Publisher
Silver Publishing
http://www.silverpublishing.info

TRADEMARKS ACKNOWLEDGEMENT

The author acknowledges the trademarked status and trademark owners of the following wordmarks mentioned in this work of fiction:

Red Bull: Red Bull GmbH
Biro: BIC Corporation
Coke: The Coca-Cola Company
Advil: Wyeth Healthcare, Inc.
JD (Jack Daniel's): Brown-Forman Corporation
Durex Play: Reckitt Benckiser

IN MY DARKNESS, I FOUND A LIGHT

Thursday. Holding onto the rail, I leaned my head against it as the train thundered away from the station, the shudders under my feet making my body sway.

Only one more day to go after today until the weekend and forty-eight hours of blessed seclusion and solitude.

Dinner tonight then? Pizza or frozen lasagne? Decisions, decisions. Then after? Read or watch a movie? Maybe even get some porn on cable and find the energy to jerk off when it's all I can do to carry on breathing the air of this miserable world.

Moving closer to the side of the train, I flinched as someone brushed my shoulder, dismayed at the sheer number of bodies packing the carriage. It wasn't like every morning wasn't the same. Sure, if I got my lazy ass out of bed on time and was first on the platform, I could get a seat, take out my book and read. Otherwise, like most every day, I was condemned to be just another sardine on the morning commute. I hated it. I hated those perfect strangers jostling and knocking my body, the only human touch I ever got from day to day. I hated the smell of the unwashed, those who'd eaten garlic the night before and those who'd doused themselves in sickly perfume. Truth be told, I hated people in general, which explained why I worked in a little cubicle all day for a pittance, talking to the bastards on the phone, not having to see them face to face, keeping myself to myself, friendless and watching the clock for eight hours non-stop.

The doors opened as the train made its first stop,

and I stepped aside a little. The new arrivals would expect me to move down the train and into the melee, but as usual, I battled with them as I did every morning. No way would I give up my precious few inches of personal space by the door to move along the carriage and into the morass.

I was looking away as a man in a long, dark overcoat got on, a broad shoulder brushing mine. As the train set off with a lurch, he stumbled a little and grabbed at the rail I held, inadvertently touching my hand.

"Sorry," he said quickly.

I kept my eyes averted, inwardly seething at being touched even though I murmured some platitude in reply. As usual, I was hostile to people on the inside and let them get away with murder on the outside. No balls, that had always been my trouble.

As the train picked up speed, I became aware of the stranger's shoulder pressed against mine and his scent started to make my nostrils twitch. Something expensive, something I'd sniffed in a department store but couldn't afford to buy. My eyes drifted to his left hand on the rail. Long, delicate fingers, short neat nails. No wedding ring. I glanced down. He wore dark trousers and black, highly polished shoes on small feet, briefcase held by his side.

I liked people watching even though I hated them all, and I wanted to look at this man's face now. I could just about see him out of the corner of my eye, and his face was turned away. Boldly, I lifted my head.

I saw him in profile. Shiny, black hair fell over his eyes, a startling contrast to his milk white skin, the most flawless skin I'd ever seen in my life. His nose was strong, too big if you were feeling unkind, but I wasn't, and his lips were pink and full. He stared straight ahead through the doors and I could see one eye, the lashes blinking over it thick and graceful like a doe's. The eye itself was a pale, startling green. It looked almost unreal, like a gemstone or a marble.

I realised I was staring. Christ on a bike, he was beautiful. He turned his head suddenly, and our gazes met. I saw the whole of his face and both of those stunning eyes. I looked away instantly, lowering my head, my cheeks flaming with a scorching blush. Sure, I liked to admire beauty on my morning commute, but I was usually more discreet. I didn't often get caught with my tongue hanging out by the object of my attention.

My heart beat a little too fast, my palm slippery on the rail, his hand only a few inches below it. How come I had never seen this man before? God, I would have noticed, wouldn't I? Or maybe my studied shell has blinded me even to beauty. The train swayed and his briefcase hit my legs. Usually this would have me flying into a frenzy, and I would think of all the ways I wanted to kill the inconsiderate person and their offending luggage, but today I welcomed it like he had stroked me with his hand.

I bit my lip, eyes on the floor, gaze sliding sideways to his shoes once again. Get a grip, I told myself fiercely as my prick started to stiffen, but I couldn't because I was imagining how those pale eyes might darken with desire and what he looked like with those heavy winter clothes stripped off.

We were coming up to the next station but not slowing down. I was on the direct train, the one which missed some of the little shitty stations on the way and got me to my dreaded job even quicker than I would like. I always watched the people standing on the platform of these stops and shuddered a little at how fast the train would plough through these stations and how much turbulence it must create. I never understood why the train didn't slow a little, for safety's sake, even though it wasn't stopping, and I always wondered why I gave a shit when I hated people. Maybe it was because I had once stood on one of these platforms when a train had thundered past without stopping and it had scared me badly. I'd had all sorts of ideas in my head about what it would be like to step out as it hurtled through the station and how one's death would be, without doubt, immediate. At how the other people on the platform would be sprayed with brains and blood and it would probably be all over the station roof. I had wondered if anyone would care.

I stood at the front of the first carriage, and I could see the people on the platform clearly as we approached. They kept well back, but one moved with intent to the front of the group, directly to the edge. It was like watching it unfold in slow motion. I didn't even have time to realise what was happening as the man—and it *was* a man, I could see his suit and his short, blond hair—didn't stop at the edge as I expected him to but merely carried on, not hesitating for one moment, but stepping out into oblivion.

I heard the green-eyed stranger next to me give a gasp of absolute horror as he, too, realised what was happening before his eyes.

The man's body looked like the mannequins they use in the movies as it bounced off the front of the train, a huge splattering of crimson raining right against the door in front of us. The man beside me flinched back, his shoulder knocking into me hard so I stumbled against the back of the seat next to me.

The train lurched, metal screeched against metal as the brakes were applied, and we came to an agonisingly slow stop, people clutching in desperation for handholds to avoid being thrown about like marionettes.

Only when we came to a complete stop did I hear the true commotion in the carriage. Women screamed and cried, and men shouted in disbelief. I turned my gaze to my beautiful travelling companion. He had his eyes closed and head bowed, hand still clinging to the rail. A soft moan of horror escaped his lips, and a light sheen of sweat covered his face as though he was seconds away from puking. I stared at him, feeling emotion and empathy towards another human being for the first time in a long, long while.

As I opened my mouth to offer some platitude, the door to the carriage slid open and he almost fell out onto the ground below. We had come to a stop some distance out of the station, and it was a long way down. Railway employees helped people down, and sirens blared in the distance. As I climbed carefully down, gripping some guy's hand with thanks, my gaze sought the stranger who weaved haphazardly towards the bushes at the side of the tracks.

He fell to his knees, dropping his briefcase as he vomited. Even doing one of the most humiliating things you can ever have an audience for, he still retained a certain sort of grace. He didn't do it with that noisy drama some people did, but with a quiet, almost exhausted kind of resignation, his hands on the ground, bent over, the vomit pale and liquid and sparse, like nothing much had gone into his stomach in a while.

Maybe he was as tired as I was, because I could imagine myself puking with the same lack of energy. Maybe he was as lost as I was, adrift on the sea of life with no destination in sight. I sternly told my romantic heart not to get the better of me. Seeing an attractive man and feeling compulsively drawn to him did not make him my soulmate, even though, empty and lost as I am, I still pitifully hope for that with every pair of eyes I meet. Even as far down the line as I am, lonely, isolated and withdrawn, I still dream of that soulmate. I still dream of curling myself up into a warm body at the end of the day and crying my troubles out to someone who understands. Someone who wouldn't fuck me once and never call me again.

I studied the stranger with a pang of sympathy in my poor, criminally underused heart. He wasn't the only one doing this. There was a line of people all along the tracks puking. I never understand this human reaction. The only time I puke is when I've drank too much or there's something physically wrong with me. I never feel the urge to puke at things I've seen, and the suicide's broken body hadn't driven me to it either. Did that make me a callous bastard? Well, I am anyway, I already know that and yet, as much as the sight of someone puking is abhorrent to me, I had no intention of walking away from the stranger.

I approached behind him as he sat back on his heels, shuddering a little and catching his breath, his face covered with sweat and tears running from his eyes. I reached for a handkerchief from my pocket, the one with the initials RG that my mother had bought me last Christmas. I held it over his shoulder silently.

He took it without a word and held it to his mouth a moment, eyes closed, taking some deep breaths. I put my rucksack down on the ground, opened it up and took out a bottle of water, and handed that to him too. He said, "Thank you," his voice deep and hoarse. Uncapping it, he took a mouthful and then spat it out into the bushes, repeating this twice before swallowing some.

He held the bottle a moment, head bowed, the other hand wiping the sweat and tears from his face. I stepped closer to him, not distracted by the calls from cops who had just arrived on the scene and were rounding up the passengers. I put my hand hesitantly on his shoulder, feeling how soft the wool of his overcoat was and murmured, "Are you okay?"

He nodded, teeth biting his lower lip, startlingly white against the pink flesh. "Thank you," he said again, and he held the bottle out to me.

"Keep it," I said, because no way was I going to drink from it now that his puke mouth had been against it, even if he was the most divine creature I'd ever seen in my life. I handed him a stick of gum. He took it, thanking me yet again.

I stepped back as he stood up and retrieved his briefcase, turning around so our eyes met for the second time. Those peridot eyes had the same effect on me as they had on the train. They turned my bones to water, and I felt like I was falling into the sweetest of abysses with no safety harness anchoring me to reality.

There was no way he couldn't have seen the desire and adoration in my eyes; my pupils were probably like saucers, but he didn't look away, only held my gaze as the air became thin and I struggled to get enough oxygen to my brain. The spell was broken abruptly by a cop striding towards us.

"Guys, if you could walk up to the station, we just need a few minutes of your time for a statement."

My travelling companion and I started to follow

other people along the track, walking side by side in silence until we reached some steps leading up to the platform. There were no seats left so we both leaned against the wall, shoulder to shoulder. I turned my head, my eyes seeking his again. But the stranger had his closed, and I could bet he had visions of blood and guts beneath the lids which would haunt him for a very long time to come.

I imagined I would think about this day, too, when I lay down to sleep that night, but I didn't expect that I would have nightmares about it. I was made of stronger stuff. I didn't know this jumper, so I wasn't going to grieve over him. People like that were selfish, affecting others with their misery. Some of the people on this train might suffer post-traumatic stress disorder the rest of their lives. I mean, take my companion here, look what the jumper had done to him. It made me angry just to think about it.

The sweat had dried from his face, but his skin was still a ghastly shade of grey. He opened his eyes, as if he felt my gaze and looked at me a moment. I smiled at him, a tender smile which the world never saw, which only came out on special occasions—for animals, for children, for my mother.

He returned it tiredly, teeth kept behind his lips, eyes fixed unblinkingly on mine. And my dead, cold heart began to sing. It rose up, banged the table, and made an announcement.

Hello?

Yes.

Don't write me off just yet because at the age of thirty-four, sick and done with life and on a spiral downwards, I'm still alive. You hear me, motherfucker? I'm still alive.

I reddened under his gaze, convinced all my thoughts were blatantly displayed on my face and even worse, I felt tears pricking my eyes. I told myself it was the emotion of the day. That maybe the suicide had got to me after all and it would be okay to cry like dozens of people up and down the platform were doing. Abruptly, I moved a couple of steps away, trying to regain my composure, in case I made an idiot of myself and declared myself in love with him at first sight, asked him to marry me in any state which would take us and run away to a desert island.

Willing myself back to the business at hand, I pulled my cell out and dialled work. As I waited, I saw a splash of blood on the ground a few feet away from me, an eyeball nestled in the middle of the congealed puddle. To my horror, a flood of acid rose scorchingly up my oesophagus. I ducked behind an advertising board and leaned against it, breathing heavily, my hand over my mouth, the taste of bile strong. So evidently I *was* one of those people who puked at extreme sights after all. Obviously, I hadn't yet witnessed anything shocking enough before today to warrant it.

"Hello?" my boss said.

With eyes closed, I took my hand a few inches away from my mouth and said, "It's Robert. I'm going to be late. Someone jumped in front of my train, and I have to talk to the cops."

"Jesus Christ," exclaimed my boss, an asshole with a Hitler complex. "Are they dead?"

I let out a high-pitched laugh, the wave of nausea subsiding. "Yes, dude." I bit my lip at the accidental slip of calling my boss *dude* like he's some sort of friend to me.

But my boss let it slide. "Are you okay?" His voice

was low and concerned.

I was taken aback. For the second time, I got tears in my eyes. Maybe my problem was that I wrote off everyone as worthless without ever giving them the opportunity to prove themselves to me. I shut them out and kept myself cocooned in my own world and told myself I didn't need them because they didn't understand me and didn't give a shit. My boss, with his gruff exterior and rigid work ethic had never shown this side of himself before, but maybe that was because I had never looked.

"Yeah," I responded unsteadily.

"Well... you don't have to come in, Rob. I wouldn't expect you to."

I was even more nonplussed to the point of speechlessness. "A-Are you sure?" I stammered finally. My boss was as hard-assed about sickness as he was about everything else. He wanted to know the ins and outs of every single day missed, what your doctor was doing about it, and if it was work related in case he got his ass sued for it.

"I'm sure," he said. "Look, I'll call you tonight. Go home, have a drink, don't think about it."

"Thank you," I replied almost dazedly.

"Bye." He hung up.

Remembering where the puddle of blood and its eye was, I walked around the opposite side of the advertising board. The stranger had found a bench and now sat a few feet closer to the station entrance, talking to a cop with a notebook. His head was bowed and he held my handkerchief tightly in one hand, my water in the other, his briefcase by his feet.

My heart contracted at his obvious distress. He

looked so forlorn and lost sitting there that I longed to take him in my arms. I loitered, watching until the cop had finished with him, the same cop who had moved us off the tracks. I watched him put a hand on the stranger's arm and murmur something to him before he left and headed towards me.

"Hi, can I get your name and address, please?" He was in his early forties, swarthy and heavy-set. His eyes, so dark as to be almost black, glittered in the wan winter sunshine.

I glanced over his shoulder. My travelling companion drank from my bottle of water before putting his head back against the wall, eyes closed as though meditating.

I recited my details to the cop, and he asked me a few more questions, my place of work, where I was standing on the train, what I had seen. I glanced at the name badge on his shirt. *Officer Ramirez.*

"Do you know him?" The cop asked, flicking a thumb over his shoulder when my gaze strayed back to the stranger for the dozenth time.

I shook my head. "I was standing next to him on the train."

"He seems shook up. I was going to take him for some coffee, but I've got a load more people to interview..."

Nice guy. I was surprised again at discovering humanity in the last place I would have looked.

"... maybe you could do it?"

Closing my gaping mouth, I nodded quickly.

The cop smiled at me and moved away.

I stood looking at the stranger. He had taken his cell

out and was staring at it almost in dismay. I moved with purpose towards him, and he glanced up when I got there.

"I can't get a signal. I need to call work." He was anxious and agitated. "I'm due in court..."

I frowned. If this had been a tongue-in-cheek movie, I would have slapped him across the face to control his rising hysteria and told him to pull himself together. Instead, I silently handed him my cell.

"Thank you," he said, taking it, then stood up and moved away.

I glanced towards the puddle of blood with fear clenching my insides that he would stand in it, or kick the eyeball and start screaming the whole station down until I had to knock him out to shut him the fuck up.

I heard him on the phone, voice low and barely controlled, pacing the platform, getting closer and closer to that blood. He ended the call finally, and as his shoe came to rest on the edge of the pool, he glanced down.

I went to him swiftly, catching his arm hard and pulling him towards me as he turned away with all colour once more gone from his face. To my surprise, he clung onto me instantly, arms around my back, face hidden in my shoulder, great wrenching sobs spilling from his throat. I stared down at his raven-black head, his scent and warmth overwhelming me. I put one hand up to cradle his neck and the other around his waist. He felt solid against me, only an inch or two shorter than me, a little thicker than me around the middle, his shoulders and arms muscular. I glanced around uneasily at embracing another man in public but no one paid us the slightest mind, mainly because everyone else was indulging in similar acts of comfort along the platform.

For a moment, I allowed myself to luxuriate in the feel of another person's touch after so long. How long had it been? I knew very well how long it had been, but I tried to play these games with myself so that if I didn't break it down into years and months, I wouldn't look like the sad bastard I knew I was. It had been five years since I had been kissed, touched, or fucked, and I craved the feel of skin on mine like nothing else.

He lifted his head and let go of me, bringing that handkerchief of mine to his nose, those pretty eyes of his red and swollen. "I'm sorry," he muttered, moving away, back to the chair where he had left his briefcase.

I followed him. "It's okay."

He picked up his briefcase and held my cell out to me. "Thanks," he said, and he started to walk away.

For a moment I stood staring in desolation before that heart of mine, which had jumped up and announced its obituary was premature, took a hold of me and shook me hard. *What the fuck are you doing? Are you going to just let him walk away, when you don't even know his name, least of all his number? Are you going to let him walk away when he's crying and upset, and you promised the cop you would buy him coffee? If you allow this, that man jumping in front of the train might be you within a year.*

By the time I'd had a lengthy fight with myself over my usual lethargy and inability to act on anything, he was long gone. I ran into the station, cursing myself, my heart so strangled in a vice at the idea I would never see him again that it hurt just to breathe. I darted up the steps to the exit and back into the miserable winter light.

There he was, just climbing into a cab.

"Wait!"

He stopped in surprise, sitting inside, his hand on the door. He looked up at me questioningly as I made my way over.

"Where are you going?" I asked him, leaning on the door.

"Work," he said, those reddened jade eyes fixed on mine.

"You're not in any fit state to go to work."

"I have to," he protested.

I shook my head. "Let's go somewhere." I knew what I meant in that moment and I wondered if he did too. I couldn't believe my own ears.

He stared up at me for the longest time.

"Hey, are you taking this cab or not, mister?" An irritated male voice came behind me.

I turned around and glared at the interloper and then jumped into the cab, forcing the stranger to move over. Leaning forward, I gave the driver the address of a hotel in the city before I sat back and stared out of the window.

Neither of us spoke until we got there, my companion thrusting a bill at the driver before I could even reach for my wallet. We got out and went up the steps, through the lobby and into the bar. When we were seated in a quiet table by the window, I asked him, "What do you want to drink?"

He hesitated a moment, gaze straying to the top shelf of the bar behind us. "Is it wrong to have JD at ten o'clock in the morning?"

"Hell no," was my reply as the waiter came over, and I ordered two, along with two coffees.

In the silence, I studied him covertly while he looked out of the window. I was not going to get riveting conversation here, but I could be honest with myself and admit that I hadn't brought him here for that anyway.

When the drinks arrived, I stood up. "Be right back."

I walked out into the lobby and up to the reception desk, where I asked for a double room. I handed over my credit card, inwardly gulping at the price but knowing without doubt he would be more than worth every cent, and pocketed the key card. I couldn't quite believe what I was doing. This wasn't me. I didn't bring strangers to hotels at ten o'clock in the morning on a work day.

Then I returned to the bar and took my seat. He had finished his drink and started on his coffee, both hands wrapped around the cup, staring down into the dark liquid. I sat there a moment in silence, debating what to do.

I felt curiously like Benjamin Braddock in *The Graduate* as I said, "I got a room," like *he* was the one in control even though I was the one who had done all the chasing so far.

The stranger didn't look too shocked, even though he reddened and took a quick drink of his coffee.

I downed my JD and started on my coffee, hoping for a quick buzz of alcohol and caffeine before we went upstairs. Our eyes met over the rims of our coffee cups, and I trembled with both hope and fear.

He put his cup down decisively and stood up, taking his briefcase. I almost stumbled to my feet in my haste and excitement. I was so uncool, like a virgin desperately hoping to get it right. He strode out of the bar and across the lobby, and I trailed behind him. What exactly did he see in me?

The elevator was empty and he got in, me

following, jabbing the button for the seventh floor. He stood there in silence, both of us looking up at the numbers while I shook with sweet anticipation and thanked whatever God had not smiled down on me for thirty-four long years.

When we came to a stop, he was first out, turning to look back at me as I got my key card out, looked at it, and examined the nearest door before setting off. He followed me until we arrived outside room seventy-seven and I swiped the lock open. Then I stood back and allowed him to enter first. He thanked me, stepped inside and set his briefcase down on a chair. For a moment, he looked around before turning to face me as I closed the door and let my bag drop to the ground.

I stood, leaning against the door with my heart in my mouth and a tent in my pants. Our eyes met for only a brief second before he came to me. I stepped forward, and he was in my arms and under my mouth.

I can't even describe what kissing him was like. I can't do justice to that warm, sweet, achingly soft mouth and the way it played every single string on my heart until each one vibrated with desire. He moaned a little as my tongue found his and his fingers tangled in my hair, pulling it, pressing his body to mine.

I gasped for breath against his mouth. I couldn't help it; I thought I was going to suffer the sweetest suffocation ever, right there. My hands moved under his coat and I felt the heaviness of the wool, saw the silk lining and the expensive label inside. I slid it off his shoulders, tossing it to the nearest chair and missing. Then I pulled his suit jacket off too, another designer label inside that. My heart sank a little at how he might compare the labels in our clothes as he undressed me, but I ploughed on, hands pulling his tie open, caressing the silk material a moment as though it were his skin before I shed it and pulled the tails of his shirt free from his pants.

His breathing got heavier against my mouth, and he clung to me as I fumbled each button free and drew the material open. His torso was pale, a line of dark hair tracking down it and past his belly button. I slid the shirt slowly down his arms, taking my time to examine each freckle, each mole, the stark black dragon tattoo on his right biceps.

I ran my hands slowly up his torso, over his chest, to curl my arms around his back as I dipped my face against his neck and kissed the delicate curve of it. Goose pimples rose on his soft, scented skin everywhere my lips touched. I sucked, licked and bit lightly, trailing my way over his clavicle while I manoeuvred him backwards to the bed.

He allowed me to push him down lightly on the edge, and there I had full access to his torso as I dropped down between his knees and fastened my lips around one rosy nipple.

He gave a groan of delight as I sucked it stiff, my tongue flicking over it, my hands tracing the bones of his ribcage and moving over his stomach, one deliberately brushing over the bulge in his pants so he drew his breath in.

I let go of the nipple, leaving it glistening, and moved onto the other, tonguing it and generally worrying it until my partner was virtually writhing against me, one hand gripping my hair while the other fumbled at the buttons on my shirt.

I sat back on my heels a moment and tossed off my

coat before removing my shirt. I was right about what his eyes would be like during sex. They had darkened to emerald as they darted over my torso, the pupils huge. He licked his lips, his mouth swollen and pink with my kisses.

He quickly unfastened my belt, popped the button and drew down the zip before delving into my boxers and drawing me free. If I'm honest, I thought I would blow my load right then at the feel of those fingers around me. Groaning in sheer bliss, I leaned into him again and kissed him hard.

Our tongues tangled, and one of his hands roamed my chest, rubbing and twisting at my nipples while the other jerked me off. *Fuck*, I thought, *how do I make this last when I'm going to come my brains out into his sweet hand any second?*

My hands went desperately to his pants, and I pulled them open, reached into tight fitting boxers and drew him free. Once I had him in my hand, I broke the kiss to look down at him. He dwarfed my hand, a big boy with the most perfect cock I had ever seen. I slid down and took him in my mouth.

He hissed a little, and once more his hand yanked at my hair. I took him down as far as I could go and played with his balls while I did it, drawing back to run my tongue around the head, watching how his eyes fell shut and his tongue came out again to lick those pouting lips.

Fuck, he was beautiful. He was so fucking beautiful, I wasn't even worthy. He pulled my head back from him suddenly, and shook his head breathlessly before he stood up and began to fling the rest of his clothes off with determination. I did the same, kicking my shoes away, peeling my socks off and stepping out of my pants and boxers. I paused to go in my pants pocket and take out my wallet as I watched him crawl naked onto the bed. I looked in the secret pocket which had so little use I expected to see cobwebs over it. No condom.

My heart sank, but I didn't give up hope. He was lying naked against the dark red covers of the bed, the tattoo startling against his snow white skin, his eyes like burning jewels. He looked anxious, holding his hand out to me as I crawled up between his legs and settled myself against him, skin to skin, naked as the day we were born.

We kissed again and he lifted himself from the bed, arching into my arms, pressing every inch of his delectable body against mine. One leg wrapped around my hip and our erections rubbed agonisingly together. I cursed a little under my breath and bit at his neck too hard. I murmured an apology, but he only writhed beneath me more and brought my hand to his mouth, sucking on two of my fingers slowly and sensually, eyes fixed on mine.

Oh Jesus, I thought, staring into those jade eyes and my reflection in the huge pupils. Each suck of his mouth on my fingers sent a reciprocal jolt of pleasure to my dick. I pulled them free, reached down between his legs and pushed one, then both, into him.

He gripped my shoulders with bruising hands and whimpered a little in what sounded like both pain and pleasure. I stifled those sounds with a kiss, and he sought my tongue, jerking against me and moaning as I curled my fingers forward and pressed against his inner walls.

I smiled against his mouth because at least I still remembered how to please someone in my increasingly selfish and solitary life. At least I still had something to offer. And my God, I was going to blow his head off if it killed me. He pulled back, grabbing my wrist. Evidently he was as close as I was and wanted to advance straight to the main event.

The fact of the matter dampened my enthusiasm though; with no lubricant and no condom it would hardly be a smooth ride.

"I haven't got a condom," I spoke for the first time, brushing some hair out of his eyes. "Have you?"

He shook his head solemnly and bit his lip. We were still and in our own worlds with all this desire and nowhere for it to go. I read the thoughts in his eyes before he turned his head, spat on his hand, and rubbed it along my shaft.

I tried to protest, because that was the morally correct thing to do, but it died in my throat as he repeated the action and then gripped my hips, lifted his legs, and drew me to him. I grabbed myself, and before I had consciously thought about it, I was buried inside him.

He gave a cry which he smothered with his hand, turning his face away. I stopped immediately and leaned down to press soft kisses to his face. He was tight, really tight, and I was scared to move in case one thrust sent me over the edge.

I balanced myself on one arm while my other stroked over his hip before moving into his groin and taking hold of his erection. He sucked his breath in as I slid him firmly through my hand. As I did so, I moved further inside. The dryness wasn't comfortable, but it hardly mattered when I was having the time of my life with the man of my dreams. It would be over soon enough anyway, before we both got too sore; that wasn't in doubt.

I continued to jerk him off and slowly move inside

him. His breathing became heavy and erratic. He let out a moan and lifted his hips to me, throwing his head back when I penetrated him ever more deeply. I buried my face against his neck, and he clutched at my head, fingers in my hair.

The sensation of being inside him was indescribable. The sensation of him beneath me, pliable and writhing against me was something else. All I knew was that I was right there at the edge, and I didn't want to come before him. I tried to hit the area I professed to know, from other men and other times.

I struck gold. Watching his face, I almost smiled as he wrapped himself hard around me, nails scratching at my back, moaning, "Please, *please...*" His voice was hoarse with passion, the first words he had spoken to me since down in the bar.

I jerked him off more quickly and thrust into him hard, over and over. He trembled beneath me, shuddering convulsively, eyes closed and tears, to my consternation, snaking out from beneath his coal-black lashes. But I understood why. I was his catharsis for what had happened that morning. It saddened me to know that maybe that was all I was.

I couldn't last another moment. My stomach tightened with my impending release, but I didn't need to hold off because he arched up at me, mouth open, cries spilling from it as he came, wringing my climax from me, semen forming pale puddles on his own stomach.

I gasped a little and moaned. The orgasm, like nothing I'd had in such a while, left me utterly wiped out, only able to fall forward onto him, my face against that sweet neck of his.

His skin stuck damply to mine as my heart pounded against his chest and his against mine in return. He uncoiled his limbs from around me stiffly, and I took his hands, lifted his arms above his head, and held my fingers entwined with his as I kissed him.

He responded with lazy satisfaction, sighing against my mouth in such pleasure that my heart swelled with pride. We kissed gently for the longest time until I finally eased myself free of him and shifted my weight off him to his side. He immediately turned on his own side facing me and buried his face in my chest, holding me tightly.

We remained like this for some time, with no words exchanged until finally he disentangled himself, saying regretfully as he slid from the bed, "I have to go to work."

He went into the bathroom, and I heard the sounds of running water and the toilet flushing. Then he came out and I lay still, watching the pale skin and the intricate dragon tattoo disappear beneath those expensive clothes. He took something out of his pocket and bent over for a moment before he turned to look at me finally, with his coat on, fingers raking quickly through his dishevelled hair.

He leaned down over me, one hand on the pillow by the side of my head. "What's your name?" he murmured, jewelled eyes fixed intently on mine.

"Robert," I said.

"Robert," he repeated in a whisper. "Thank you so much from the bottom of my heart." He kissed me with velvet soft lips. I didn't speak. His hand slid against mine a moment, fingers entwining and releasing, leaving something behind.

As he turned away to pick up his briefcase, I brought the card to my face to read. *Bradley Robinson.*

Attorney at law.

As well as a printed address and office number, there were two more numbers scribbled on it, a cell and a home number. I felt a stupid smile lighting up my face like I was sixteen again and in love.

He opened the door, hesitating at the threshold as I lay watching him from the bed with my heart both singing and weeping.

He sighed. He bowed his head and leaned it against the doorframe for a moment with eyes closed. "Fuck it," he said suddenly, lifting his head decisively and dropping his briefcase. "*Fuck work.*"

He slammed the door, and my thawing heart jumped into my mouth as the long coat fell from his shoulders and I watched him strip for the second time.

He smiled as he drew the covers up over the both of us and fitted himself perfectly into my waiting arms.

It was a sad smile, but one tinged with hope. The smile of someone who had been lost but now, just maybe, was found again.

A TALE OF TWO HALVES

The noise coming from the Kop was deafening—drums banging, whistling, shouting, chanting—and star striker Luke Adams lapped up the adoration from his home crowd. Three points away from winning the English Premier League football championship for the second year running, this should have been the sweetest of days for his team.

There was the rub.

Their opponents today were the only ones who could stop them. This grudge match was more than personal.

Luke's gaze strayed to the other end of the pitch, searching red and black shirts and finding the tall, elegant figure of his nemesis, Dieter Müller.

He'd crossed swords twice with the twenty-seven-year-old *wunderkind.* At Dieter's home ground, Ravensberry FC had beaten Luke's team one-nil. Luke had been sent off that day for a tackle on Dieter. He'd decided Dieter had indulged in a little continental acting, and in the tunnel afterwards a scuffle had ensued where Luke had told Dieter he would kill him next time he saw him. Dieter had merely smirked at him.

Later on, they'd knocked Rainton Athletic out of the FA Cup, beating them two-one in the semi-final. Dieter had scored both goals, one of them the coolest penalty Luke had ever seen. Sent off for almost punching the ref for his decision, the last thing Luke had seen as he left the field was Dieter smirking.

"You're a dead man!" Luke screamed viciously

from the touchline. "A fucking dead man!" The outburst cost him a month's wages and a three-match ban.

Luke sat down on the grass, legs spread, ostensibly stretching his thigh and groin muscles, his gaze straying down the pitch. Dieter was bent over, touching his toes, shorts pulled tight over a pert, muscled backside. Luke licked his dry lips. God, he hated Dieter.

Somehow, the man had kept his credibility in the male-dominated homophobic environment of English football even when a tabloid had exposed him as gay. Where once Luke had been the darling of the English press, the angelic-faced Dieter had taken the mantle. He could do no wrong.

Dieter straightened up and turned around as though he felt Luke's gaze on him and their eyes met. Dieter smiled slowly and winked. Luke stared. The papers hadn't told tales of rent boys, orgies, or gay bar cruising. Instead, there was one solitary man who'd had a five-year relationship with Dieter and could not speak highly enough about him.

Dieter seemed beyond reproach, and something about him appealed dangerously to Luke. His angelic, boyish face, plump lips, and pearly teeth could make him millions should he ever quit football. His eyes were nearly black, his closely cropped hair dark brown. Almost translucent in nature, his skin was pale and beautifully smooth like a peach.

Dieter strolled to the away team's dugout and discarded his sweatshirt. His cheeks hot, Luke glanced around to see if anyone had seen that wink, but the other players were too busy. Seeing as they were being watched by fifty thousand people, though, it was a reasonable presumption to think *someone* had seen it. Hopefully not a photographer with a nice long lens.

Luke stood up and turned towards the Kop. He let the noise of his fans wash over him a moment and then retreated to the side lines. The vitriol they directed towards Dieter almost embarrassed him. It almost made him feel sorry for the jokey, flamboyant character who enjoyed playing to the crowd.

If it wasn't Hitler salutes, it was the vilest homophobic abuse. Some of the fans on the front row today wore porn moustaches and leather.

Dieter was never put off his game. He didn't complain to the press about his treatment, and for this Luke almost admired him because *he* usually threatened to fight the entire crowd when they got on his back. He glanced over at Dieter again. How exactly could you be pelted with pink feather boas and women's underwear and mince around the pitch modelling them instead of losing it as Luke would have?

Dieter strolled onto the pitch as the clock approached three. Luke looked at his muscular legs speculatively as the German prepared to kick off. A tackle, judged just right, could break both tibia and fibula. A tackle from behind, catching the Achilles' tendon, would be worth a few months off. It might have been the last game of the domestic season, but the World Cup qualifiers started that summer. Luke didn't intend to face Dieter again playing for his country. He intended to give Dieter an injury to keep him out of action for the next year.

Luke glanced around the ground again. He noted how cool Dieter was, how he didn't seem to hear the abuse screamed at him. Dieter wasn't effeminate. He didn't seem gay. Were Dieter's teammates scared to get in the showers with him now that they knew? Did they ration their cuddles and kisses after scoring goals? It didn't seem so, and Dieter certainly didn't. Luke had seen him plenty on *Match of the Day*, hugging his team mates after scoring. He obviously wasn't afraid to be interpreted the wrong way.

The referee blew his whistle. It was about time Luke forgot his grudge and concentrated on winning the league for the dedicated fans who chanted his name.

His team started off badly. The away team had the lion's share of possession, were swift to mount an attack on goal, and soon forced a corner. Luke came up to defend, growling at his defenders who ignored him as they always did.

One of the midfielders, an England teammate of Luke's and a good drinking buddy, took the corner for Ravensberry FC. Dieter, the goal poacher, loitered in the penalty box, not put off by the elbows and sly boots which flew his way. The German often scored the most astonishing goals Luke had ever seen—direct from free kicks, from the half way line, and around four defenders from inside his own half.

The cross was whipped in. Dieter leapt to connect with it. Luke dived in to beat him, hit Dieter hard, and the two of them crashed to the ground. *Oh Jesus no, I've given away a penalty*, was Luke's first thought as he lay on top of his nemesis. But no, the ref motioned for a goal kick, and Luke wasn't even booked.

The body lying beneath Luke's was hard with muscle. Panting for breath, Dieter turned his head. "You're clearly enjoying this position, but want to save it until later?" The German's thick accent wrapped exotically around the words. Dieter lifted his pelvis, pushing his buttocks into Luke's groin.

Luke gasped. He scrambled up. Making sure the ref's back was turned, he aimed a sly boot into Dieter's side.

Dieter grunted. He flew to his feet and shoved Luke back, halfway across the penalty box. Luke stalked back, squaring up to him. Dark eyes bored into his, Dieter flushed and furious. Luke felt an undeniably sexual thrill run through him. *Jesus*. The electricity which crackled between them at that moment could have powered the stadium floodlights.

Two players were quick to break up the confrontation before the ref could book either Dieter or Luke, and Luke stalked back down the pitch, glaring across it. Dieter never lost his temper. He had never been booked in his career. Luke collected red cards like women collected shoes, and at this rate he was going to get the angel of English football sent off. He smirked viciously to himself.

Ravensberry FC continued to dominate. The home crowd grew testy. They booed Dieter every time he touched the ball, and chanted a filthy ditty, the gist of which seemed to be that Dieter was a slut who got fucked by all this teammates at full time. Even Luke thought it was cruel and he noticed Dieter starting to become ruffled for the first time ever by the abuse. He shouted something at the first few rows as he took a throw in. Luke kept up his own intimidation. He bumped into Dieter a few times. He took his legs from under him and stood on his hand while he was down on the grass. When he couldn't get close, he threw Dieter evil glares across the pitch, and Dieter threw them right back. All joking was gone.

The ref seemed blind to what was going on. Luke

was leading a charmed life. He hadn't forgotten his threat to kill Dieter. Hadn't forgotten Dieter was his nemesis, his most deadly enemy, the man who by his very nationality and his international team's record against England should have been every English person's enemy.

Despite this, he still couldn't forget that contact with the hard muscles of Dieter's body, the way his plump buttocks had been pushed into his groin. Christ, did Dieter actually want him, or was he just a terrible slut? Would he put out for Luke if Luke wanted him? He almost shivered, and his lack of concentration caused him to miss a pass from one of his teammates which saw him in acres of space with a clear run on goal. Behind him, some of his own fans jeered. The worm had turned.

Someone patted him on the back as he watched Ravensberry FC mount their own attack. "Concentrate," Dieter said, "and not on my arse." With a blatant wiggle of the aforementioned backside, Dieter burst into a run, received the ball from one of his teammates, charged into the box and put it into the top corner of the net past the despairing Rainton goalkeeper.

Luke stood staring as Dieter ran towards his own fans, arms aloft, his teammates chasing him, mobbing him so Dieter disappeared in a sea of bodies.

Luke spat on the ground. He turned his back on the celebration, keeping his head down against the boos of his own fans. It was a moment from half time. Luke needed to step up a gear. He needed to score a goal and cripple Dieter. Not necessarily in that order.

The ref blew the whistle, and Ravensberry FC filtered towards the tunnel still buzzing with excitement while Rainton Athletic were dejected and sullen, heads bent. Dieter arrived at the tunnel entrance at the same time as Luke. He smiled, pursed his lips and blew a kiss. Luke lunged at him, pinning him to the wall by his neck.

A furious skirmish followed between both teams before the two men were separated and the referee loomed up between them. "You've got one more chance, and then you're off," he told Luke coldly. "Your choice." Luke curled his lip at him and stalked off down the tunnel.

The manager roasted him. He threatened Luke with immediate substitution at the beginning of the second half. Luke sat half-listening. He was used to this. At times, the dressing room walls shook with the weight of his manager's anger and disappointment. Luke lost the England captaincy after going out to a nightclub the night before a big match. He had received a drunk driving ban a few years ago. Women and alcohol were his downfall. Often, his off-the-field exploits featured more heavily in the tabloids than his on-field activities. Even *he* wasn't sure why his manager didn't sell him.

The second half kicked off in a war of furious fouls and name-calling. It was end to end stuff, near misses by both teams, played at a breathtaking pace. Then came the breakthrough, finally. Rainton got a corner. It whipped in across the face of the goal, and Luke shoved off every defender in his path and rose towering above them to head the ball right into the back of the net past the helpless goalkeeper.

Screams came from the crowd behind the goal. Luke whirled away, ran with arms outstretched and stopped just as suddenly when his teammates failed to join him and cries of anger erupted from the fans closest to him.

His heart sank as he turned around to see his

teammates remonstrating with the referee. He didn't know why, but his goal had been disallowed. Perhaps it was off side, perhaps the way he'd climbed above the defenders had been judged illegal. He stared a moment, hands on hips and then he let his head drop in defeat and trudged back to the half way line. He couldn't believe it.

A red and black shirt flashed in his periphery, close by and getting closer. Luke lifted his head and at that moment, Dieter smiled at him. Luke charged across, fist raised, a red mist upon him, and knocked the German down with one punch.

Thousands of fans reacted, hands pulled him back and the ref tried to get in the middle. Dieter jumped up, cheek red and already swelling, and threw a punch in return. Luke danced back so the fist caught him a stinging blow on the temple, almost making him see stars. For a gay guy, Dieter sure knew how to fight.

The fight was over as soon as it had begun. Firm hands held him while the ref dug in his pocket and brandished a red card in Luke's face before he turned around and did the same to Dieter. Dieter spat on the grass, cursed loudly in German, and shrugged free of the teammates holding him to stalk towards the tunnel.

Luke followed him screaming. "German arsehole! I'm going to fucking kill you!"

Dieter turned back. "Blow me," he told Luke, thrusting his groin in his direction.

Hands caught Luke as he tried to run down the tunnel after Dieter. His manager and his teammates off the subs bench restrained him.

"I don't think so," said his manager. "Let him go."

Luke struggled, swearing at the disappearing man,

trembling with fury. Only when Dieter had disappeared completely was he released, and he clomped clumsily down the tunnel in his boots, trying to pull himself together. He glanced at the door of the visiting dressing room as he walked past. Of course, he could go in and kill Dieter now as promised, but already he was feeling calmer. His anger had turned cold and deadly. He was thinking of what he would do to the man next time they met on the pitch. He went into his own dressing room, stripped off his kit, and plunged naked into a cold shower.

But the water riled him in a different way. His anger was redirected. The spray hit his aching skin, and suddenly his body was alive with need. His cock hardened, and shameful thoughts grew within him.

Innocently perusing a titty mag a few months back, Luke had been almost hit in the face by the picture of an undressed Dieter reclining on a bed in a pair of tight, white Calvin Kleins. Now, the man was beautiful, even Luke would grudgingly admit that, but he had hardly expected Dieter to be hiding such a body under his football kit. Not only were his pecs and abs sculpted and hard, but he filled those shorts to eye-popping status. Did he have a pair of socks down there or what? Luke stared and stared. That image had to be the most interesting in the magazine. He had put the magazine away but taken it out several times since.

Luke glanced out of the shower towards the door. At the moment, Dieter was widely regarded as the hottest man in the country by both men and women. Luke needed to get himself a piece of that.

He lunged suddenly from the spray, leaving it running, and grabbed a towel which failed to disguise the growing erection beneath.

He pulled the door open and stepped into the cold air of the tunnel, then looked back and forth before he pushed his way into the visitors' dressing room. His heart hammered in his chest. He had no idea if he was going to kill Dieter or fuck him senseless.

The dressing room was silent apart from the sound of running water. As Luke approached on damp, bare feet, the sound merely made him grow harder. He stopped at the threshold of the large walk-in shower and feasted his eyes on the sight in front of him.

Dieter stood naked under the spray, pale and muscular, hair wet, rubbing himself furiously with shower gel, suds flooding down the drain around his feet. He had his back turned, and Luke's gaze travelled down the perfect curve of his spine to rest on his backside. Dieter was God's gift to mankind. What women had lost was man's gain, and today this was going to be Luke's gain. Luke, who had never contemplated fucking another man in his life.

Dieter turned around suddenly, startled. His cheek was kaleidoscopic with bruising from Luke's fist. For a moment he stood staring, then allowed his gaze to drop slowly down Luke's chiselled torso, lingering on the outline of his arousal in the towel.

"Well," he said lazily with a smirk. "Come to kill me with a large, blunt instrument, Luke?"

"Something like that," Luke replied tightly as he dropped his towel and stepped into the shower.

Dieter was clearly all talk, though, because he actually shrank back as Luke stalked towards him, looking unsure and afraid. Luke didn't much care. He was going to take what he wanted, regardless. Dieter gasped as Luke crushed him against the wall and kissed him hard.

That smart mouth drove him insane. It was soft, sensual, and juicy. It turned him to putty. Dieter moaned almost reluctantly and tried to slide away but Luke held him there by the neck and the waist and kissed him furiously.

Dieter soon relented. He sagged against Luke as though exhausted, hands seeking his body, touching him everywhere, chest, shoulders, back, buttocks. Luke squirmed under his firm hands, the sensation delicious and so, so different than a female touch. His mouth moved to Dieter's neck. The German cursed as Luke bit, sucked, licked, and then trailed down his torso to capture one nipple after another, wetting and sucking them stiff.

"Oh, my God," Dieter groaned. He ground his erection against Luke's, hands greedily on his backside, pulling Luke closer. "Take me, take me…"

Luke lifted his head. "Have you got a condom?"

"Yes, in my bag. And lube."

Luke smiled wryly. "You're well prepared."

Dieter glowered at him. "I'm not a slut."

"Did I say you were? Let's go, then." He took Dieter's hand and pulled him out of the shower behind him. Once they got back onto the tiled floor, Dieter veered off, their hands separating, and Luke followed him around the back of one bench, hung with clothes, to a bank of lockers.

He watched as Dieter pulled a door open and rummaged in a bag, producing a pump-action dispenser of Durex Play and a foil square. The German was rock hard, his considerable erection curving up to his belly, small drops of water and creamy fluid pooling at the tip.

Luke lunged forward, almost losing the plot such

was his desire. Dieter grunted as Luke pushed him face first into a row of jackets above one bench. He gripped the coat hooks with both hands and spread his legs, bending over, deliberately presenting his ripe, plump backside to Luke with a grin over his shoulder.

Luke slapped one firm cheek and watched it vibrate. *Christ, he was going to eat Dieter alive.* He fell to his knees, seeking between Dieter's spread legs with his mouth, drawing one ball between his lips, sucking.

Dieter hissed in pleasure. He reached behind him, his fingers tangling in Luke's wet hair. Luke found his cock, pulled it back between his legs and sucked at the head, tasting the tang of semen.

"Fuck... oh God..." Dieter moaned, pushing himself into Luke's mouth.

Luke straightened up. He pushed Dieter further forward, his legs even wider apart so the German was spread for him and Luke could see the prize, a tight little hairless hole. He twisted the lube open and pressed the dispenser, letting the liquid fall between the plump cheeks.

Dieter flinched, groaning as Luke used the tip of his index finger to rub the lube slowly over and around his entrance, before pressing inside. His partner pushed back with a gasp, fucking himself on Luke's finger shamelessly while stroking his own cock.

Luke pulled back. He tore open the condom with his teeth and told Dieter, "Why don't you lube yourself up a bit more?"

The German didn't need telling twice. He grabbed the lube and squirted it onto two fingers. While Luke rolled his condom on, he watched Dieter play with himself, opening his hole up with his fingers.

Luke groaned, already trembling on the edge. He couldn't remember the last time he had been so aroused. Pushing Dieter's hand away, Luke gripped his firm cheeks and rested his cock in Dieter's arse crack, rubbing up and down slowly. Dieter squirmed, pushing back, trying to impale himself.

"Thought you said you weren't a slut?" Luke teased. "You're gagging for it."

"Shut up and fuck me," Dieter growled.

"Beg me."

"What?"

"Beg me to fuck you."

"Fuck off, you want it as much as I do," Dieter ground out.

"I can take or leave you," Luke replied as nonchalantly as he could manage with all the blood deserting his brain for his cock. "You're just a hole."

Before he could even anticipate it, Dieter whirled around and slapped him hard across the face. "Fuck you!" He shoved a shocked Luke backwards and stalked away behind the bench.

Luke stood a moment in contemplation. Perhaps Dieter wasn't a slut at all. Maybe he objected to giving his favours away cheaply. Hadn't the man from the five-year relationship said as much? Luke bit his lip. Insulting his partner wasn't going to get him anywhere.

He stepped around the bench and saw Dieter at his locker with a towel around his waist. "I'm sorry," Luke muttered.

Dieter ignored him. In the silence, a mass cheer echoed around the foundations of the stadium. Luke froze. It was loud but not that loud. Not the voices of the home team's fans but the voices of the lesser away fans.

Dieter turned to face him. "Oh dear," he said with a smug grin. "We've just won the league."

Snarling in fury, Luke grabbed him by the arm, shoved him face first against the row of coat hooks over a bench and thrust into him all the way in one smooth stroke.

Dieter cried out. The bench rattled beneath him as he grabbed hold of two coat hooks to steady himself, moaning loudly as Luke drew back, then pushed in again before starting to fuck the German swiftly.

Oh God, it was amazing. Luke had had this type of sex before with women but no one had ever felt so good. Dieter seemed to fit him perfectly, hot and tight and just beautiful.

"Oh Jesus, oh God..." Dieter sounded like he was begging for help. Luke smiled wryly. He put an arm around his partner's waist and pulled him back, sealing his torso to Dieter's back, wanting to feel the German's skin against his own. They slid together damply. Dieter's skin made Luke tremble. It was hot and satin soft. He sought Dieter's neck, kissing and nipping, feeling the shudders it provoked in his lover's body.

Dieter panted hard. He moaned and groaned with every thrust inside him, masturbating swiftly. Luke felt around him. He batted Dieter's hand away and replaced it with his own, because he wasn't in the habit of leaving his partners to get themselves off, be it male or female.

Dieter thrust eagerly into his hand and then pushed himself back on Luke's cock. They had a perfect rhythm going, moving like they'd been lovers all their lives, and the heat consumed Luke whole. Dieter was something else. *This* was something else. There was nothing about this which could ever add up to a one-night stand, Luke knew that now. Nor did he want it to. Dieter had caught him effortlessly. Luke, the ladies' man, was converted.

He bit Dieter fervently on the neck, lapped at little at the bruise, tasting sweat and aftershave. God, he was beautiful. In the distance, cheering began. Luke lifted his head, glancing at the clock on the wall. Full time and his team had lost. It didn't matter. It all took second place to the ecstasy of being inside Dieter.

The away team would be back in the dressing room within minutes though. Luke didn't intend to be interrupted at his task. He doubled his pace and Dieter doubled his moaning.

His body tightened around Luke, his limbs shuddering, clearly moments away. "*Ja, ja...*" he chanted.

But Luke wasn't quite ready for Dieter to finish without him. He clamped his hand hard around the base of his cock.

Dieter howled. "What are you doing, you English bastard?"

Luke's teeth nipped at his ear, not pausing in his thrusts. "Abusing me isn't going to get you your orgasm. You come when I say so. Now what's the magic word?"

"Arsehole," Dieter spat then groaned in torment, trembling. "Please, okay? Jesus, just you wait till next season..."

"Looking forward to it," Luke growled. He was close now. Dieter's insides were spasming around him, gripping and releasing him hard, milking him all the way. Luke let the waves wash over him. He released his death grip on Dieter and jerked him off hard, listening to the fireworks.

Dieter came with him perfectly, crying out, cursing in German, bucking back against him. Luke held him close, not letting their skin lose contact for a moment, allowing the orgasm to turn him inside out and upside down. He heard his own cries of ecstasy and felt the semen on his hand, and then he slumped against Dieter, holding his lover hard.

Beneath him, Dieter whimpered and clung to the coat hooks with trembling hands. He turned his head over his shoulder, and Luke kissed him fiercely. Dieter returned it breathlessly, and it went on and on for what seemed like an eternity.

The clattering of studs on the tiled floor penetrated Luke's brain. He pulled free of Dieter, almost slipping on the damp floor as he slid around the bench to where he'd dropped his towel in the mouth of the shower. He dragged it on just as the door flew open and the ten other men of Ravensberry FC burst in, singing and laughing.

Everything stopped. Silence crashed over the room as the team saw Luke standing by their showers grabbing at the towel which threatened to slip from his hips at any moment.

"What the fuck are you doing in here?" asked the captain, eyes narrowed before his gaze swung to Dieter as he appeared from behind the lockers.

Luke's eyes met Dieter's. Luke smiled slowly, and he knew the fondness wasn't hidden. "One-nil England," he told Dieter. "See you for the replay."

Dieter was flushed, the redness extending down his neck and across the top of his chest. He tried to glower at Luke but failed, the smile twitching at his mouth.

"Excuse me gentlemen," Luke said as he pushed his

way through the group of men at the door and stepped across the tunnel, back to his own dressing room.

His heart was light, way lighter than it should have been on this most terrible of Saturdays. It was filled with nothing but Dieter Müller.

GUILT

The club's dark and sweaty. I feel the bass thumping in my chest like an extra heartbeat as I move through the throng, eyes expertly tuned to every male form in the place. I've developed cat vision in here. I can spot a hard body through the dark and the dry ice at a hundred paces. And there he is.

Leaning against the railings surrounding the dance floor with a drink in his hand, he stands about six feet tall, lean and subtly muscled, his limbs long and strong and elegant. He wears a black T-shirt which clings to pecs and biceps and tight blue jeans which emphasize everything inside them—strong thighs, pert ass and decent package. His dark hair is cut razor short, and his profile is beautiful. My tongue must be hanging out. I put my empty glass down and close in for the kill.

"Hi there, buy you another?"

He turns to look at me, having to angle his gaze downwards to my five nine. His eyes are a smoky grey, lit by a spotlight behind me, his lashes lush. His gaze moves soon enough from my face, travelling down my body impudently to linger on my crotch.

He smiles slowly, his mouth wide and sensual, his teeth perfect. "Sure," he says. "Jack and coke."

Of course. What else would a man like him drink? I can't stand the stuff myself. That alone should tell me that I'm far too uncool for this man. I'm not usually so lacking in confidence but I'm not yet drunk, and he's unnerved me with his beauty. I know I'm good-looking but I feel rather like a moth next to a beautiful butterfly at the moment. I nod to him, stepping off to the bar, hoping he's not gone when I get back.

Glasses clutched in clammy hands, I head back. I've chosen vodka, which doesn't agree with me, but I'm hoping for Dutch courage.
"Thanks." He takes his glass, clinks it against mine. "Cheers." He swallows half in one go.
I sip at my vodka. "So what's your name?"
"Steven."
"Nice to meet you, Steven. I'm Evan."
"Hello, Evan." He finishes the rest of his drink. "Let's get another." He heads off to the bar. Real conversationalist I've chosen here, but then why pretend that I'm after that? I come to this club for one thing and one thing only. Often I get it in the bathroom; rarely do I actually get a name. Never do I see them again.
I approach behind him, getting a good eyeful of his ass. Perfect. I imagine him naked, face down. Yeah right, as if he takes. If I want him tonight, I'd better be prepared to have a sore ass in the morning. I don't mind taking, it's just most times I top.
He turns his head to me. "Vodka?" He gestures to my glass.
I squeeze in next to him, bare arm brushing his. Electricity, swift and sudden, shocks me. "Yeah. With Red Bull this time." I hold his gaze.
He smiles slowly. "You'll need it," he tells me brazenly.
My breath catches in my throat. A rush of blood stiffens my cock. Oh my God, all my Christmases have just come at once. I can't remember the last time I hooked a guy as gorgeous as him.
He pushes a glass to me, done up with a pink

umbrella and straw, and grins. I smile back wryly and drink. Jesus, that's strong. He's put a double in it. I don't let on, just pretend I'm the hardened drinker that this isn't going to affect. Unfortunately, after one slug, I feel the alcohol in my blood. I need to take it easy. I don't want to pass out in a puddle of my own vomit before he can fuck me.

I grope for conversation as he shoves his wallet back into his back pocket and turns away from the bar.

"So, you from around here? I haven't seen you before."

"Yeah, I just don't come out much."

It really is my lucky night. "Why's that?"

Grey eyes like steel turn on me. "Do I need a reason?"

I stumble over my words, flushing. "No, but someone like you shouldn't hide himself away." Shit, I've offended him.

"Someone like me?" He arches a brow, looking amused.

"Yeah, someone as... *hot* as you." Fuck, now I know why I don't do conversation with my fucks.

He chuckles. "Are you always so lame?"

I glare at him. "You know what, if you're just going to..." I make as though to walk away. A firm hand grabs me by the arm. My drink slops over my shirt.

"Where are you going?" His voice is only just audible over the music. He holds my gaze steadily.

As I fumble for words, he says firmly, "Drink up, we're leaving."

My cock's rigid against my jeans as I follow him from the club, my head swimming with the vodka. He hires a cab at the curb and holds the door open for me. I hesitate.

I'm always wary about leaving with strangers after a friend of mine got drugged and gang-raped.

"Come on," he says impatiently. "I don't bite." Under the street lights, I catch a better look at his face. His skin is paler than anyone's I've ever seen in Southern California before. It's almost translucent, completely without blemish, almost as white as his teeth. I bend my head and climb into the taxi.

He climbs in next to me and gives the driver an address in the hills. As he settles back, I get an intoxicating whiff of expensive cologne. My cock hardens further. I imagine his weight on me, his cock driving hard into me. I almost moan.

A hand rests on my knee. He smiles at me in the dark.

Steven's house is average sized, with a well-tended front garden. I follow him into a large kitchen, looking around. It's tidy, the fridge cluttered with magnets. On the wall next to it is pinned a calendar which is densely written on, most of the figures being numbers.

"Want a drink or have you had enough?" He grins.

"I'll take a beer if you have one." I resist the childish urge to stick my tongue out at him and sidle closer to the calendar. There are numbers written on every day, seeming to be times with strange, cryptic abbreviations under them like TRU, RTV and DRV.

I glance away and see the fridge is full of fruit and vegetables and not much else. I smile, trying to pretend I wasn't looking at the calendar.

He moves to the drawer with two bottles and finds a bottle opener. He's polite, I'll give him that. I expected to be bent over the kitchen table by now. He hands me a bottle. I thank him and take a swig. He's right that I don't need any more though. I'm just sober enough to be on the right side of appreciating tonight, just sober enough that I won't be all night trying to get off.

"Why don't we go upstairs?" he suggests.

I follow him upstairs on unsteady legs and into a dark bedroom. He clicks a bedside lamp on, and I see a king size bed with dark red covers, an arty print of a naked man on the pale wall opposite. A dressing table against another wall is crammed with hair styling products and cologne. I'm still looking at this as he takes the bottle from my hand and as I turn towards him questioningly, he grips me by the neck and kisses me.

Fuck, Steven kisses like an angel. His kiss belies the strength of the hand holding me. It's passionate, but it's almost tender too. It has real need in it, and I feel a jolt of something inflame my stomach. Christ, I realise, he doesn't do this all the time, like me. Not at all. I don't know how I know this, but I'm sure of it.

I let loose a moan as his tongue finds mine. Strong hands slide up my back, pulling a shudder from me before they wrench the shirt from my body. I put my arms up to allow him to strip me, and then he shoves me backwards suddenly. I fall to the edge of the bed, and he's on his knees in front of me, hands on my belt buckle, lips seeking one nipple. He drags it into his mouth, using teeth and tongue.

"Jesus," I hiss. I kick off both shoes while he's unfastening my pants. A large hand reaches inside, into the fly of my already damp boxers, and withdraws my cock.

"Someone's excited," he observes smartly as his thumb smoothes over my wet slit. A groan issues from my throat. He smiles up at me. "Want me to fuck you?" His hand slides into my pants, under the leg of my boxers, fingers seeking between my cheeks.

"Yes," I moan helplessly and spread my legs, shuddering as his fingers part me, one stroking my entrance teasingly.

He leans forward, still smiling. "You said I was hot. I think you're hotter. I think you're the hottest man I've had in some time."

My heart almost stutters to a halt. His face is serious and composed. He's not playing me, and he has no need to butter me up when he knows he's going to get laid. I smile hesitantly at the ego stroke.

His smile widens. His hand caresses my neck. "Beautiful," he murmurs as he kisses me.

I sink back onto the bed, and he climbs onto me, one hard thigh between mine, pressing against my needy cock, almost driving me insane. I clutch at his back and slide my hands up his shirt, feeling every muscle shift under my palms.

He sits back on his heels. He discards his shirt, then starts to unfasten his pants with such a hot, blatant look of promise in his eyes that I writhe in desire on the bed. Oh my God, if he touches me just once more, I swear I'm going to come. I don't know how I'm going to last at all.

His torso is hard and chiselled, his abdomen flat and defined. He pushes his pants and boxers down his thighs and releases a long, thick cock. I push my knuckles against my mouth. He laughs softly. "Like what you see?"

"Yes, God, give it to me." I'm utterly shameless. I'm not in the habit of begging for cock. Not ever.

He grins. He pulls my socks off one by one, then he drags my jeans down, with me lifting my hips to help him, before following with my boxers.

He runs his palms up my thighs, studying my naked

body. I have the feeling he's not going to undress any further, but I don't much care. I only care about his cock at the moment.

"Turn over."

I scramble onto my hands and knees as I'm told, briefly disappointed that I can't see his face as he's fucking me. He reaches for the bedside drawer, withdraws a condom and a tube of lube.

The lube he squeezes right between my bare ass cheeks. I flinch, letting out a soft moan, and follow that up with a louder groan as large fingers probe my cleft, massaging the lube in, pushing gently.

"Fuck..." I pant as one finger penetrates me.

"More?"

"Yes... God..."

A second finger enters me and I almost squeal. I push back. I've clearly forgotten how good it is to receive. I should do this more often. His fingers fill me like heaven. I might just pass out when he puts his cock in me.

He fucks me slowly but firmly with his fingers, then takes them out and lubes them up again. He works me open so thoroughly I can hardly breathe.

"Please... please..." I start to beg, head hanging down, trembling all over.

"Please what?" There's a smile in his coy words.

"Fuck me, God please, fuck me."

His other hand strokes my buttocks. He withdraws his fingers. I hear foil tearing and the roll of latex. I look over my shoulder. He reaches for the lube, squirts more on me, puts some on his condom, running it over the latex, covering his shaft thickly.

Holding his cock, he rests it between my ass cheeks and rubs slowly. I groan and move back greedily. He continues to rub, parting my cheeks, pressing against my entrance until I feel myself start to give.

As I draw in my breath on a gasp, he stops. "What's the matter?" I glance back at him, and see him looking down at his cock, staring at it as though mesmerised. "Jesus, Steven don't stop!"

He glances up at me. His face is closed and serious. "Are you sure? Are you sure you want it?"

"Yes, God!" I'm confused and unsettled by his expression, his hesitance, but I'm drunk and desperate to be fucked. I won't analyse his behaviour too closely.

"All right then," he says in a murmur, and he spears me so suddenly, gliding right into my depths all the way, that I cry out in shock.

"Mmm..." He rocks slowly against me. "God, you feel good."

I pant for breath, trying to get used to him, fighting back the urge to come, the urge to scream, the urge to tell him to stop, that it's too much. I feel dragged a thousand different ways. The pain-pleasure of it is such that I feel I might pass out.

His hands run up my sides. He takes it slow, in long, smooth strokes. A hand closes around my cock.

"Oh God..." I buck into his hand. I'm going to shame myself disgracefully fast. I push back even though it hurts, white-hot heat surging through me.

"Good?" One hand is firm on my hip. I can't even articulate a reply. I moan out something which might be his name. I'm on the cusp of coming. He starts to pummel me, hitting that spot over and over, and I'm lost.

Bright stars dance before my eyes. I cry out loud. I hear him laugh and then I'm coming into his hand, clenching around his cock, convulsing over and over again before I fall forward onto the bed with his weight crushing me.

It's some time before Steven moves out of me, rousing me from almost unconsciousness. I lift my head to follow him with bleary eyes as he disappears into the en suite. Jesus, when was the last time I was fucked into near unconsciousness? Try never. Fuck. The covers are wet under me. I glance at the clock on the bedside table. Two in the morning. Is he going to let me stay? He's going to have to because I can't even move. I don't think I can even feel my limbs. I let my head drop back down.

The bathroom door opens, and soft footsteps pad across the bare floorboards. Steven clears his throat, and I turn my head to look at him.

"So, I've got an early start tomorrow…"

I stare at him in incomprehension.

"If you'll excuse me." He stands pointedly staring down at me. His cock is still half hard to my astonishment.

I try to speak, wetting my dry lips. "Come on," I say, "you just fucked me senseless. You can't expect me to…"

His voice is as hard as his expression. "Get out."

I sit up with cheeks flaming. I can't remember the last time a man treated me quite so badly, although there's been a few. I stand up on trembling legs, casting around for my clothes. "There's no need to be such an asshole," I spit back at him.

"Then take the fucking hint," he growls and hurls my boxers at me.

Seething, I scoop my belongings up into my arms, drop one shoe and bend to retrieve it again. What a bastard, what a fucking bastard. I'm cold and trembling, all post-orgasmic glow gone, and in that moment I actually wish I could take back all the glorious fucking of a few minutes ago. Fuck him. I've never regretted something as much in my life.

I stalk for the door and hurl myself down the stairs, almost falling when I get tangled up in my jeans. There, naked in the hallway by his front door, I dress myself. My heart beats furiously hard and my face burns with shame.

When I'm done, I stand still and listen a moment. It's completely silent upstairs. Tears prick my eyes unbidden. In fury at my weakness, I drive my fist into the wall leaving a sizeable dent in it and my hand screaming in pain. Still there's no sound from upstairs. I slam the door behind me and storm off down the driveway, not even knowing which way I'm going.

It's months later. After my humiliation at the hands of Steven, rather than drive me away from my lifestyle, it only pushed me deeper. I crave more and more men to stroke my ego, to reassure me that I'm attractive and desirable. But I leave with no one. I fuck them here in the club or not at all. No one's going to do to me what Steven did. I've never seen him again, and I guess he's staying away. Surely he knows I'd knock him out if I saw him again. It wasn't the throwing out as such which hurt me, because Christ, I never expected more than a one-night stand, I never do, but it was the *way* he did it. Humiliated and shamed me so much, when if he'd done it politely and nicely, he could have coaxed me from his bed no problem. But instead he treated me like trash. Something on the bottom of his shoe. A hole which had just massaged his dick to climax. I won't ever be treated that way again.

I scan the club. There's a guy I fucked a couple of

weeks ago giving me the eye, but I turn my gaze away firmly. I don't do repeats. Not for anyone.

And then through the smoke and the spotlights I see him. My body goes rigid as I watch him at the bar lifting a drink to his lips, scanning the bodies on the dance floor.

I start to tremble. I turn away. *Please don't let him see me.* Then I turn back and suddenly the injustice of what he did rises to consume me whole and I'm back in that room, naked and holding my clothes, being told to get out by the man who just fucked my brains out. No way is he going to get away with this.

"Hey asshole!" I cry before I'm anywhere near him, and he turns his head, just like everyone in the vicinity, his eyes registering recognition before he looks away.

"Hey! Don't fucking ignore me! I've got a fucking bone to pick with you!" I catch hold of him as he tries to walk away.

He shoves me back hard. "Fuck off."

"Hey! Hey!" I'm so mad my vision's blood-red. I want to kill him. I want to slam him against the ground and open his throat with the glass in my hand. "Don't tell me to fuck off, you treated me like shit."

He turns back again and this time he grips me by the throat and slams me into a pillar. My glass falls to the ground and shatters. I squirm furiously in his grip. "I fucked you. End of story," he snarls into my face, grey eyes blazing. "What exactly do you want from me? A fucking marriage proposal?"

My fist slams into the side of his head and he falls back with a grunt. "I didn't want anything from you. I just didn't want to be treated like some kind of whore you picked up."

He regards me, eyes flashing, a hand to his head. "If

the cap fits," he suggests dangerously.

I throw myself at him and we crash to the ground in a tangle of limbs, flailing, throwing punches, me screaming abuse, screaming that I'm not a whore although I'm not sure I believe it myself.

Rough hands separate us, lift us from the ground, drag me through the club with my feet barely touching the ground. Then I'm outside on the sidewalk, a couple of boots in my side for good measure before silence descends, broken only by the occasional car on the boulevard.

I crawl slowly to my feet, touching my mouth where it's bleeding. I see him up ahead of me, veering into an alleyway unsteadily, where he sinks down onto a stack of packing crates, holding his abdomen as though injured.

I stand at the mouth of the alley staring at him. He lifts his head slowly to look at me, then lowers it, shaking his head almost imperceptibly.

"I'm sorry, okay?" he says. "That asshole wasn't me."

Something grips my stomach. I step closer to him. "Oh no?"

"No. That wasn't me who took you home and fucked you either. I don't normally do that. It was wrong of me. I'm sorry."

I'm utterly taken aback now.

"I just... wanted you," he says helplessly. "I should have had more willpower."

Alarm bells go off in my head. Why was it wrong of him? What was wrong about it? "Jesus, you're married!" I blurt out.

He looks up at me and a small smile crosses his face. "No, I'm available. There's no one else."

"You're straight then."

"No, I'm queer."

"Then what?" I'm exasperated. I step closer, putting my hand on his shoulder. "I don't know about you, but I had a fantastic time. There was nothing wrong about that, Steven."

Steven shakes his head. "It was wrong."

"Stop saying that. Tell me why."

Steven lowers his gaze again. He swallows audibly and runs a hand through his hair. "Shit, Evan, you were right to try and kill me just then. So fucking right, you have no idea. I'm HIV positive."

I stare at him. My hand falls from his shoulder. I wrap my arms around myself, stepping back, shaking my head. "No. No."

He nods. "Yes."

"I don't... understand..." I stammer. "You... fucked me, and you didn't... how could you..." I start to scream. "How the fuck could you do that to me? How could you just take someone home like that and not tell them? You've got a duty to *protect* people!" I slap him hard across the face.

He doesn't react. "I wanted you," he repeats. "I know I was wrong. I wasn't looking to pick anyone up."

"Then you should have told me! We could have done something else. A blowjob or..."

"Bullshit," Steven interrupts. "If I'd have told you, you would have been out the door like a shot. Staying for a blowjob? I don't fucking think so." He laughs bitterly.

I ignore him. "You *fucked* me! I didn't fuck you, which might not have been so bad, *you fucked me*! You chose the riskiest sexual practice you could think of and you went ahead and took that chance with my *life*!"

"I used a condom." His voice is sullen.

"So? So fucking what? Condoms break. They've broken on me plenty of times."

"It was extra strong. I never had one of those break before."

I stumble back and sit on some crates opposite him, laughing incredulously. "I can't believe my fucking ears. It's okay to lie and deceive me and play Russian roulette for kicks with my life because you used a condom. Oh, that's okay then!"

Steven sighs. He dabs some blood off his bleeding lip. "I tried to minimise the risk to you. I didn't let myself get anywhere near you until I had the condom on. I didn't let you touch me. And I didn't come."

"What?"

"I didn't come."

I stare at him. "You didn't come?"

"No."

I'm completely astonished. Had that taken the willpower of a saint or was he just not that into it that night?

"I know what you're thinking, and yes, it nearly killed me not to blow my load when I felt you coming," he says. "But I held it back until I got into the bathroom."

"You jerked off in the bathroom?"

"I didn't jerk off; just the action of taking my condom off made me come."

I stare and stare, and then suddenly a wave of such pity and sorrow hits me that I lower my head and start to cry.

"Shit, Evan, what are you...?" His voice trails off in confusion and unhappiness. Standing, he moves to kneel before me. "Come here." He takes me by the back of the neck and holds me against his shoulder.

His scent is familiar even all these months later, and so is the feel of the body which drove me out of my mind with passion. I clutch him and hold him hard.

"I'm sorry," he says again helplessly. I realise that he thinks I'm crying because of what he did to me and I am, but I'm also crying *for* him. Because I feel sorry for him. Because he had to go into the bathroom to come. I hope he doesn't know that. I imagine he would be offended.

One of my hands smoothes over his closely cropped hair. My touch is tender. My heart is broken open by him. "Take me home," I whisper.

He pulls back suddenly, gaze fixed on mine. "No. *No.*"

"Please."

Steven stands up, paces the alleyway agitatedly. "Jesus, I don't deserve anything from you, nothing at all. How can you..."

I ignore him, rising to my feet, holding out my hand. "Let's go."

We're silent all the way home, just like that first time. When he goes into the fridge for beer, I look more closely at his calendar, at the numbers and letters. "This is your drug regime isn't it?"

He nods, looking uneasy as he pops the caps and hands one bottle to me.

I drink from it. "How long have you had it?"

"Five years."

"How many men have you had in that time?"

"Just one."

I swallow. My gaze strays once more to the calendar and then back to him. "You must have really wanted me," I try to joke.

"I did."

"You were so cool about it too."

"Was I? I didn't *feel* cool. I felt like a desperate dick. In both senses of the word."

I laugh. "Let's go upstairs."

He watches me for a long while, his face serious and unsure. He steps forward, cradling my neck and kisses me.

I'm sober this time, and it's just as good. I want more. I want that first time again. No matter what.

We're stripped and naked beneath the covers. We lie face to face, our right hands joined, his thumb stroking mine.

"Don't throw me out this time," I warn.

"I won't, but God... do you know what you're doing?"

"I like you, Steven. I never once stopped thinking about you."

Steven sighs. He kisses me. "I can't make love to you again. At least, not yet. I feel too guilty."

He's hard though. I touch him. "There's no rush," I tell him.

Steven's eyes are dark with desire. "I want to get you off." He slides beneath the covers, kissing me all the way down my body, a wet tongue running over my balls before he sucks me into his mouth. I groan, clutching at his hair.

We end up sixty-nining, me on top, leaning over to suck him off while his tongue probes my ass, wet and wicked. He tries to stop me blowing him first though. I tell him, "It's okay. I don't have any sores or cuts in my mouth. There's no risk." Still he's reluctant until my mouth encloses him and his protests die away.

When I'm close, he throws me onto my back. He kneels over me, stroking his cock. Then he reaches for the bedside drawer. He takes a dildo out. It's brand new in a box, still sealed. I don't speak as he opens the packaging, takes it out, lubes it up. Then, with me on my back and knees open, he fucks me with it.

As he does, I jerk off, moaning, writhing, watching him as he jerks off too. We come together in pale puddles on my stomach and I look at the white fluid mingling together. Sweaty and exhausted, I drop back, smiling.

Steven is careful to clean me up with a wet cloth. He curls against my body and I hold him. "Next time I think you should blow me with a condom on," he murmurs. "If you want a next time."

"I do want a next time," I reply, stroking his hair. "Very much. And whatever you want. I'll get some flavoured ones."

He smiles against my chest. "I'm very lucky."

"No, I'm lucky. Don't treat yourself like a leper, Steven."

Steven hides his face. Soft sobs escape him. I pull him closer and whisper that it's going to be all right. That I'm not going anywhere.

ROMANCE

Fox Reed parked his car and backed slowly out of the space to straighten up. A blur of movement caught his attention, a car travelling recklessly fast, before it slammed into his rear end.

Fox threw himself from his car and furiously confronted the idiot behind him. He was taken aback to recognize the man he'd come here to meet—Jamie Warner, porn star extraordinaire and soon to be Fox's co-star.

Jamie Warner was up and coming, in both senses of the word. He was the newest thing at a rival studio and was causing quite a stir in the porn world. Fox knew him of course. He didn't often watch porn in his down-time, but he made an exception for Jamie. Who wouldn't? Fox had jerked off to him more times than he could count. When his director had suggested that they approach the exclusive top to be a one-off bottom to Fox, Fox had about come in his pants on the spot. He had never expected Jamie to agree, but then the fee *was* considerable.

Jamie, lean with copper-coloured hair and eyes like flame, lifted his hands apologetically, his expression conciliatory. "I'm sorry, man."

"You fucking prick." Fox had just blown any civil working relationship they might have had with those words.

Jamie's pretty face turned cold as stone. "Why don't I just get you my details?" He ducked back into his car. Fox watched as he scribbled something on a bit of paper before he got out and wordlessly handed it to Fox.

Fox snatched it, locked his car and stalked away

without another word.

Ten minutes later his director was introducing him to Jamie Warner, enthusiastic to have his two stars together in his office, clearly hoping it was love at first sight or something equally ridiculous. What it was, was hate at first sight.

Fox was major league when it came to porn stars. He worked exclusively for the RoMANce studio with artistic say-so on everything. He and his director Martina had an understanding. Both disliked the mechanics of porn films, the concentrating on the cock penetrating an orifice to the detriment of the actor's faces, the way the man on bottom was often degraded just like the woman in straight porn. If the man on the bottom showed obvious signs of pain and wasn't hard, then filming was halted; and he didn't have to get himself off later because his partner got him off during the sex. Fox had a list of things which were absolutely forbidden during his films and any other film made at the studio. Barebacking was an absolute no, as was coming on someone's face, one of the most derogatory things you could do to a person as far as Fox was concerned. While some group sex films were made at the studio, a group of men using one man for their pleasure was a no-no.

Fox believed in a story, dialogue and romance, not meaningless sex. He was derided for it, but with his bank balance he didn't much care. Working with a female director suited him just fine, and he appreciated the perspective she brought to the films.

He glanced over at Jamie again. Perhaps he could forgive him for almost writing his car off because just looking at his co-star made Fox hard. Jamie was a little shorter than him, about five-eleven, his body lean but toned. His face, unlike some porn stars, wasn't the let down of the package. His cheekbones were high, his jaw strong. He was beautiful all over too, Fox remembered that from watching his films. Jamie was immaculately waxed, his cock on the big side of average, as was to be expected.

Jamie studied him in turn, his expression cool. He obviously still harboured a grudge over Fox's anger in the parking lot, when it had been *his* fault. He stood up, and Fox was helpless not to move his gaze slowly up his body to linger on the package in his tight jeans.

"See you later," Jamie told Fox in a slightly condescending tone.

"Looking forward to it," Fox replied frostily. *More than you know.*

Fox's palms were damp. After having sent his fluffer away, much to the man's astonishment, Fox stalked the dressing room, the belt of his robe tied tight, holding his hard-on against his body.

It was a carefully kept secret that Fox had trouble getting an erection before a shoot, which wasn't as rare a problem in the industry as some might think. Put simply, Fox's co-stars didn't turn him on. The clinical environment of voyeurs and lights didn't do it for him. Sadly though, this tended to extend to real life. Fox couldn't remember the last time he'd had a satisfactory sexual encounter either on camera or off. He fucked faceless men whom he never called afterward and faceless actors who gave theatrical moans which left him cold.

Now here he was, minutes away from getting to grips with Jamie Warner, and he was hard as a rock and virtually panting with excitement. He tried to calm himself down. He'd only ever seen Jamie on top in movies. Who said he would be as sensual and arousing when he was getting fucked? Clearly he didn't do it often, so it might be a tight, uncomfortable fuck for them both rather than the warm butter Fox normally slid into. It might be long, frustrating foreplay followed by an aborted mission because Fox had defeated several inexperienced men in his time. He wasn't the sort of actor a virgin should pick for his first time.

He chastised himself for his thoughts. How could Jamie be a virgin? He was gay wasn't he, so he must have been fucked at some point, right? Not necessarily. And who said Jamie was gay? Fox had met gay porn stars in the past who preferred women and had only swapped genders because they hadn't been able to get the work.

It didn't matter. Fox was about to get to grips with Jamie Warner, the only man to get Fox's loins twitching in many a long year, and for that he was grateful. Never mind that the bastard had almost written his car off.

The film was called *Strangers in the Night*, no stealing of the famous film noir intended. Jamie's character, Philip, shows up one night at Fox's (Joe's) door. His car's broken down, he's wet through and Joe is instantly aroused. Charitably, he invites Philip to spend the night, offering him food, dry clothes and the spare bed. He doesn't know how he manages to control himself, but he does. It's different next morning though, when he encounters Philip in his kitchen, wearing nothing but his bath robe.

The first scene they were going to shoot was scene two in the kitchen. Martina never shot in order, preferring to wait until it rained for scene one, so she didn't have to go to the expense of creating rain herself. She would get the take; it was forecast for later in the week.

Fox paused to speak to Martina and then strode on set. Martina had given him a knowing look which meant the fluffer had told her Fox was towering and erect with no help from him at all. Martina better hold onto her panties, Fox thought, because he and Jamie were about to blow her away.

Jamie loitered in a white bathrobe by the sink, barefoot, his hair carefully tousled as though fresh from bed. He eyed Fox coolly.

I'll soon be wiping that look off your face. Fox scowled at him. Unbelievably, his cock was leaking against the soft material of his bath robe.

"Okay, positions," Martina called. Fox retreated to the edge of the set. Jamie turned his back, as though looking out of the window. "Scene two, take one, action."

Fox strode into the kitchen, the camera following him to focus on his face as Jamie turned around.

"Hey there, sleep well?" Fox's voice was soft. The blood pounded in his veins as he stepped closer.

"Hi, yeah, great thanks. Your bed's really comfy." Jamie smiled and dimples sunk deep around his mouth… and that was Fox lost to desire. *Christ.*

"That's good. And you found the coffee?" Fox gestured to a mug behind Jamie.

"Yeah, hope you don't mind."

Fox shook his head. Both actors allowed the uncomfortable silence to grow as dictated by the script. Fox counted to ten slowly in his head before he moved in for the kill.

He took Jamie firmly by the back of the neck and kissed him, and at the first touch of velvet lips on his, fireworks exploded behind his eyes. Oh God, he thought he was about to come just from the kiss. Jamie clung onto his neck, returning the kiss with passion, touching Fox's tongue with his own, pressing his erection against Fox's purposefully.

Fox panted for breath. Breaking the kiss, he looked down into Jamie's eyes for a moment. To his shock, he saw his own desire mirrored there. This was real. There was no acting for the camera. With a groan, he lifted Jamie onto the kitchen table and pulled open his bath robe.

Lounging there with thighs apart, cock hard against the belly of his exquisite body, Jamie stared up at Fox with an expression which told Fox all he needed to know.

Fox pushed the robe off Jamie's shoulders. He trailed his hands down Jamie's chiselled torso, then fondled his cock and balls a moment before he sank to his knees. Jamie groaned as Fox swallowed his cock, sucking smoothly and slowly, using plenty of saliva. The cock in his mouth made his own prick throb, and Fox parted his robe with one hand, making sure the camera could see him stroke himself.

He gave and received blowjobs equally. He wasn't the top who lay there getting blown for fifteen minutes and giving nothing in return. That wasn't his style at all. And besides, he didn't mind giving a blowjob. It made him hot.

He found Jamie's smoothly waxed balls, sucking each one into his mouth before he lifted them out of the way and tongued the soft skin behind them. Jamie shuddered, squirming on the table, his hand on Fox's head, playing with his hair.

"Move it to the living room," Martina said softly behind them. Fox did as he was told. He stood, discarded his robe, then lifted his partner off the table, legs around him as he carried Jamie out of the room.

A soft, roomy couch awaited them, and he lay his partner down gently, kneeling between his knees. Jamie sat up, giving Fox an eager kiss. Melting once more, Fox pushed Jamie back, attacking his neck with fervent kisses, moving down his torso greedily, sucking at nipples until they were wet and hard. All the while Jamie showed his appreciation, moaning and writhing beneath each kiss, his hands on Fox's shoulders and back, stroking and caressing and driving him out of his mind. He could hardly wait to be inside Jamie. He didn't know how he was going to last that long.

He settled back between Jamie's thighs and sucked his cock. He licked his balls and pushed Jamie's legs further apart so he could bury his tongue between his cheeks. Jamie groaned, fingers tangled in Fox's hair, and pushed himself into Fox's face.

Fox lifted his head. His partner was flushed, eyes bright and cock leaking as Fox licked the semen from the slit. Jamie swore under his breath. Fox reached for the lube conveniently placed down one cushion. With firm hands he turned Jamie over onto all fours and spread him open, letting the camera see what delights awaited Fox. He almost moaned at the sight of the tight, little, hairless hole and hoped, yet again, that he didn't hurt his partner.

Jamie squirmed under his hands, almost squealing as cold lube hit him. Massaging it in firmly, Fox penetrated him with one finger. Pushed back wantonly against Fox's finger, Jamie's breath caught. Martina moved her camera around to capture the action of Fox's finger-fucking.

He rolled his condom on one handed while he pushed two fingers into Jamie. Below him Jamie sounded like the porn star he was. It was enough to almost make Fox blow his load.

He leaned forward and whispered in Jamie's ear for him to turn over. Martina hadn't discussed which position she wanted Fox to take Jamie in first, but only the missionary would satisfy Fox right now. He wanted to see his lover's beautiful face as he made him come.

Jamie settled onto his back, knees up and open. Fox knelt there, holding his cock. He bent his head to once more tongue Jamie's cock and then he nestled between Jamie's cheeks, pushing.

Jamie lifted his legs, wrapping them around Fox's back and Fox slid right in, smooth and slick.

Oh God. He sat still a moment in bliss, gripping Jamie's hips. Below him, Jamie panted in clear excitement, his cock twitching against his belly. Fox was sure Jamie was long enough to suck while he was fucking him. Nestled within Jamie, he leaned down and sucked the head of his cock into his mouth.

Jamie cried out in excitement. He pushed his hips forward, fucking Fox's mouth and then fucking himself on Fox's cock.

"That's hot," Martina whispered from nearby. "Suck him some more, Fox."

Fox did as he was told. He sucked and sucked and fondled Jamie's balls, keeping his cock buried to the hilt, loving the way Jamie pushed against him.

Jamie was close, Fox realised, and he stopped sucking him. Instead he leaned forward and started to fuck his partner. Jamie hissed beneath him. He clung to Fox with both arms and legs, arching up, undulating with each thrust.

Fox moaned helplessly. He kissed Jamie, and his fellow actor responded eagerly. They kissed, mouths never breaking as they fucked. Fox gave his co-stars their fair share of kisses. After all, romance was the point of RoMANce studios. He didn't like porn without kissing, it was cold and clinical. He wanted two men to show that they actually *liked* each other while they were fucking. That said, if he wasn't attracted to his co-star, he didn't kiss him too much, just as much as duty dictated.

But this was different. He wanted to keep his lips on Jamie's until they both came—together if he could possibly manufacture that.

He felt his partner shuddering, squirming under him, nails digging into his back. God, Jamie was close again and Fox was too. In fact, too close. It rushed upon him all of a sudden.

He groaned, coming to a complete stop. He lay down on Jamie with gasps for breath, eyes squeezed shut.

"What's the matter?" Jamie moaned beneath him in clear disappointment.

"What are you doing?" Martina demanded by their side. "Cut!"

Fox lifted his head. "I'm going to come. Just give me a minute."

"Jesus, what's wrong with you, minute man?" Martina asked scornfully.

Fox glared at her as she stalked away. *Jamie* was what was wrong with Fox. Usually he went all night or however long his director wanted him to go, coming on demand. Not today. His body wanted its due. It wanted to worship at Jamie's altar.

He looked down at a flushed Jamie, their gazes meeting intensely.

"Right, take a break," snapped Martina across the set. "Have a cold shower or whatever the fuck you do to calm yourself down. I want you back here in twenty with your dick hard and ready to go all night, got it?"

Fox scowled. He knelt back on his heels and made to withdraw himself, finding Jamie clamped tight around him. He looked down at his partner. "Come on," he said in an undertone. "Let me out."

"I'm trying." Jamie's face screwed up with concentration.

"Try harder."

"I am. Fuck." Jamie groaned. That groan shot straight to Fox's cock, caught in a vice.

"Let me out or I'm going to fucking come," Fox growled.

Jamie took some panting breaths, resting his hands on Fox's hips. A shudder swept down Fox's spine, and suddenly it was too late.

He couldn't fight it, his body took over. He fell back over Jamie and pumped into him three times, desperate and lost. Jamie cried out, one hand clutching the back of Fox's head, his muscles furiously clenching around Fox.

Fox moaned out his pleasure as he came, collapsing on his partner. Jamie's thighs tightened, holding him hard, and he continued to spasm around Fox.

Fox pressed his mouth to his partner's neck, kissing in adoration, senses lost. Behind him came a frustrated shout.

"What the fuck? Do not tell me you just came,

Fox!"

Fox ignored his director. He was concentrating more on the trembling body below him, the soft moans that heaved the chest beneath him. Christ, Jamie was right on the edge. Fox thrust a hand between them, feeling for Jamie's cock.

"What are you doing?" screamed Martina. "Get up right now! Do *not* get him off!"

Fox turned his head, glaring at Martina while his fingers still caressed Jamie's leaking cock.

"What do you think this is?" Martina slapped him on the shoulder. "In case you don't realise, you're getting paid for this! You don't waste my time and money getting off and getting him off when the camera isn't even fucking rolling! If you want to fuck him off camera, you do that on your own fucking time not mine!" She was livid with rage, her face red.

"Fuck off," Fox told her and slipped from his lover, climbing from the bed, pulling off his condom.

"Asshole!" screeched Martina as Fox yanked his robe on and walked off set. As he went, he turned back to look at Jamie who lay there motionless as though dazed, cock rigid against his belly. Their eyes met, and Fox's cock, unbelievably, started to stiffen again. *Christ*.

He hurried for his dressing room. *God, what had just happened?* He wanted to run back to the set and swallow Jamie whole, milking his glorious cock until Jamie had the orgasm he deserved. He felt bad for leaving his co-star high and dry. He felt bad for his own lack of control.

He climbed into an icy shower and scrubbed himself with shower gel and sponge, reliving every short moment of his tussle with Jamie. When he got out, he was towering once more and desperate for round two.

Fox walked right into a lecture from Martina. She took him to one side of the bedroom set and laid the law down.

"I get that you're hot for him, that much was obvious as soon as you both met and it's what I hoped for when I hired him, but Jesus, play by the rules, Fox! I say cut and take a break and I mean it. I don't mean carry on and fucking come and ruin the first come shot! I don't mean try to get him off when the cameras aren't even rolling."

Fox glared at her. "You know what, Martina? Just leave the cameras rolling and leave me and him in here all afternoon and we'll give you something to fucking cream yourself with over and over."

Martina smiled coldly. "You and him can have your private time after this movie's finished. For now, we're all watching you."

Fox rolled his eyes. Martina caught his arm as he made to stalk away. "And I mean after the movie's finished, Fox. I don't want you two fucking off camera during this movie and emptying your fucking balls."

"Yeah whatever," Fox said because he hadn't seriously considered fucking Jamie off camera yet. He expected to be so satisfied by the end of today that he wouldn't be able to pop a boner for the next twenty-four hours.

"All right, we're moving into the bedroom. Jamie, on your back please. Fox, between his legs, sucking his cock.

Jamie walked onto the set, tossed his robe off and lay down, legs spread, cock hard. Fox shuddered in anticipation. Christ, was he actually getting *paid* for this? If there was a better job in the world right now, he didn't know what it was.

He threw his robe over a chair and climbed onto the bed. Leaning down, he kissed Jamie softly. Jamie's arms curved around his back, pulling Fox down onto him. They rolled across the bed, kissing passionately. They were supposed to have started at a blowjob, but Fox didn't much care. He just wanted to kiss and kiss until neither of them could take anymore. The script was out of the window. He wanted to make love to Jamie as though he belonged to Fox, even if it was temporary.

Beneath him Jamie panted for breath, hands gripping flesh hard, muscle and skin undulating like sleek rivers. Oh God, Fox was going to lose it again. Jamie was exquisite. Divine. God-made flesh. He kissed him harder and harder and they worked each other and themselves up into fever pitch, the kiss lasting for what seemed like hours.

"The blowjob," Martina said irritably. "The fucking blowjob or do you two want to just get a room and fuck the film?"

Yeah, that was pretty much what Fox wanted to do. Get a room and fuck Jamie until this desire was sated once and for all. He didn't see how it could ever be. It was like Jamie was made to fit him. He lifted his head, looking down at Jamie below him. Their gazes caught and held with powerful intensity, Jamie's pupils huge, his eyes almost black with lust. Slowly, he smiled at Fox almost shyly. Fox returned it, something huge and warm blossoming in his chest. Jesus, he didn't know what love was, but he could have sworn he was looking at it right now.

He kissed Jamie hard. Then he slid down his body, kissing every inch. Trembling beneath him, Jamie moaned, gripping the sheets and hissing as Fox sucked Jamie's cock into his mouth. The feel of Jamie's hard flesh made his own cock throb. He put his hand down to stroke himself and groaned around Jamie's erection.

"That's nice," Martina said appreciatively. "That's very fucking nice."

Fox moved to Jamie's balls, tonguing, sucking, playing with them in his hand, lifting them to lick behind them.

Jamie writhed and spread his legs wider, giving the camera a nice shot of the treasure. Fox stroked the tight little hole for the viewers, tickled and teased, probed and rubbed. Wetting his finger, he brought it back, slid it inside and fucked Jamie with it. Jamie arched off the bed with a loud moan, grabbing at Fox's hair and pushing him back to his dick.

Fox did as he was told and went back to blowing Jamie while fingering him. He hated to see the bottom doing all the work. Not in his films.

And besides he would have done anything Jamie wanted at that moment. Anything.

He sat back, reached for the handily placed condom and rolled it on. He lubed it up and rubbed some lube over Jamie's entrance. Rising to his knees, Jamie kissed Fox while manoeuvring him around until Fox was on his back and Jamie was astride him but facing away, a favourite porn position. The camera could see what was going on just perfectly. It was the position the script had asked for.

It was fine with Fox, but he wanted a little more intimacy with his partner. Moving Jamie with him, he slid up so he sat against the headboard, and then he held his shaft steady as Jamie sank down on him.

Oh God, Fox was going to blow his load again in record time. He groaned loudly, arms around Jamie's waist and clinging to him, chin on his shoulder. Meanwhile, moaning softly, Jamie rode him enthusiastically, using his hands on the bed to aid his movements.

His back slid damply against Fox's torso. With a moan, he leaned back, letting Fox take over the work, throat exposed so Fox could sink his face into his neck and kiss desperately. He looked down at Jamie's bouncing cock and balls. His hand cupped them and he stroked, feeling how Jamie shivered against him.

Fox forced his climax back, wanting the perfect shot of Jamie coming while he was getting fucked. There was nothing Fox liked more in his films than to capture the bottom partner in ecstasy, coming with a cock buried in him.

He put his mouth to Jamie's ear. "Good?" he whispered.

"Oh God, yes," Jamie moaned, loud enough to be picked up by the cameras, but the words were appropriate and Martina murmured something in satisfaction, zooming in on Jamie's flushed face.

"Are you going to come for me?"

"Yes... yes..."

Jamie sagged back as though exhausted, breathing loudly. Thrusting up into him, Fox held Jamie tight with one arm while jerking him off with his free hand. He saw them reflected on one of the monitors, his cock firmly embedded between Jamie's spread legs, the pleasure on Jamie's face.

He bit Jamie on the neck, shuddering, his pleasure so great that Fox was afraid when he did come, he would pass out.

Jamie cried out. He arched back into Fox, Jamie's cock swelling ever harder in his hand, and Fox felt his own prick clenched in undulating waves as Jamie came, spurting upwards onto his own chest and belly, covering Fox's hand in copious white cream. Oh God, it was poetic. Fox thought about watching this scene again later, and it tipped him over the edge.

He clung to Jamie as he came, breath in loud pants, body contorting, straining, bucking up. Fox buried himself over and over as the orgasm rolled through him, scattering his senses, wiping him out.

He slumped back against the headboard, gasping, holding onto Jamie hard.

Fox and Martina didn't have rules about the evidence of the top coming. Fox hated the tradition of the top withdrawing before orgasm and jerking off over his partner. Let the evidence of his face and his moans be enough. Fox couldn't fake it if he tried, nor would he want to. Often he pulled out shortly after and stripped his condom off, so the camera could see the semen in it. His partner might touch his still hard cock, coax the remaining drops from it, taste it. He didn't need to jerk off over anyone. It was offensive.

"That was quicker than expected guys," Martina said disapprovingly as Jamie climbed tiredly from Fox's lap. "We'll keep rolling though if you want to kiss and touch a bit."

Fox very much wanted to kiss and touch a bit. Jamie turned around and lay himself down on Fox's body, one leg over him, backside spread for the camera and his half-hard cock visible between his legs.

Fox put an arm around him and kissed him. With his other hand he removed his condom and fondled his cock a little, the wet head still leaking. Jamie reached behind him and placed his own hand over Fox's, stroking. Fox took his hand away and let Jamie play with him.

Soon Jamie slid down his body and took Fox in his mouth. He was sensitive, and he squirmed a bit but found himself growing instantly back to full hardness. This was unheard of for him. He usually needed twenty minutes and a fluffer to be ready again.

"If you want to go again, we can do this as one long take," Martina said. Going from one scene to another continuously never happened on set. Actors needed time to recover and clean up. Fox needed nothing more than Jamie now though. Again.

He gripped Jamie under the arms and pulled him up his body. Fox slid down so his head was on the pillow and then he manoeuvred Jamie's knees over his shoulders. With Jamie on his face, he sucked his cock down.

Jamie moaned softly, pushing forward, and Fox, with lips wide open, let Jamie slowly fuck his mouth. Oh, it was good. Fox liked a man on his face providing that man didn't try to choke him, and Jamie was gentle and considerate about it. Jamie soon moved into a more mutually beneficial position though, and Fox's pulse rocketed with excitement as Jamie turned around, straddled Fox's head and bent down over him to suck his cock.

Now *this* was one of his favourite positions. Having access not just to a man's cock, but his balls and his ass too, *and* getting his own cock sucked. It didn't get much better than this. Fox sucked and licked at Jamie's dangling balls. His finger probed Jamie's still wet asshole. God, he wanted to be back inside that gloriously tight cavern He wanted to fuck Jamie until neither of them could take anymore.

He gripped Jamie's buttocks and pulled him right onto his face, thrusting his tongue inside.

Jamie groaned around his cock, sucking furiously, a hand squeezing Fox's balls. It was all too much. It was only minutes before Fox groped for Jamie's head and pushed him away as he came. Jamie grabbed his cock. He milked Fox until he was done, then he sank down on him once again and sucked the remains from him.

Fox breathlessly sank back onto the bed, gasping for air. Then he grabbed Jamie's ripe ass again and continued his job, tongue wetting, licking, burrowing. Jamie came soon enough, Fox's hand around his cock, semen spurting over Fox's chest.

Jamie collapsed forward. His mouth pressed gentle kisses to the inside of Fox's thigh.

"Come here."

Jamie turned around at Fox's prompting. He slotted himself into Fox's arms and lay with his head against his shoulder, motionless.

Fox looked over his shoulder at Martina. "Cut," said the director. The crew started to disperse. Fox and Jamie remained where they were, almost comatose.

"My office five minutes, Fox," were Martina's departing words.

Fox sighed.

"What've you done?" Jamie asked against his shoulder.

Fox tightened his arms around him, stroking his

back. "Come in about five minutes every time," he said dryly. "This isn't like me. Usually I'm at it until my partner can't take anymore."

Jamie laughed softly. "I don't mind. Suits me just fine." He lifted his head and their eyes met.

"Yeah well, it's going to do me out of a job," Fox said gruffly. "If you weren't so hot..."

"So it's my fault?"

"Yeah." Fox disentangled himself from Jamie and sat up, looking around for his robe. Even now his dick was half-hard. He knew without doubt he could go again.

"I'm sorry." Jamie sounded contrite, but when Fox turned around, his partner was smirking, lounging against the bed with knees open and such a wanton look on his face that it was all Fox could do not to pin him down and fuck him to death.

"You're not sorry. You're enjoying my misfortune. We can't go on this way. The film's going to last about fifteen minutes if I don't get my act together."

Jamie's face became more serious. "So what do you suggest?"

Fox bit his lip. He got up, pulled his robe on and tied it. "I think we should call it a day. Get your part recast with someone else."

"What?" Jamie sat up, his face flushing in anger. "Are you fucking serious?"

"Yeah."

Jamie got off the bed, pulling his robe on furiously. "Asshole," he spat.

Fox sighed. He turned away.

"You fucking prick. Just because you can't handle your attraction to me doesn't mean I should get the fucking can. Dickwad!" Jamie stalked off the set and down the corridor. A moment later, his dressing room door slammed.

Great. Just fucking great.

"So," Martina said when Fox took a seat in front of him. "You two are the hottest couple I've ever seen. Even just seeing you kiss makes me wet."

Fox folded his arms and regarded her stonily. "So what's the problem?"

"You know what the problem is. You're desperate for each other. The level of passion is too much. You're coming as soon as you touch each other."

Fox bit his lip. He looked at the floor. "I told Jamie we should call it a day. Recast him."

Martina sighed. "I don't know, Fox. We'd be throwing away footage that's one of a kind. I've never seen you fuck anyone like it actually means something to you."

Fox stood up. "Pay him whatever he wants. Cancel his contract and recast him. Give me a call when we're ready to go again." He walked out of the office.

Heading for his dressing room, he took his bag and car keys and left the studio. Out in the car park, he saw Jamie getting into his car.

For a moment their gazes met before Fox climbed into his car, started the engine and pulled out of his space. He couldn't believe he'd just thrown away the most amazing man he'd ever met.

That night was hard in every sense of the word. Fox lay tossing and turning in bed with his cock hard as rock, refusing to jerk off over Jamie. What had he done? He could have guaranteed himself another week of fucking

Jamie three times a day until he had the man out of his system, and instead he was gone. But wasn't it something more than that? Damned right it was. Jamie was under his skin, and he'd known him less than a day. But Fox *wanted* to know him. He wanted to know him in every single sense of the word, inside and out. He had never been smitten like this in his life. Jesus, what was he going to do? Jamie wasn't someone he could just forget.

It was one in the morning in a never ending night when a knock came at the door. Heart in his mouth, Fox went downstairs in his boxers. The shape through the frosted glass door looked familiar. Fox swung the heavy door open.

"Hey." Jamie looked unsure and nervous. "Look... I'm sorry about today. I overreacted. And I'm sorry about your car." His face was earnest, anxious.

Fox smiled slowly as his insides lit with warmth, and he swore his heart surged with glee. "You'd better come in."

Kicking his shoes off on the mat, Jamie followed Fox through to the kitchen.

"Want a beer?"

"Sure."

As he took two bottles out and opened them, Fox was more than well aware of Jamie's eyes on his ass, on the bulge in his boxers neatly profiled. Even flaccid Fox packed shorts to overflowing, and right about now, Jamie's proximity was causing severe overcrowding.

He handed Jamie the bottle. Their gazes met as they drank.

"I didn't want to get fired, Fox. There's got to be

some other way." Jamie smiled a hesitant, almost shy smile. Not the porn star smile captured on camera at all. There were hidden depths to this man. "I was enjoying myself."

Fox put his bottle down. He turned away from Jamie with a sigh. "Fuck. I know." He almost shivered with need. Strong fingers closed around his bare neck, causing Fox to shiver with need. With a moan, Fox turned into Jamie's arms.

Jamie's kiss seared his mouth just like that first time. Jamie held him tight, backing him up against the fridge, pinning him there.

Fox felt deliciously dominated, an unfamiliar feeling. He wanted to give in to whatever Jamie wanted to do to him.

Jamie lifted Fox's arms above his head and held him against the fridge by his wrists. Fox nearly gasped with excitement.

Jamie, flame eyes almost black with lust, spoke. "I want to fuck you. Are you going to let me?"

Fox's cock twitched. His ass ached with need. He hadn't been fucked in years. Most partners knew better than to ask. But most partners weren't Jamie. He swallowed, nodding hesitantly.

Jamie dragged him away from the fridge. He threw Fox face down over the kitchen table and yanked his boxers down. Fox stepped out of them obediently and glanced over his shoulder to see Jamie unfastening himself, freeing his cock.

Fox groaned. He bent further forward, deliberately spreading his legs.

Jamie drew in his breath. A wet finger sought Fox's

entrance, rubbing, spearing him, making him curse.

"Wider." Jamie kicked his ankles further apart.

Fox did as he was told, presenting himself. He breathed heavily, face against the table, so excited he didn't know how he could control himself.

"Now," Jamie said. "Let's make our very own porn film. Just for us." He took his phone out and propped it up on the table in front of Fox.

Fox stared into the lens. A condom packet floated onto the table. Cold liquid between his cheeks made him jump. Hard flesh pressed against him, and Fox cried out in ecstasy as Jamie entered him.

"Fuck." Hands gripped Fox's hips. A tongue licked the sweat from his back. "You feel so good."

Fox pushed back with a moan. "Fuck me."

"My pleasure."

Jamie took him masterfully, just like Fox had seen him do a dozen times on screen. But nothing could have prepared him for Jamie. The way he fucked Fox almost out of his mind, dragging him up off the table, holding him close and jerking him off while he rocked into him.

Fox was helpless putty. Jamie pushed him back down, and Fox writhed on the table as Jamie fucked him harder and faster, each thrust sending shudders of white-hot pleasure through his body.

"Oh God, Jamie, fuck... please... please..." Fox was out of control. He begged for more. He begged for Jamie never to stop, to make him come, to fuck him harder and harder and harder.

And Jamie's hand jerked him faster and faster with each thrust until Fox exploded. He cried out in his pleasure, showering the table, bucking against Jamie, incoherent words spilling from his lips.

He fell forward onto the table, groaning as Jamie's hands tightened on him and his lover used Fox's prone body for a few more strokes before he came.

Gasping and groaning were the only sounds for several minutes.

"Fox?"

"What?"

"Did you just say you loved me?"

Fox lifted his head. "No."

"I think you did."

"I didn't!"

"What did you say then?"

"I... don't know." Fox squeezed his eyes shut in mortification. He was still hard. Already he was thinking of round two.

Jamie laughed softly. He drew himself free. Straightening up off the table with difficulty, Fox located his boxers.

Jamie threw his condom into the trash and fastened himself up. He washed his hands at the sink and then retrieved his phone.

Fox flushed as Jamie played the video back and their moans filled the air. "Oh God," Jamie said. "I can see my cock going into your ass. I'm going to jerk off to this until my dick falls off."

Fox smiled. "Send me a copy."

"I will." Jamie took a drink of his beer and pocketed his phone. The two stood looking at each other. Jamie looked unsure now. "Well... I should go."

"I don't think so," Fox said.

"What?"

"I haven't finished with you."

Jamie raised one eyebrow. "Haven't you?"

"No. I want to handcuff you to my bed and rim your tight ass until you come everywhere. Have you any objections to that?"

Jamie gulped. "No."

"Good boy. Get upstairs."

Jamie smiled. He took his beer and walked out of the kitchen. Fox followed him up, watching his ass. He wasn't thinking about the film anymore. Whoever replaced Jamie in the lead didn't matter because Fox had the real life man in his bed, no pretence, no voyeurs. Just him and Jamie.

He hoped it would never end.

They made it to the bedroom and Jamie put an arm around his neck and kissed him. "I think I love you too, Fox." He grinned crookedly.

"The beer's gone to your head."

"No, *you've* gone to my head." Jamie unfastened his jeans.

Fox sank to his knees in worship.

THIS WAVE ALWAYS BREAKS

I lost the love of my life when I was twenty-one. I looked around for quite a while in an attempt to replace him. For that, read, *screwed* around, because that's what I did. Then I came to accept that no one would replace him. I'd had my one chance and blown it.

Now I live quietly alone, in virtual celibacy, going to work, coming home, spending far too long on the internet, keeping a few people close and holding all the rest at arms' length. I have accepted my lot, and I know this is how it will be for the rest of my life. I don't even mind any more. Once I was bitter and resentful when I saw my friends married or living with their soulmates and I wondered what was wrong with me that I didn't get that too. Now I don't think about that, I just concentrate on getting through one day at a time in a life that I know deep down will not be very long. I don't know how I know that, but at nearly thirty-seven, I feel like I'm already winding down.

Little do I know as I arrive for work that Monday morning, that the worst day of my life is about to be thrust upon me.

I work for Tim. He owns a chain of shops in Orange County called *Beauty Without The Beast*. Kind of self-explanatory—lotions and potions and make-up without animal testing or ingredients. He's been my best friend for ten years now. He accepts my foibles and my reclusiveness, and he doesn't try to change me. There's never been anything sexual between us even though he's hot and as bent as I am. He has been with Blake for five years. Blake is jealous of me and I have no idea why.

I'm drinking my coffee when Tim arrives. He smiles, far too cheerfully for eight-thirty in the morning, on a Monday fucking morning of all things. I am surly and withdrawn until at least ten, which he has come to expect. He takes his briefcase and laptop into the back and then he comes out, rubbing his hands, looking around in pleasure, like he expects something to have changed in the immaculate displays of body butter and elaborate pyramids of soap.

I eye him in irritation and then go back to putting the float in the till.

"He's not here then?"

I look up at him from my stool behind the counter. "Who?"

Tim has spiky white-blond hair and a nose-ring. His eyes are the colour of a stormy sky. He's beautiful. It's probably a crime that I've never fucked him. There must be something wrong with me that I don't want him.

"Daron," Tim says.

I stare at him a moment. That name still makes me shudder even now. Like there's only one Daron in the fucking world. And there may as well be.

"What?" I ask stupidly.

"Daron." Tim's impatient now. "The new assistant manager."

"Oh, right. No, he's not here."

"I can fucking see that."

"Then why did you ask?"

He stares at me blankly for a moment before turning on his heel and stalking into the back.

I shake my head and slam the till shut. I move from

my seat and traverse the length of the shop. I reach the door, my hand on the sign to flip it around to open, just as a figure looms up on the other side and I find myself face to face with my past.

I recoil in horror with a gasp, my heart lurching so hard within my chest that I instantly feel vomit rising into my throat. I put my hand out to clutch onto something and only succeed in knocking down a display. A cascade of body scrubs and shampoo clatter to the ground.

My legs are like rubber and don't seem able to support my weight, and I'm trembling violently all over.

He stands on the other side of the glass motionlessly and stares back at me. He's hardly aged. His dark hair is cut shorter and more severely than I remember, those eyes of the darkest chocolate exactly the same as I remember in my dreams. He looks just as shocked as I am. I can't move. I'm torn between vomiting and fainting, whichever might come first.

"What the fuck?" asks a voice behind me. "You clumsy fuck, Karl."

I'm galvanised suddenly into action. I whirl around, slamming directly into Tim, pushing him aside and running for sanctuary like a man possessed. Once locked into the bathroom, I fall to my knees and vomit, sobbing out fifteen years of anguish as I do.

I'm sitting on the floor shaking, with my head in my hands when the outer door opens. "Karl," Tim says cautiously outside my cubicle.

I don't reply.

"Shit, I didn't know. How was I supposed to know it was *that* Daron? I'm sorry."

In the silence he gives a sigh. "I can't fire him, Karl. He told me he still wants the job. You're going to have to come out here and face him."

I give an involuntary groan of terror.

"Fuck," Tim says. "Open the door."

I climb unsteadily to my feet and do as I'm told. As I step out, he enfolds me hard in his arms. "I'm fucking sorry. I wouldn't have done this to you for all the world."

I cling to him a moment, eyes closed, praying for the courage to face my worst nightmare. When he moves back, I go to the sink and splash some water on my face, swilling my mouth out.

"I can let you go home," Tim says quietly behind me. "I'll run the shop today."

I look at him in the mirror. "And let him think that I'm a coward? And that I give a fuck? I don't think so."

When we go back into the main area, Daron is standing looking at a display of men's products, holding a moisturiser in one hand and sniffing with that button nose of his. "That's for combination skin," I tell him stiffly. "You would be better with the normal to dry." Like I've ever forgotten the feel of his skin for one moment.

He turns to me and reddens as our eyes meet and I redden too, and it's like some sort of competition to see who can turn the most crimson, and I imagine I win hands down.

Tim coughs. "Come and put your stuff in the back, Daron, and get a coffee."

Daron follows him, glancing back at me as he reaches the door, those dark eyes of his solemn.

I look towards the exit. I have the urge to charge

from the shop and keep running, until I'm so far away I can never be found again. I don't want to be brave. I don't want to stay here and face my demons. I just want to curl up into a ball and weep until there are no more tears left.

It was three weeks before Daron and I slept together after we became an item. When he moved into me, I felt complete. I lay beneath him, not in submission but as an equal partner, my legs around him, my hands clutching at his back, feeling the taut muscles beneath the satin soft skin.

When we made love, it seemed to be something beyond sex. Something which transcended the physical act, like our souls joined. Like we had been made for each other before we were even born. Obviously Daron thought differently because he found it easy to dump me after a mere three months, when I was head over heels in love with him, sunk so deep into him that I wasn't sure where he began and I ended.

He didn't give me a reason. He did it by letter, and then he moved away.

I slink back to the counter and retrieve my coffee, putting it to my lips with a trembling hand and sipping. I sit down and bow my head over a catalogue, a pen in one hand, pretending to be busy as Tim and Daron return.

They walk around the shop, Tim leading, commenting on products, giving Daron a thorough talk on each one. I bite my lip and stab the page with my Biro over and over again, wishing it was those chocolate eyes.

"Okay, I have to go," Tim says suddenly.

My head snaps up, and I stare at him in horror, panic-stricken.

"Karl, I was supposed to be in Long Beach ten

fucking minutes ago."

My eyes silently plead with him not to go.

He shrugs and goes into the back room for his briefcase. "I'll be back later." He looks a little shame-faced as he nods to Daron and hotfoots it from the shop.

My gaze moves to Daron, who stands there like some sort of rabbit caught in the headlights, looking as terrified as me. Hang on a moment. I'm his boss. I can make his life so miserable that he'll leave within the week. It will be my ultimate revenge on the man who ruined mine.

"Has Tim shown you the stock room?" I ask coldly.

He nods warily.

"It needs tidying. Get to it."

He regards me a moment confrontationally. Daron never liked taking orders from anyone—except in bed, which he quite enjoyed—and it doesn't look much like that has changed.

I hold the eye contact while a thousand memories overwhelm me. He's the first to break it, turning to walk away, with a short shake of his head and a sigh.

I slump back onto my stool and let my head fall onto the desk. I fight not to weep because the shop is open and any moment the first customer will be walking in.

The bell rings. And there they are. I lift my head, a smile on my face.

The stock room is a mess. Tim doesn't complain about it to me because he knows that there's method in my madness. I know that Daron will be in there until at least lunch-time and then maybe I can send him out for a two-hour break. In fact, send him home if Tim isn't around and the shop is quiet.

Unfortunately the shop doesn't stay quiet, because it's a Monday. Daron should really be out here mingling with customers and generally helping out while I serve but I would rather struggle and bust my balls than call him out here, even if his dazzling smile would charm the fucking birds out of the trees.

It's an hour and a half later when the shop is momentarily empty and I look fearfully towards the back, listening to the sounds of boxes being moved. I want to use the restroom, but I'm scared to even move past the stock room to reach it. Then the bell rings again, and I turn to see a familiar customer.

Cameron, of course. I should have known.

Tim calls Cameron my stalker, much to my embarrassment. He comes into the shop once a week and always buys something, sometimes from the women's range, sometimes from the men's. Usually it's only one thing and yet it often takes him half an hour to choose this. Tim jokes and says Cameron probably has enough of our stock at home to open up his own branch of *Beauty Without The Beast*. He knows Cameron's name because Tim always chats to him whenever he's in the shop. Often he's invited him to stay for coffee, clearly mocking me when asking Cameron about himself and indiscreetly mentioning my availability.

But Cameron has never hit on me once and he's been coming here six months, so Tim has it all wrong. It's more likely that Cameron comes for Tim himself, not me. Cameron hardly speaks to me at all, just hands cash over and mutters thanks as I give him change and his bag, keeping his eyes lowered as he leaves the shop, suddenly in a hurry after spending half an hour browsing.

Tim says he's still gathering the balls to ask me out. Cameron has a body like some sort of Greek god. He's over six feet tall and he ripples with muscle. He's most peoples' wet dream come true, and I would be lying if I said I hadn't jerked off over him a few needy times. His hair is dark and cut very short, and his eyes are a pale blue. He has a smile which could blind you if you were unprepared.

My face heats at my thoughts as he nods to me and moves to the men's section. I study his ass for a moment in his jeans and then dip my head back to my catalogue. His ass is something people should write poetry about.

His nervous voice brings me from my reverie. "Hey, er..."

I look up. "Yes?"

"Do you have any more of this aftershave balm?" He points to an empty spot on the shelf.

I realise I've been too much in a lather over Daron that morning to stock up properly, and I'm momentarily disappointed in myself. I nod and quickly move from behind the counter. As I reach the entrance to the back, my footsteps slow. Wait a moment. I stop and look back at Cameron, who's still in the same place, studying the products like he doesn't know them like the back of his fucking hand.

I'm suspicious. He's a shoplifter. That's why he comes here once a week. It's nothing to do with me or Tim. He's a kleptomaniac who's been stealing from us on a regular basis. But I've never caught him. He looks up questioningly when he catches me staring, and I duck quickly into the back, moving down the corridor to the stock room. Wouldn't I have noticed him stealing by now? No matter. If I did catch him red-handed, would I seriously tackle this brute of a man? No, I fucking wouldn't. I would tell him to take all Tim's stock and just leave me with my face intact, thank you very much.

My thoughts are suddenly replaced as I reach the open stock room door. My anguish returns full force as Daron turns to face me from his position at the back. I stand there a moment as the hurt washes over me once more, that familiar, once-beloved face watching mine. Often I would imagine Daron was dead. I knew it would be easier that way. My grief would be bearable by now if that was the case, instead of this limbo I find myself in, still not knowing why he did what he did when I thought we were soulmates.

After several seconds standing there staring at each other, I say quickly, "I want some aftershave balm. The aloe and chamomile."

He ignores me and instead starts forward. "Karl," he says, his voice soft and his eyes so impossibly tender that confused tears burn my eyes.

This is not how it's supposed to go. I glare at him and instead of running away from the danger, I plough headlong into it. I know where the men's stuff is kept and I veer past him to the back, plunging my hand into a box, grabbing a bagful of bottles, dragging them out and turning around only to find he's right behind me, my exit cut off.

"Karl," he says again.

"I don't want to listen to anything you have to say!" I almost scream, my composure gone completely.

He shakes his head, and to my horror, reaches out a hand as though he would touch my face. I slap it away viciously and shove him back. As I stalk past him, he grabs my arm and pulls me back.

I fight furiously with him, struggling, lashing out with fists, yelling, but even he knows as well as I do that it's half-hearted. I fall against a shelf and a cascade of products rain down as I sob.

"Why did you do it? Just tell me fucking *why*! That's all I want to know."

His eyes are gleaming. They're intent on mine as he moves forward, so I'm virtually pinned to the shelf. "I was unfaithful to you," he says in a low voice.

I stare at him with heart hammering and tears streaking my cheeks. "What do you mean? You fucked someone else?"

He shakes his head. "I kissed someone."

"What? You kissed someone?"

"Yes."

"A-And, and..." I stammer over my words, "And you put me through this because... you *kissed* someone?" I'm not sure I can even understand. I'm sure I'll wake up from this nightmare very soon.

"Karl." He moves closer so his body is against mine, and he very slowly and gently cups my face. I tremble, unable to push him away this time. "How could you trust me when I couldn't even trust myself?"

A wave of such anger runs through me that for a moment I'm sure I'll lose it, take the nearest heavy object and bludgeon him to death with it. Something like a wail escapes me. My fist collides with his chest and clutches hard to him, almost ripping his shirt from his body.

His hand moves to the back of my neck and tightens on it. I smell his still-familiar scent and feel the warmth of his much loved body as he bends towards me, and I stare up in fright as he kisses me.

His lips sear me. I remember this kiss like it was yesterday. I remember the lovemaking it would lead to. I remember never having another kiss like this since. I whimper with need against his mouth, and he only kisses me harder, holding me tight, his tongue seeking mine, finding it, caressing it, claiming it.

The kiss deepens, so my hands go around his back, touching, feeling, seeking, pulling him closer, so he pushes me firmly into the shelf, body pressed hard against mine. I moan, the electricity between us exactly as it always was. My eyes flutter open to look at him as the kiss breaks momentarily and I see a flash of metal on the hand holding my cheek.

Oh my God, he's married. On his left hand he wears a band of some silvery colour, something which tells me he now belongs to another, the way he once briefly belonged to me. Or so I thought.

I shove him away, meaning it this time so he doesn't try to fight me again. I stalk from the store room with him calling me back and move quickly down the corridor on trembling legs, wiping the tears from my face. Only as I reach the shop do I remember Cameron is still there waiting patiently.

He's just moving away from the counter and when he sees me, he reddens a little. I'm too distraught to care that maybe he's had his fingers in the till. "There's no more aftershave balm," I say tonelessly.

"Are you okay?"

I move back behind the counter as though it's my shield from the outside world and look at him, taken aback by the concern in his voice. I realise then that this man would probably go beat Daron senseless if I wanted him to.

I nod, gulping down tears.

"I heard shouting out back. Is Tim there?"

"No. We have a new guy." I lower my head, hands braced on the counter because I'm about to start sobbing. "If there's nothing else," I add pointedly, making it clear I want him to leave.

There's silence. "Sorry," Cameron says quietly, like he really has anything to apologise for, and I hear his footsteps moving towards the door. The bell rings, the door closes and I sink onto my stool and weep.

I try my hardest to do it quietly in case Daron comes out of the back. I wouldn't give him the satisfaction of hearing or seeing this. I put my hand over my eyes and cry like it's that moment all over again, when I received that letter and my heart was buried in the ground for all time. I scrabble for a tissue in the drawer, doing my best to stop, knowing a customer could walk in at any moment, only wanting to give full vent to my agony until it's all purged and I'm drained.

I wipe my face quickly and blow my nose, fresh tears falling as soon as I brush them away. As I do, my eyes fall on the catalogue on the desk and the small white card sticking out between its pages.

I slide it out with trembling fingers. It's one of our own business cards which we keep on the counter. On the blank side is scribbled a phone number, written by my own Biro. I stare at it in disbelief for the longest time.

There are seven people in the shop when Tim returns, and he sees my red eyes immediately. He takes my arm, leading me to one side. "What's happened?"

With my head lowered, I mutter, "He kissed me."

Tim gives a sigh. "Okay look, go to lunch. He'll be gone when you get back."

I lift my eyes to his. I don't want him gone. I only want him here. Instead, I nod. I go into the back to get my jacket and then I leave, those sounds of moving boxes still coming from the store room because evidently Daron finds it easy to just get on with his job, even though he's just kissed a fifteen-year-old memory.

I move through the shoppers to the front door, smiling half-heartedly at a couple of regulars and step outside gratefully into the sun, making for my usual café.

On my return, the shop is quiet; a young couple browses in the corner, the man looking bored, the woman cooing over the products. Tim comes over to me quickly, and I can tell by his face that it's going to be bad news.

"He wouldn't let me send him home early. He wants to do a full day's work."

"Fine."

"I have to go out again."

I nod and move back to the counter. I can do this. I can make Daron stay in the stock room all day.

"I'll be back at four and then you can go home. But Karl, we need to talk about this."

I perch on my stool and look blankly at the catalogue still open on the desk.

"And what's this?"

I look up to see Tim holding out the white card with the phone number scribbled on. I redden and try to stammer something.

"Is it Cameron's? Cameron finally gave you his number?"

"I don't know. He left it there when I was out back. Maybe it was for you."

"Come on," Tim snorts. "I don't know how many times I have to tell you that he comes here for *you*, not me. Now you listen to me, you fucking call this guy tonight and you make a date with him, okay? He's a nice guy, Karl, and it's taken him six months to get the balls to do this, so give the guy a break and stop fucking living in the past." He jerks his thumb derisively towards the back of the shop. "Got it?"

I keep my head down as I take the card and push it into my pocket, biting my lip. I don't give him an assent because I have no intention of doing what he wants.

Tim gives an aggravated sigh and takes his briefcase, leaving the shop.

Silence falls. The couple make their way to the counter. I smile at them.

It's three o'clock, and the shop is empty. There's no sound from the back. Only an hour, I tell myself, and then Tim will be back and I can go home. Cautiously I make my way into the corridor, heading for the kitchen to get a drink.

I'm dismayed to find Daron there. He's sitting with a mug of coffee in his hands, his head bowed over it, his shoulders slumped. How dare he look so sorry for himself! He looks up.

"Karlo…" he says quietly, which used to be his pet name for me and now drives me wild.

I stalk over to him and slam the coffee cup from his hand. He gasps as he's splashed with hot liquid, and the mug shatters against the wall. I grip him by the collar and drag him from his chair.

I don't even have any words to spit at him. I just want to hurt him. Tears are streaming down my face, his hands are on my shoulders and we are struggling and shoving and he's winning, pushing me against the wall.

I gasp as he kisses me, and I don't push him away, only cling harder to him and kiss him back desperately, in the hope that this might be enough for him, the way it wasn't fifteen years ago.

We kiss and kiss and kiss, and I realise he's crying with me, our hands moving up each other's shirts to touch skin, pressing needily against each other, our lips burning.

His face drops into my neck and he covers it with kisses. I groan, clutching at his hair. "We can do this," he says. "Just one more time."

I draw back and stare at him in incomprehension even though I know exactly what he means. With his thumb he smoothes the tears from my cheeks.

"Go out front. Put the closed sign up and find something to act as a lubricant."

My mouth falls open. I stare into his glossy eyes, fathomless like ink-dark water. Am I going to let him take me apart again like this? Where is my strength to refuse? I don't want to refuse. I want to feel whole and complete again, the way only he could make me feel. I want these memories again, just once. I want to feel alive again.

I turn around and walk out front on violently trembling legs. I go to the door and turn the sign around, and then I stand staring blankly at the products for a while, because I've never considered which one of them would make the best lubricant.

Then I remember Tim confessed to me drunkenly a couple of months ago that the Monday nights Blake helps him cash up here, usually end up in them fucking over the counter. Tim told me they often forget to bring lube and so had ended up trying out most of the products. I gravitate towards the body lotions and pick up one containing orange blossom and bergamot, the one Tim rated as the best. Then I return to the back, with my heart in my mouth.

Daron already has his socks, shoes and shirt off, and to my surprise is sitting on the couch, taking a condom from his wallet. I put the lotion down on the coffee table and hover there as he stands up and comes towards me. He's much more muscular than I remember, his skin glowing with sun. His body is simply stunning. His hands move to my tie and slowly he unknots it and slides it from my neck. Then his fingers move to the buttons on my shirt and unfasten them to the waist. He pulls it free from my pants and slides it off my shoulders.

When he embraces me, I shudder at the feeling of our naked torsos together. His hands move down my back and knead my ass firmly. Against my ear, he says, "Take me, Karl."

My blood heats to the temperature of molten lava. Never in our short history did I ever fuck this man. I was always the one bending over for him, lying beneath him or riding him. Not that there was anything to complain about, but I often fantasised about how it would feel to be inside him.

I wonder if this is his way of apology, to let me do this to him, but I'm not going to question it, only do it, before he changes his mind.

We fall onto the couch, kissing frantically, writhing against each other, hands fumbling belts and buttons and zips open, pushing pants and boxers down, dragging them off and tossing them aside. Then Daron presses me onto my back, slides down my body and takes me in his mouth.

My head falls back and I groan, my hand tangling in his silky hair, tears once more burning my eyes, pleasure warring with grief inside me. His mouth is so hot around me, his tongue wicked as he licks up and down my shaft, before moving to suck at my balls. As he does this, a wet finger works its way inside me and I gasp, because it's been far too long. He probes, seeking, until he presses on my spot and I arch up into his mouth, almost choking him.

He presses me back down and then lifts his head and slithers up my body. With his face over mine, he watches my expression as he keeps his finger in the same place, stroking. I grip his hand, torn between wanting to remove his finger before I come and just letting him do it.

He solves my dilemma by drawing it free and presses the bottle into my hand, making it clear that we're now getting down to the real business in hand. He rolls me over so he's below me and then he lies with knees open, looking up at me through dense lashes.

For a moment I look at him, taking in his beauty. Then I sit back on my heels and tip the bottle up.

I grip one muscular leg by the calf, hook it over my shoulder, then I delve between his buttocks with my fingers, circling the outside of his entrance, working it open slowly. He's so tight. I wonder if I was the last man he slept with before he got married. He was never comfortable with the queer side of him, and that was probably why he never allowed me to fuck him. For all I know, maybe no one ever has.

I get two fingers in and I move them backwards and forward, stretching slowly. His eyes fall shut and little gasps escape him. I remove my fingers and tilt the bottle slowly, allowing lotion to dribble down onto him. He likes the feel of that, likes it even more when I work it all around his ass and then inside once more. I seek his prostate, taking my time to find it, my fingers pressing and searching until he jerks beneath me and groans loudly.

I bend my head and suck lightly on the head of his cock. Then I sit back and reach for the condom which is lying on the arm of the couch. His eyes open with a look of disappointment when my fingers leave him, but soon focus on me rolling the latex onto myself.

I let his leg fall down. I hold myself, rubbing slowly against him before I push forward. He catches his breath in undeniable pain but I continue, watching how he turns his face away, eyes closed. I haven't fucked many men in my time, but certainly, none were as tight as he is. I get myself all the way in and then I stop, because I'm scared that I'll come as soon as I move.

Daron's eyes open, he clutches my shoulders and breathes, "Come on, Karlo."

My face crumples, and I start to cry again. I think this may be the pinnacle of my life, buried inside Daron this way, and I don't want to feel like this. I don't want him to still exercise this effortless control over me. His hands move to my ass and as he pulls me forward, deeply into him. His lips seek mine.

I sob against his mouth and he makes shushing noises as I move within him slowly, his hands caressing my back, his lips glued to mine.

Slowly we build a rhythm, exchanging these kisses so I taste his tears as well as my own. I know he enjoys it. I can tell by the feel of the electricity running through his body, in every tightening of his muscles, by every stifled cry like he's trying to keep his pleasure inside, lest he betray himself to me.

I know I shouldn't care about pleasing him. I should get off and fuck whether he does too, but I can't. I want him to remember this day for the rest of his life. I want him to remember it when he thinks about how he threw me away.

So I wrap my hand around him, and he hisses his appreciation as I jerk him off. I bury my face in his neck, moaning with each thrust I make as I come closer and closer to my end. He lifts his pelvis to mine, his back arched, his head thrown back. His nails dig hard into my back, but I don't tell him to stop because I want these visible reminders on me when he's gone.

He starts to pant hard. He's going to come. "Karl..." he moans. "Karl..." He grasps my head, forcing me to look at him. "I'm sorry," he says with swimming eyes. "I'm sorry."

I'm crying so hard that I can hardly force myself to keep moving into him but I do because my orgasm is almost upon me. "I love you," I gasp.

"I know," he groans as his eyes fall shut and he bucks up at me, semen coating my hand. He clenches so tight around me that I'm coming too, falling onto him, trembling uncontrollably with an orgasm so powerful it's almost painful.

In the aftermath, he doesn't disentangle himself from me and get up immediately like I thought he might now he's had me. He only holds me as I lay with my face against his neck, his arms around me, one hand stroking my hair.

I still weep because now it's all done. I had Daron back for the briefest of times and he's lost again. I don't know why I've done this, when all it's done is open up the wounds again and douse them in salt.

We turn on our sides finally on the cramped couch and embrace, kissing awhile, long, leisurely kisses like they're not the last ones we will ever exchange. And then he holds me again like he did after that very first time when we laughed together at how amazing it had been.

There's nothing to laugh about now, because this isn't the start of something amazing, but the end of fifteen years of torment and misery. I wonder about his life. I wonder how long he's been married and whether he has any children, but I don't ask because I can't bear to carry that knowledge around with me for the rest of my life.

It's ten minutes to four when he slides from the couch and starts to pull his clothes on. I remain lying naked there. I used to be shy about my body in front of him, but age has mellowed that, and I don't care much anymore about being undressed. I was a little plump when I was with him. Now I'm thin, probably too thin, but it's the way I like it. I don't have much interest in food beyond it sustaining me. I just lie and watch him quietly. My tears have dried and my head aches fiercely. I watch him fasten his shirt over his muscular torso. I will never uncover that stunning body again.

He comes back to the couch and kneels before me. One hand trails down my side, over the curve of my hip, raising goose bumps in its wake. I want him again. If he were to lie down with me again now, I would be able to get it up again no problem, and this time, I would love to lie beneath him and feel him inside me.

"I'm going now," he says, and I know he means he isn't coming back. "Don't cry for me anymore."

I can't find any words. He smoothes my hair back from my forehead and kisses me so softly that I melt into him. My hands trace the contours of his cheeks and hold his face as we kiss for some minutes.

When he draws back, my hand is clinging to his shirt. He looks at it a moment, then he bends his head and kisses my knuckles, which causes me to let go. As he stands up, I see there are tears in his eyes. He moves to the door quickly, just as I hear the outer door open and he looks back at me for the briefest moment.

I see regret, I see loss, I see redemption in his eyes. A small smile crosses his lips, and then he's gone. Outside, I hear his voice and Tim's voice and then the bell goes again and there's silence.

I've managed to get my boxers on and am sitting on the edge of the couch when Tim enters the room. Behind him is Blake, looking really sorry for me.

"Jesus," says Tim.

I have no excuses to offer him.

"I'm really fucking disappointed in you, Karl."

I nod. "I'll get my things and go."

"What?" he barks. "I'm not *firing* you. I don't give a shit that you've been fucking at work. Christ, I've only told you half of what I've done with Blake here, and most times you've still been in the *shop* while we've done it." Behind him, Blake reddens and looks uncomfortably at his shoes. "I'm talking about allowing Daron to fuck you after everything he's done to you."

"I fucked *him*," I correct quickly.

"Good," is Tim's instant reply. "I hope he can't sit

down for a fucking week."

I smile, despite myself.

Tim drops to one knee between my legs and pulls me into his arms, holding me tight. "Now listen to me. He just gave me his resignation. It's done. Okay?"

I nod, my face in his shoulder, feeling safe and warm.

His hand strokes my hair. "Get dressed and go home. Blake and I will lock up."

Tim stands up. He hands me my pants and I pull them up my legs, standing up to fasten them. "You're too thin, Karl. My place, tomorrow night, for pizza and beer. I would ask you tonight, but unfortunately I have a date with the counter and Blake's ass."

Blake grumbles his protests, and Tim merely smirks at him.

"Go home and go to bed. If you want to take tomorrow off, that's fine with me. Just… be good to yourself, okay?" The affection on his face is so palpable that I have to bite my lip to keep from crying all over again.

I pull on my socks and shoes and then my shirt. Gathering my bag and jacket from the corner, I make my way outside.

I squeeze Tim's arm and nod at Blake as I leave the shop. Then I stand outside on the sidewalk. Where do I go from here? People have to step around me as I stay there motionless, and I hear a couple of them calling me an asshole for blocking their way. If they knew what had happened to me today, maybe they would give me a break.

I turn back to the shop to see Tim and Blake standing there watching me, their faces solemn with pity, Tim's fingers seeking Blake's as though he has to hold on to what he's got to remind himself he will never be as miserable as I am.

I turn away. Crossing the road, I head towards the beach, sinking down on a bench overlooking the ocean. It's hot, but the stiff breeze helps ease that a bit, whipping up the waves. Some black-suited surfers are having a field day below me.

I didn't expect this to happen. For me to achieve closure with Daron today, some nondescript Monday in early May. For him to walk back into my life, present himself to me, allow me to take him and then retire from it gracefully, leaving only the marks on my back and the burning on my lips as his memory.

With the sun on my face, I close my eyes and sink back against the bench. I go back to that room and let myself drown in the physical sensations I felt there. Daron's limbs around me, strong and hard, the muscles of his body pressed against mine. His velvet soft lips plundering mine, his heart beating against my chest.

I sigh, my mouth a little slack with desire and remembrance. My heart is beating way too hard. I sit there for the longest while until it calms itself and my erection subsides. I open my eyes and stare at the horizon, at the sun, past its zenith and beginning to sink, the way I've been doing for fifteen long years.

A few tears escape me and I reach my sunglasses from my pocket to hide my eyes from curious passers-by. It's always been my adage that boys don't cry, at least not in public and I'm disappointed that I've shed enough tears today to fill this vast ocean before me.

But my tears are done now. I know that as I feel them begin to wane and my chest hitches uncontrollably, my head falling back in exhaustion. I know why Daron did what he did and now I know that it wasn't through any lack of love for me. I can finally draw this line, lick my wounds and allow them to start healing.

Still these tired little dry sobs escape me as I sit in the sun, the scratches on my back stinging. I lick my lips slowly so I can taste Daron one last time.

It's fifteen minutes later when I finally rouse myself from whatever dreamlike state I've managed to sink into. The sun's burning my face, and it's time to move before it does some damage. My head aches, and I long for my bed. But before I go, I have something to do which won't wait.

I reach into my pocket and pull out the white card with the phone number scrawled on the back. My other hand takes my cell free and my thumb is a little unsteady as I press the keys.

I hesitate before I press connect. Then I lift the phone to my ear and wait. It seems to take forever, and my heart is hammering against my ribs. I'm sick with nerves because I can't remember the last time I did this, if I ever did. The line rings now, interminably and my heart sinks when my call is not answered because I doubt very much whether I'll ever have the guts to do this a second time.

Suddenly, just as I expect an answering service to click on, my call is answered. "Hello?"

That voice is familiar. The soft, deep voice which asked me if I was okay that morning, the voice which I've known for six months and never taken the trouble to look beyond the muscle and the eyes and the smile into the heart of its owner. Now I want to.

"Hi, Cameron. It's Karl," I say and hesitate before

adding, "From *Beauty Without The Beast*."

"Hey," he replies, and I can hear the smile and the pleasure in his voice and my dead heart starts to sing a little. "I'm glad you called."

HAPPY BIRTHDAY

Everyone had gone to lunch, leaving the open-plan office empty. Lewis sighed and stretched, looking across the rows of empty desks in front of him. He sat at the end near the window, right under the A/C, with a view across the city. It was worth having lunch at your desk to enjoy this peace and solitude.

Lewis was shy and withdrawn. Nerdy and studious, he preferred bird watching to going out drinking and didn't socialise with the rest of the office. They gossiped about him. Lewis had never come out and said he was gay, but that didn't stop people talking about him and some of the homophobic men treating him with barely concealed disdain.

Lewis didn't do much to further his interest in men. Sometimes he took off his glasses, gelled his hair a bit and put on a nice shirt before he went down to West Hollywood in search of some company. He usually scored. Maybe it was his squeaky clean looks, which made him appear younger than his years, his golden hair or his cornflower blue eyes. Maybe it was the shyness and obvious inexperience which turned on the sort of predatory men who inhabited the bars he went to. Regardless, if he wanted it, he could get it. Which didn't stop him from feeling lonely on a regular basis.

Today he was miserable because he was working on his birthday—his thirtieth birthday—and currently sitting alone at his desk eating a sandwich which tasted like ashes in his mouth. He sighed, took a drink of Coke and then rested his head on his hand, eyes closed.

"Hi, there."

Lewis lifted his head, about to scowl at whoever had broken his self-pitying solitude. His glance turned to a stare. His mouth almost fell open.

A man of about six foot three stood before his desk wearing an immaculately tailored pinstripe suit which clung to every curve of his muscular body. A white shirt and pink tie finished the outfit. Lightly tanned with closely-cropped dark hair, the man had a strong jaw and full sensual lips. His eyes were a bright, startling green, like emeralds, large and fringed with lush lashes. He looked vaguely familiar. Lewis was sure he had seen this man before but couldn't place him.

The man smiled slowly at the expression on Lewis's face. A secretive smile as though he read all Lewis's thoughts, his pearly teeth perfect. In one hand, incongruously, he carried a small, portable CD player. Lewis stared at this and then looked back at the man's beautiful eyes.

"Can I help you?" he almost stammered.

"I'm sure you can," the man almost purred. "Are you Lewis Allen?"

Lewis gulped. He nodded, his throat tight.

The man smiled again. "I'm Chris. Happy Birthday, Lewis."

Lewis stared, open-mouthed as Chris put the CD player down on the edge of his desk and pressed play. The strains of Donna Summer's "Hot Stuff" blared out, making Lewis flinch in shock. Chris stepped purposefully around the desk, looming over Lewis, gripping the arms of his swivel chair and pushing him back from his desk towards the window.

Then in the space he had freed up, Chris stood before Lewis, smiling as he started to sway his hips seductively to the music.

Oh. My. God. Lewis clenched the arms of his chair until his knuckles went white, his eyes wide in disbelief. No, he wasn't. He wasn't. He couldn't be about to...

Chris unfastened his jacket, pulled it off and tossed it casually over Lewis's desk. *Oh, yes, he was.* Chris continued to smile. He ran his hands down his torso, stroking himself through his shirt before he pulled the ends free from his pants, flashing several lean, tanned, inches of flesh.

Lewis put his hand to his mouth, his cock stiffening hopelessly in his pants. *Oh God, oh God.* Which of his colleagues had set this up? Who had paid to send Lewis all the way to heaven?

Putting his hands to his tie, Chris slowly pulled it open. Sliding it from his neck, he stepped close to Lewis. Lewis stared up at him, frozen in place as Chris draped the tie around his neck and almost pulled Lewis up from his chair, face close to his.

Chris's breath smelled of strawberries. His neck smelled of expensive cologne. His skin was utterly perfect. Lewis hung half-in, half-out of his chair, a slave to the stripper.

Leaving the tie around Lewis's neck, Chris moved away. He turned his back, gyrating his hips suggestively as he unfastened his shirt and pulled it off one shoulder and then the other. A back rippling with muscle came into view, and Lewis almost panted with the need for Chris to turn back around.

The stripper did so, holding his shirt closed over his

chest, a coy expression on his face as he flashed a little flesh and then covered himself again, moving closer to Lewis. Lewis was half-hard. He couldn't help it. This man was the most perfect physical specimen he had ever seen in his life. Christ, he must make a fucking fortune from this job, and he looked like he was actually enjoying it too. A smirk tilted his mouth as he watched Lewis flush redder and redder with his teasing. Finally he yanked his shirt open, pulled it off his arms and tossed it away.

He stood facing Lewis, his torso so hard and so chiselled that Lewis's fingers ached to touch. Chris' smile became more knowing. He stepped close and straddled one of Lewis's thighs, thrusting his groin towards his face. Lewis stifled a groan, gaze on the bulge in the tight pin-stripe pants. Hands still clenching the arms of his chair, he forced himself not to grab.

Moving back, Chris put his hand to the waist of his pants. Lewis wondered how he would negotiate the awkward, unsexy pulling off of pants over shoes and socks. Then he noticed Chris' footwear—sparkling silver boots—and the fact his pants didn't have a belt or apparent zipper. Perhaps if Chris was a proper professional stripper he would have…

Chris's hands clutched at his hips. There was a tearing noise as he ripped his pants clean off and tossed them aside.

Those.

Lewis gave a soft squeak which the music drowned out. Chris wore the most ludicrous glittering silver posing pouch Lewis had ever seen, but oh God, he filled it to bursting. He had to be at least half-hard because the outline of his cock was so thick and turgid, the head bulbous and clearly visible, almost poking over the top of the pouch. His balls were big and heavy, barely restrained by the flimsy material, and looked like they might fall free at any moment.

Smirking, Chris swung his hips and thrust his groin at Lewis. Hard as a rock, his mouth full of saliva, it was all Lewis could do not to drag Chris to him and bury his face into that straining pouch.

Chris's package swung and bounced with every turn of his hips. Lewis wondered if he had ever lost the pouch mid-dance, or perhaps that was the point. Perhaps that was the thrill of the act for both the stripper and voyeur, that you might get a look if the pouch came loose.

Chris's hands rested on his own thighs. He dragged those hands slowly up his body, stroking, and Lewis's groin got tighter and tighter the closer Chris came to touching himself. Finally, Chris cupped his package with one large hand, fondling and unmistakably stroking the head of his own cock with his thumb.

Lewis moaned helplessly and shifted in the chair, spreading his legs. Was Chris's cock getting harder under his eyes? It seemed that way. It seemed the head of his cock was about to burst from the top of the pouch at any second.

Chris continued to touch himself with one hand, grinding against his own touch, shaking his hips, his other hand on his chest, fondling his nipples.

Oh God. Lewis wished Chris would take himself free and masturbate right in front of him. Christ, that would be the most perfect birthday ever. His gaze dropped down the bare, muscular thighs and suddenly he realised he hadn't seen the back view.

"Turn around," the croak fell from his throat before he could control it.

"I'm sorry?" Chris arched a brow, still smiling.

Lewis licked his lips, summoned his courage. "Would you please turn around?"

Chris smiled wider. He did as he was told. The string of the silver pouch was buried right between two hard, ripe cheeks which Chris now shook at Lewis.

"Oh my God," Lewis whispered.

Chris stepped back, looking over his shoulder. He bent forward, shaking his ass, so Lewis could see the balls jiggling weightily between his legs. He clung onto the chair hard. Chris reached back, plucked the silver string free from his cleft and then gyrated back against it, rubbing it back and forward between his buttocks.

Jesus Christ, Lewis couldn't take any more. He was going to come if Chris didn't stop. But Chris clearly had no intentions of stopping. He leaned over, holding onto Lewis's desk, presenting his ass, legs spread wide, and Lewis saw the tight little hole between his legs.

He almost squealed. *Oh fuck, oh God.* He saw himself reaching out, catching Chris's hips and dragging him back, thrusting his tongue right into that hole.

Chris smiled knowingly over his shoulder. One hand strayed behind him, fingers lingering on his ass, delving between his cheeks.

Lewis ground his teeth, nails digging into his palms.

Chris straightened up. He turned around and marched towards Lewis, then he put his hands on his shoulders and straddled one thigh. In time to the music, he ground himself against Lewis, heavy balls and ripe ass sliding up and down his thigh.

Lewis panted for breath. He gripped the chair arms as hard as he could to stop himself grabbing at Chris. He had never had a lap dance before, but he knew it was wrong to touch without being invited. It would be disrespectful to grab at Chris with his grubby, excited hands.

Chris slid ever closer so his bare torso was pressed against Lewis's sober business suit. He grabbed hold of Lewis's tie, holding on tight. Lewis looked down at the straining pouch. He saw dark hair peeking over the top of it and the clear outline of the head of Chris's cock rearing towards his belly. He licked his lips and stared, moving his thigh uncontrollably, unable to stop himself from deliberately massaging Chris's ass and balls with it.

Chris held his shoulder and tie ever tighter. Without moving his groin from Lewis's thigh, Chris brought one knee forward, right between Lewis's legs and rested it on his aching cock and balls.

"Fuck..." Lewis's head fell back. He pushed against Chris's knee and the contact was exhilarating.

Chris stared into his eyes as he rubbed Lewis's groin. Was this part of the service? Did Chris often attempt to bring his customers to orgasm? Christ, he was about to, that was for sure. Lewis was going to go insane from the need to touch.

Chris removed his knee suddenly, leaving Lewis feeling bereft. He sat back on Lewis's thigh, legs spread, his knee forcing Lewis's legs wider so his own bulge was clearly outlined in his pants.

Chris sat there looking at him with his hands on his own thighs, close to his pouch. The music had finished, but neither of them noticed.

"Want to see?" Chris asked in a whisper.

"Oh, God yes," Lewis said.

Chris smiled slowly. One hand drifted across his belly. He hooked a finger under the top of the pouch and pulled it very slightly away from his body.

A thick cock almost sprang from the thin material. Lewis whimpered, thrusting his groin up at thin air. Chris let the pouch go, but the rosy head of his cock, remained on the outside, flat against his belly, the elastic of the pouch nestling it there neatly.

"Ohhhh..." Lewis moaned long and hard.

"Like what you see?"

"Yes, God yes, you're beautiful."

"Thanks very much."

Lewis stared with hot eyes. He was sure Chris was getting harder still under his gaze, the head of his cock poking further and further above the silver material.

"Let me see it all." Christ, where had that come from? Lewis blushed, fit to burst at his own insolence, but Chris only smiled. He hooked the fingers of both hands into his pouch and pulled the whole lot free.

Cock and balls fell loose, the cock large and almost fully hard, the balls hairless and bouncing. Chris let the pouch nestle beneath them, cupping his package neatly.

"Oh God." Lewis gnawed at his lip, squirming in his seat. Chris put his hand down and stroked his cock and balls in one go. Then Lewis saw. As Chris let go of his cock and it bounced against his stomach, he saw it leave a pale smear against his skin.

Chris looked down and noticed it too. He put a finger down and wiped the semen off his belly. He held his finger up, looking at it.

Lewis's mouth opened, almost begging for it. Chris

moved his finger closer, while continuing to slide his body up and down on Lewis's thigh.

Lewis craned forward. He captured Chris's finger with a moan and sucked desperately. Chris's other hand tightened on his shoulder. Lewis bucked in his seat, moving his thigh furiously beneath Chris's delicious weight. He sucked on that finger, staring at the hard, straining cock on his lap and the bouncing balls.

His cock leaked and swelled and begged for release. Lewis threw his head back, and Chris's finger fell loose as he came violently.

He shuddered for long seconds, gripping the arms of his chair, completely lost. He collapsed, panting, aware of the warm weight leaving his thigh.

"What the hell's going on here?"

Lewis's eyes snapped open in horror. Chris stood before him, pouch covering his modesty once more, pants in his hand, his gaze turned towards Lewis's boss.

"I was just wishing Mr Jones here a happy sabbatical."

Lewis stared, his throat dry and closed.

"What?" Lewis's boss demanded. "This isn't Mr Jones, and he isn't going on sabbatical."

Lewis remained quiet. Why was Chris pretending he had the wrong guy? To spare Lewis's already considerable blushes? He shut his legs and pulled his chair up to the desk to hide the wet patch on his pants.

"It isn't?" Chris asked in mock horror, looking at Lewis. "This isn't the Simpson building?"

"No," growled Lewis's boss. "That's next door. This is the Moorland building."

"Oh." Chris's eyes were wide. He looked at Lewis

again. "I'm so sorry, sir. That must have been very... distressing for you." He bit his lip, emerald eyes sparkling.

Lewis stared, unable to speak.

"If you'll excuse me." Chris bent over right in front of Lewis, his hard ass causing Lewis's cock to twitch again, and scooped his clothes into his arms. As he did, he brought something from his pocket and seemed to drop it deliberately on the floor near Lewis' feet. He straightened up and hefted his CD player in the other hand.

Then he smiled at Lewis and his boss and walked away. Lewis followed the deliberate swing of his hips and the silver string between his tight ass cheeks all the way to the door, shifting in his chair as he got hard again.

He glanced at his boss who was as red faced as he. His boss glowered at him and walked away, leaving Lewis alone once more.

Lewis sagged back in his chair, almost panting. *Oh my God, best birthday ever.* He could still taste the stripper's semen in his mouth. God, he would have loved to have swallowed that hard, leaking cock and given Chris something to remember. Did he always go so far with his clients? If he did, he was probably the most popular stripper in the city.

His gaze strayed to the small, white card on the floor by his feet. He bent and retrieved it. The gold italic font read, *Christopher Crane, managing director, the Simpson Building.* An address and office and cell numbers were below that.

Lewis stared, his hand shaking. *What the fuck?* Jesus, that was where he'd seen Chris before, at a convention a few months ago with the neighbouring building. He wasn't a stripper. The *managing director* of the company next door had just stripped for Lewis and got him off! *Fuck!*

Footsteps distracted him. His colleague, Jeffrey Barnard smirked at him. "Hey Lewis, have a nice lunch?" Jeffrey was actually an okay guy and showed no interest in the gossip that went around.

"Do you know something about what just went on here?" Lewis demanded.

"You mean the hot guy who just gave you a lap dance?"

"Jesus Christ, Jeffrey, that was Christopher Crane from next door!"

"I know who it was. He's had the hots for you for months, since he saw you at the conference."

"W-what?" Lewis stammered.

"You need to get your glasses checked, dude. He watches you every day when you sit in the square with your coffee. I ran into him yesterday, told him it was your birthday today. He asked me to make sure you were alone at lunch. I didn't know what he was going to do until I just saw him walking bare-assed down the corridor!"

Lewis stared, his face so hot he thought he would explode. But the warmth in his chest, his stomach and his groin rivalled it. Christopher Crane. The man who had given him the birthday treat to end all treats and then blatantly left his card. Oh God. The man who behaved like the hottest stripper *ever* wasn't even a real stripper. Christ.

"I hope you're going to go over and thank him," Jeffrey said with a smile as he sat down at his desk.

"I could," Lewis murmured, thinking what sort of pouch he could wear and how ridiculous he'd look in it. He imagined striding into Chris's office, putting the CD player down and wrenching off his jacket, swinging his hips as he started to strip. He imagined Chris leaning back in his executive leather chair, hard cock outlined against his tight pants as he watched Lewis shed his clothes. He smiled to himself because even as the thought of stripping for a stranger terrified him, it also aroused him beyond belief. He'd sit on Chris's knee, grinding himself on one strong thigh and then he'd say to Chris, "Want to see?" And Chris would groan a yes.

But it wouldn't stop there. This time Lewis would make sure there was touching involved. And this time Chris would be the one coming his brains out.

THE LONG ROAD HOME

The hot, dusty road stretched out into the distance, winding down to the harbour. It may have been only wide enough for two vehicles to pass each other snugly, but for Kester Kemel, it was a vast, yawning chasm which had separated him from the love of his life for five years.

He peered from the window where he sat reading his book like he did every day, looking directly opposite into the shop across the road, where Melek Keskin was talking to a female customer, bestowing that devastating smile on her, no doubt seducing her money out of her purse with ease.

Kester had run his little bookshop since time began, old tomes towering precariously to the ceiling, threatening one day to bury him forever in words, which to him, would be the death to rival all deaths. Sometimes he thought he had loved Melek Keskin for an equal amount of time, although it was actually only five years, a mere seventh of his life.

Melek had moved into the premises across the road at that time and started to sell crystal. The window of his shop winked ferociously with blues and greens and dazzling purples when the sun was at its zenith, blinding Kester when he looked across, the display almost as beautiful as its owner.

Kester was a man of passion with a few failed love affairs behind him, who hadn't known he liked men until he set eyes on Melek Keskin. His reclusive little world had been rocked when he had seen the new owner setting up a few trinkets outside, crouching on the pavement and looking up as he sensed Kester's gaze.

Kester's glance had turned to a stare and his heart had surged within his chest so powerfully that he had trembled in shock, convinced he was having a heart attack. Then Melek had got up and gone into his shop, closing the door and sealing Kester's heart in there with him for the next five years.

During those eighteen hundred plus days, Kester had not acted on his feelings in any way, shape or form. To his utter shame, he had never so much as spoken one word to Melek Keskin. He had never even crossed the street to the other side. Instead, he had slid towards forty and remained resolutely alone. The longer time went on, the more difficult it became to even contemplate making a move over there. After five years, it became impossible.

If Kester had to explain in all honesty what had prevented him from doing something about the unrequited love he felt for someone who was still a stranger to him after five years, he would have summed it up in one word: fear.

He knew from bitter experience that fantasy was always better than the reality, and he knew without doubt that Melek would never be able to love him in return the way Kester loved him. The way he saw it was this: Melek kept him alive. His love for Melek helped him face these days which were all the same. If his dream was realised, he would have no reason to go on living.

That was why he had never yet crossed the road to the other side. Little did he know that a catalyst was about to arrive, someone who would give Kester a push out of his own self-obsessed world before another five years passed and forty came and went.

The vacant premises next door had had a let sign on it for some weeks before a dirty cart arrived and a tall, slender man with radiant, almost white-blond hair started unloading boxes. Another even taller man helped him, his hair as jet as the first man's, but longer and scruffier. The two men worked hard at their task for a couple of hours, until finally, they dragged two chairs outside the door and sat themselves down with satisfied smiles, drinking beer from bottles dripping with condensation. Trapped in the hot little shop, surrounded by paper containing words about other people's lives, Kester watched.

He could almost taste the crisp, ice-cold bitterness of the beer on his tongue, feel the rush of it as it went to his head. The blond man glanced into the shop, cocked his head and beckoned with one finger for Kester to come out.

Kester, startled, almost put a quizzical finger to his own chest and mouthed the word *me?* before he stopped himself. Of course his new neighbour meant him. He put his book aside, forgetting the bookmark in his nervousness and leaving it carelessly face down where the spine would get broken. He got up off his stool, opening the door.

The blond man was up on his feet, showing a truly stunning set of teeth in a smile which caused the flesh around his mouth to dimple like a schoolboy's. Here was a smile you could trust, Kester thought, instantly relaxing and taking the stranger's hand as he held it out.

"I'm Xas," said the man, the radiance of his smile jostling for attention with his rather startling crystal blue eyes. If Kester hadn't already been in love, he may have lost his heart again at that moment.

"Kester," he almost stammered.

"Nice to meet you, Kester," Xas said, letting go of his hand. "This is Yalon."

Kester leaned over, taking the other man's hand.

"Want to join us for a beer?" Xas asked.

Kester nodded with that taste still on his tongue.

They sat there for the longest while as the sun set and darkness caused the shopkeepers to put on their lights. When they were not talking, the three of them gazed idly across the road, some more intent than others on the scenery. Melek's shop was empty, and he came suddenly into view, crawling on hands and knees into the window, taking some crystal out and replacing it with other pieces, glasses and vases and animals and flowers. His milky skin, an anomaly in these parts, was accentuated by the ebony hair which fell across his face. Even from this distance his eyes were green jewels as he lifted his head, arrested by the three men studying him.

Yalon, Xas and Kester were perfectly still, beer bottles poised in hands, lifted to lips. Xas was the first to speak discreetly under his breath. "He's *beautiful*."

Kester's head turned to him. His cheeks grew scarlet. Xas's eyes met his own, way too knowing for someone he had just met. Kester stood up quickly, mumbling his thanks for the beer, retreating to his shop, closing the door, placing the closed sign on it. When he glanced back across the road, Melek was gone from the window.

Kester would deny that he stalked Melek, but he took notice of the man's movements. Melek lived above his shop, just like Kester lived above his. He went out and brought back boxes of merchandise for his shop or paper bags of fruit and loaves of bread from the market. Melek didn't seem to go out all that much at night. When he did, he went out at sunset alone and came back alone an hour later. Kester didn't see any visitors to the shop other than customers, who only stayed as long as it took to buy some wares.

At night, Kester lay on his bed in the darkness facing the window, watching the soft glow of light from Melek's bedroom, imagining what the love of his life was doing over there. He wondered if Melek read books when he was alone and came to the conclusion that he didn't, because he had never once been across the road to buy from Kester, and he was pretty much the only purveyor of literature in town. It made him sad that Melek might not be a bookworm like himself and oftentimes he thought that he had done the right thing in never getting to know the other man, not wanting to be disappointed by finding out he was ignorant of the Brontë sisters and Shakespeare and Poe.

Kester had stopped wishing a long time ago that Melek would present himself at his shop. Why should he? What was there remotely intriguing within?

Xas came into the shop the next day around mid-morning while Kester sat in his usual place behind the counter, devouring a leather-bound edition of Charles Dickens' *Bleak House*.

He looked up nervously when Xas fixed those blue eyes of his on him. "About last night, Kester..." he began, and Kester was already blushing like an idiot. "I was inappropriate. I didn't realize you and he..."

"We're not!" Kester exclaimed and then reddened

further, lowering his eyes to his book, one damp hand smoothing the page compulsively. His gaze darted across the road to the crystal shop and found solace in the picture of Melek setting out a display on the pavement.

"It's all right," Xas said. He put a box on the counter, opening it to reveal sweet, pistachio-filled pastries. "I brought you some baklava. I thought you might want to talk."

Kester almost stared at him, so taken aback was he by this kindness from a virtual stranger. He stood up. "I'll make tea."

When they were seated at the counter with tea and baklava, his new acquaintance smiled in that charming way of his and asked, around a mouthful of the pastry, "So how long have you been in love with him, Kester?"

Kester reddened and flailed for a response before mumbling in shame, "Five years."

Xas lifted one eyebrow. "Does he know?"

Kester shook his head, longing to sink into the ground.

"Let me get this straight, you've harboured these feelings for five years and never told him?"

Kester nodded, eyes on his book again. "I've never even spoken to him, Xas."

"Oh, Kester," Xas said with sympathy in his voice. "You poor, *poor* man. Isn't it a good thing I came along when I did?" He smiled a benevolent smile, one which so lit his eyes and dimpled his mouth that Kester felt reassurance despite his anxiety.

When they had talked a little further, Xas stood up, wiped crumbs from his mouth with the back of his hand and straightened his shirt. "Okay. Wish me luck."

"What?" Kester said, alarmed.

"I'm going across the road to meet Melek," Xas said casually, as though Kester's guts weren't hanging out on a string for all to see.

"No!" Kester all but lunged over the counter and grabbed at one lean bicep. "You can't!"

"Shh," Xas said in that soothing way of his. "I'm not going to give away any of your secrets, Kester, trust me. I'm only going to see how the land lies, that's all."

Kester regarded him in panic. "You promise?"

"I promise," Xas said, looking into Kester's eyes steadily with that calm, relaxed demeanour of his. "I'll go back to my shop once I've met him. Leave it a suitable amount of time before you come over, so we don't look obvious."

Kester nodded although his heart hammered and his stomach churned. He watched Xas leave his shop, look both ways along the dusty road, then cross it, heading for Melek's shop.

He saw him push the door open and fancied he heard the ringing of the bell from this distance as Melek came out from the back with a smile of greeting on his face, and Xas held his hand out to him. Kester ducked behind the counter in fear and sat there until his heart regained a suitable speed and he didn't feel like he would vomit at any moment.

A couple of hours later when the sun was sinking into a fiery grave beyond the horizon, Kester put his closed sign up and crept the few steps into Xas's shop, his gaze flickering over to the crystal shop. There were three or four customers inside, and Melek stood chatting to one, side on so Kester saw the curve of dark lashes and the bow of a pink, almost heart-shaped mouth which seemed made for kissing. Xas's shop was cool and dark, and he stood up to greet Kester from behind the counter as he entered, smiling a smile which told Kester the encounter had been satisfactory.

"I presume the most important thing to you is that I tell you Melek is a nice person?"

Kester nodded, because of course, it was.

"Well then, he is. Charming and funny and very polite."

Kester nodded in satisfaction.

"And he likes men," Xas added.

Kester's brows drew together into a frown. "You asked him that?"

Xas shook his head. "I just knew."

Kester was naive of course and continued to be perplexed until Xas gave an embarrassed half-smile and confessed, "I could see he found me attractive."

Kester knew his expression darkened. He didn't like that at all.

Xas laughed lightly. "Relax. I'm here to help you. I wouldn't steal Melek from you or I would be a very poor friend."

Kester lowered his head, blushing. "He's not mine to steal."

"He is," Xas said quietly. "He owns your heart, and I promise you that you shall own his."

Kester looked up at him. Something about the way Xas spoke was a trifle odd, but he didn't wish to question any good fortune which had befallen him after these five barren years of unslaked desire.

"I established a few things about him," Xas continued. "He's single, and his family is many miles away. He likes to walk on the beach, and he's content running his shop." He smiled. "Already he sounds like your soulmate, Kester."

The blood rushed to Kester's face, mainly because he too had been thinking about how perfect Melek sounded. He could not help but return Xas's smile and drift off into that dream world he had inhabited for the last five years.

The next day, Xas and Kester sat outside Xas's shop in the early morning sun, the awning above protecting them a little from its rays when the first customer of the day came calling. He looked in the window of Xas's shop a moment before stepping into the dark interior. Xas didn't rush to interfere with the man's browsing. Like Kester, Xas must have known there was nothing worse than a salesman breathing down your neck, plus he seemed easygoing enough to be philosophical about shoplifters.

He waited until the man reappeared at the door, glancing to his left and then his right, eyes alighting on Kester and Xas.

"I'm looking for the owner." A man of good height and build, he wore a white linen shirt, unfastened a little way to show gleaming, sun-kissed skin. His hair was glossy brown and his eyes were a shade of hazel. The freckles across his nose and cheeks softened what was an attractive but rather hard face, the mouth cruel and sarcastic.

He held a large, black bag, the type merchants carried in that area. Kester stared, and when he looked at Xas, he saw the other shopkeeper did too.

The merchant's eyes had moved to settle on Xas,

and a slow blush rose on his cheeks at the way he was being studied.

"That's me," Xas said, standing up slowly and stretching his lean body up to its full height, so the stranger's eyes moved over it in a somewhat obvious way.

The man stepped forward. "I'm Datan. I have some hand-carved marble chess pieces for sale. I was told you sell them in your shop."

"Correct," Xas replied with a smile, holding eye contact steadily. His smile didn't convince Kester. It didn't reach his eyes, and Xas held his body rather tensely. Did Xas already know this man?

"Why don't you step inside?" There was something predatory about this offer, Kester decided, watching the exchange. If he had been Datan, he might have felt a little like a fly entering the spider's trap, but the merchant merely nodded and went back into the shop while Xas followed. Sending Kester a smile, he closed the door behind him and the merchant.

Kester settled back into his chair and let his gaze drift across the road and into Melek's shop, where the other man was busy with customers.

It was only a few moments until he was distracted by a commotion coming from Xas's shop, a raising of voices. He turned his head in alarm as the voices became louder and there was a thud and a crash, like ornaments being scattered from shelves by a body falling against them. The door was flung open violently, making the wind-chimes above it shudder in shock.

Datan appeared at the door, propelled there by Xas's hand, which held him by the scruff of the neck like a dog.

"I have nothing to say to you, just like last time,"

Kester's new friend growled, teeth bared in a snarl.

Kester saw a flash of Datan's angry face and a shocking bruise on his cheek before Xas hurled him into the road and stalked back to his shop, slamming the door. Kester leapt to his feet and stared in horror at the man lying groaning in the gutter, eyes flickering to Xas's shop, scared to be seen to be helping the stranger when clearly he had done something very wrong to offend his friend. As he hesitated there, a flash of movement made him lift his head.

Melek Keskin was crossing the street for the first time in five years.

Kester remained rooted to the spot in absolute terror as the man of his hopes and dreams drew close to him. Melek's green eyes flickered over to him once, before he focused all his attention on the man picking himself groggily from the gutter.

Tender hands took Datan under the arms, and helped him to his feet. Melek murmured soft words which Kester didn't hear above the distant calls of sea birds. Melek's arm went around the man's back, supporting him as the two of them walked back across the road to the crystal shop.

Melek guided Datan in through the door, then turned to close it, flipping around the sign to closed. His gaze flickered first to Xas's shop, then along a few steps to Kester who was still standing and staring. Their eyes met for long seconds before Melek turned away.

And Kester thought to himself, Melek is a better man than I will ever be.

Towards evening Kester finally plucked up the courage to push the door to Xas's shop open and enter its dimly lit interior. The first thing he saw was the mess, piles of broken china and glass lying beneath the shelves, while the man himself crouched beneath with brush and pan, sweeping up.

Kester bit his lip and hesitated, afraid to provoke the temper he had seen earlier. "Xas," he said finally when his friend did not acknowledge him.

Xas gave a sigh and sat back on his heels, putting the pan to one side. "There was a misunderstanding," he muttered, avoiding eye contact. "Something and nothing."

"What was it?"

Xas hesitated. He seemed to fumble for words. "He... tried to sell me ivory chess pieces. I would no more buy those than I would go out and murder the elephant myself."

Kester didn't speak. Something about this tale was strange. "Have you met him before?"

Xas's gaze moved to his. His blue eyes were unsettling for the first time. "I've had some dealings with him in the past."

The way he kept his gaze on Kester's seemed like a direct challenge. A challenge for Kester to keep going in this direction. His spine prickled with unease. "Melek took him in," he said quietly.

Xas looked alarmed. "What?"

"Melek took him into his shop. I haven't seen him come out yet."

Xas's gaze moved beyond his own door, across the street and to the shop opposite. His body language suggested agitation and annoyance. He reached a decanter and two glasses from behind the counter and poured them both a glass of the local liqueur, a fiery aniseed concoction, fatal to the head the morning after. Kester accepted it gratefully because his nerves were oddly rattled.

Xas drank his own down quickly, then he squared his shoulders and said, "I'm closing up."

Kester nodded. There were questions he wanted to ask, but he didn't dare. He left the shop, glancing back when Xas stepped out behind him, closing the door but not locking it. His new friend glanced both ways across the road and then crossed over it.

Kester watched with that troublesome heart of his once more in his mouth. Twice he had seen Xas cross that road now. How easy he made it look, as though it wasn't infested with sharks and alligators and all manner of things which might hurt and destroy Kester before he could get to Melek. But Xas was there on the other side with ease and pushing the door of the crystal shop open.

Kester hurried into his own shop and hid behind his counter, spying as his beloved came out to greet Xas. This time Kester saw no smile on Melek's face for his new friend. He watched Xas's body language, still tense, body held stiffly as though preparing for battle and noted the reciprocal tension on Melek's face as Xas spoke.

Finally, Melek nodded, turned away, and disappeared into the back of his shop.

It was only a couple of minutes before the merchant Datan entered alone. The two men faced each other across Melek's shop, Xas doing the talking, Datan listening. What was he saying? Whatever it was, Datan looked defensive, that cruel mouth curling sardonically. Xas clenched his fists as he spoke. Datan laughed, and Xas stalked forward so they were almost nose to nose. He glanced to the back of the shop and then gestured across the road towards his own shop.

Melek reappeared, and Kester's poor heart sang as he drank in the beautiful sight. Xas turned to go out of the shop with Datan following. Kester ducked further behind the counter as the two crossed the road, and Xas opened the door to his shop and held it open for Datan.

Kester stepped out from behind the counter and exited his shop. He began stacking up the boxes of books he had on display outside, casting a look into the dim interior of Xas's shop as he did so.

Datan had Xas pinned to one of the shelves, hands around his throat. Kester gasped, torn between wanting to help Xas and being afraid to intervene. The two men yelled at each other, but it was in some language Kester had never heard before, some strange, arcane language not spoken in the district. Then Xas pushed Datan back and a moment later, a vast cloud of smoke filled the shop. Kester stared, still hesitating, and when the smoke cleared he saw Xas was alone. Datan had vanished.

Kester crept back into his shop and closed the door. He was tormented all night. Just what had he witnessed next door? Who exactly were Xas and Datan, and what was their history?

He fell asleep gradually and when he awoke, he was in hell. He awoke choking and coughing, squinting through thick black smoke to see his bedroom ablaze, the flames licking around the end of his bed, the ceiling slowly sagging above him.

He cried out in horror, slithering onto the floor, crawling along it where the air was cooler and sweeter. His head swam with lack of oxygen as he tried to make it to the door, not sure where the door was anymore.

His vision darkened, his lungs were bursting and right about now, his time was ending. He imagined hands lifting him before he surrendered to sweet oblivion.

He was lying in the street when he came to his senses, and the first thing he saw was his shop and his home ablaze, a human chain passing buckets of water along. The heat seared his face and the sound of crackling reached him as thousands of books went up in smoke. Any tears which may have come at this sight evaporated speedily with the heat and Kester could only look on in absolute desolation as everything he owned was destroyed.

He only became aware gradually that he was being held in someone's arms, that someone's solid chest pressed against his back and his head rested on a broad shoulder. He looked down at the pale hand which rested possessively over his heart, and his breath caught in his throat in confusion. Slowly, he turned his head and looked up into the green eyes he saw in his dreams.

Melek's expression was solemn, sorrowful. His hand came up to cup Kester's head gently. "Don't be sad," he said quietly. "You will rebuild your shop even better than before, you'll see. I shall help you."

And Kester couldn't think, couldn't breathe, couldn't do anything, only allow his eyes to close as those lips, those perfect, beautiful pink lips, the thing he craved most of all in this whole, wide world, lowered to his own and kissed him.

He was certain he had died in the fire and gone to heaven and Melek Keskin was welcoming him at the gates. How else to explain being kissed by an angel? His heart beat hard in his chest. Soft fingertips touched his face hesitantly. Melek was real and warm and his lips seared Kester's like no fire ever could. They seemed to melt flesh from bone and mix Kester all up into confusion and softness before putting him back together again with his head on back to front and his heart right there on the outside of his pyjamas being held in the palm of Melek's tender hand.

Their lips parted, and he dared to open his eyes. Melek smiled, and Kester knew then that he was in heaven, that heaven was right here on earth.

He had once thought he didn't want this dream to come true. He had told himself that getting his wish would mean the end of wanting to live. That the fantasy was always better than the reality, that Melek would never love him the way *he* loved Melek. He knew now that was something he had just told himself, to justify his reasons for never crossing that road. For never tasting what could have been his before Melek crossed that road and came to him.

An epic of time wasted. His chest burned with both aching sorrow and poignant regret.

He allowed Melek to help him to his feet, and then Melek guided him slowly across that road for the first time in five years, like a ferryman steering him from the rocks, away from the wreckage of his life and into his wildest dreams.

Kester sat drinking tea gratefully in the kitchen while Melek ran a bath. He was blackened with soot and he smelled dreadful. He leaned on Melek's arm and moved slowly to the bathroom, unsure of his steps, not because of shock at the fire, but shock at the kiss.

He allowed Melek to undress him without protest,

and he shivered as his naked body was uncovered before he slid with a sigh beneath hot, scented water. He looked up at Melek a moment and then his breath caught in his throat as the crystal merchant started to shed his clothes too.

He was beautiful beneath them, as Kester had known he would be, his skin like rich cream, every curve and line of it seemingly fashioned by a craftsman. He climbed into the bath, and in delirious delight Kester slid forward so Melek could sit behind him and hold him the way he had done in the street.

The two sank as deeply down into the hot water as they could get, and Kester held onto those arms which were around him, eyes closed, a sigh passing his lips. His heart both hurt over the loss of one dream and sang over the realisation of the other. Steam rose from the water and soot darkened it, and Kester sank into such relaxation he was barely conscious.

Finally Melek's gentle hands urged him out when the water began to cool and wrapped him in a big, soft towel, drying every part of his body with the same care he might have delivered to a baby's sensitive skin.

Kester could not help the way he responded to Melek's proximity, the way he towelled him so gently dry between his legs and a need rose in him so sharply that it was all he could do to keep his hands to himself.

Melek helped Kester to put on warm pyjamas, for he still shivered a little, then he guided him to his own bed, climbed in beside him and extinguished the light.

Kester brought the warm body close to his own, and desire thrummed in his veins. His skin ached as lips turned up to his, and he kissed Melek. The moist mouth caressed his and hands spanned his waist, moving lightly up his back. He could not help the groan which spilled from his lips as Melek pressed closer to him.

"Melek," he gasped out. "I love you."

"I know, my love," was Melek's reply as his body came on top of his, clothing was shed and skin slid against naked skin.

Melek's hair hung down in his face as he bent to kiss Kester, his body shuddering as Kester's hands moved down its contours.

Their lovemaking was long and slow, synchronised perfection, limbs and minds entwined, five years of love finally spilled.

As he held Melek in his arms, his lover smiling radiantly at him, Kester could not believe five years of waiting were at an end. It seemed dreams really did come true, if you wished hard enough.

When he awoke, he was alone in the strange bed. But the pillow smelled of Melek when Kester burrowed his face into it. He pulled on a robe and left the room to find both the kitchen and bathroom empty.

What he did find, there in the tiny living room, was a tall bookshelf lined with almost every book Kester had read and adored in his life. There was Austen, the Brontës, Dostoevsky, Zola, Hugo, Poe, Shakespeare, Wilde. The list was endless. And some of these covers he recognised as editions he had once sold himself. With a trembling hand, he drew out *The Picture of Dorian Gray*. There was the price on the first page, written in his own hand. These books had come from his shop.

Slowly, he descended into the crystal shop and hid behind a display case when he saw Melek outside on the street, talking to a customer.

He wore a linen shirt which only emphasised his creamy skin, pale trousers and soft leather shoes. His raven hair was brushed neatly back from his face and shone glossily in the early morning sun. His teeth glinted as he smiled, and then the sun caught those eyes, like the clearest, calmest ocean. Kester caught his breath all over again.

Melek turned his head as though he had preternatural hearing and that smile was bestowed on Kester. He excused himself from his customer and came into the shop. "Are you spying on me?" he questioned teasingly as he leaned in and placed a kiss on Kester's mouth.

Kester nodded mutely with what must have been adoration spilling from his eyes.

Melek smiled again. "Go back up to bed. I'll conclude my business here, and then I'll come up and make you breakfast."

Kester smiled shyly, gratefully, pressed Melek's hand with his a moment and then turned away.

Breakfast followed the more important business of lovemaking. Melek lay beneath Kester while Kester watched the slow, sensual flush of colour track up his chest, over his throat and up to make his face glow. He arched in the kind of ecstasy Kester had only ever dreamed of and now, was causing another effortlessly.

When the two were sitting side by side drinking hot, strong coffee, Melek remarked, "The man I was talking to earlier, he was the owner of the empty premises next door."

Kester's gaze turned to his in confusion.

"He accepted an offer for me to buy it. If you want it as your new shop, it's yours. We could knock through to mine and have one big book and crystal shop if you like." He laughed a little self-deprecatingly. "I know it's a silly idea, and I'm sure you wouldn't want to share with me, but it might work."

Kester was open-mouthed, and his eyes swam with tears. He clutched Melek's beloved face in his hands. "I want to share everything with you," he said, "*everything*."

Melek smiled shyly. "You know I've been in love with you for five years, don't you? Something told me it was time to do something about that. Something told me that you unequivocally returned my feelings."

Kester tried to stammer a reply. Melek's fingers smoothed over his face. "It was Xas," he said decisively.

"I know," Kester agreed. He thought about the tall man with the easy smile and the beautiful eyes.

They sat there in silence and Kester imagined their thoughts were the same.

"I saw your books."

Melek smiled self-consciously. "I was never much of a reader until I fell in love with you. And then I wanted to learn about your passion. Do you know Amias? The man who came and bought a book off you every weekend without fail for five years? The one who always asked you to recommend him something and then always bought your recommendation?"

Kester nodded, thinking of the red-haired man with the tranquil brown eyes and the easy manner.

"He was there on my behalf. Because I was too afraid to cross the road to you."

"Oh," Kester breathed. "Oh." And he pulled Melek to him and held him hard.

Later in the afternoon, the two stepped outside the shop and stood looking at the still-smouldering wreckage of Kester's shop. "We can go over," Melek said reassuringly. "Bring over whatever we can. But first..." He gestured towards Xas's shop. Kester nodded. They set off across that vast yawning chasm that had once kept them separated.

Even before they got there, Kester saw the windows were dark, the door closed and locked. He frowned in confusion. Where had Xas been last night when the fire had raged next door to him? They reached the shop, and Kester pressed his nose to the window, cupping his hand to peer within. He drew back in shock. "It's empty," he told Melek. "He's gone."

Melek, frowning, turned and peered down the street as though it would hold some answers. Then he spotted a man with a bag walking on the other side, and he ran across, waving his arms. "Mr Heber, Mr Heber, just a moment."

The short man in the suit stopped, looking harassed. He eyed Kester as he came over to join Melek.

"Where's Xas gone?"

"Who?"

"Xas, the man who let the shop from you."

Mr Heber shook his head, looking baffled. "I don't know what you're talking about. That shop's been sitting empty for months. I haven't had a sniff of interest. And now with the fire next door," he looked across in disdain, so Kester reddened, "I've no chance of letting it for the foreseeable future."

"But he was here for a few days," said Melek. "We saw him. He sold chess sets. Ask the merchant Datan; he tried to sell him some pieces." He looked at Kester in confusion. Remaining silent, Kester had a prickling sensation crawling along his spine.

"I don't know who you mean." Mr Heber was irritated now. "I don't know this Xas, and I don't know the merchant you speak of either." He tipped his hat. "Good afternoon, gentlemen." He hurried away.

Melek and Kester stared at each other. Finally, they walked back to Melek's shop and while Melek attended to customers, Kester made some mint tea and set it out on the counter.

He watched his love as he smiled and held up a crystal piece to his customer, a figure of a cat from the display in the window. He saw the flash of purple and green and blue in the glass and the pale green of Melek's eyes as he turned to smile at him, and he thought he was beginning to understand, but the explanation was too fantastical to even voice aloud.

He had a feeling blame for the fire could be left at the door of the satanic-looking merchant Datan. Kester had certain ideas regarding Datan as the antithesis of Xas's good. He hesitated to label the two men for what, and who, he thought they were. No one would believe him.

Whatever Datan's malicious motives, it had backfired. Xas had brought Kester and Melek together, and Kester owed the man everything.

He doubted he would get to thank him for it in this life, though.

THE RENT COLLECTOR

The third knock came at the door, and Jacob crouched in a corner biting at his nails. He knew who it was. The rent collector always came on the first Tuesday of the month, in the morning because he knew Jacob was out every night. He went to all of the houses on this slovenly row in the mornings because most of the tenants had the same occupation as Jacob. Although most were women. The fact that Jacob also worked in the oldest profession in the world made him lower than low in some people's eyes. He did what he could to survive in this cruel, vile city, and no one had a lower opinion of him than himself.

The knock came again, harder than the previous blow. Jacob owed three months' rent and he had nothing to give. In the dead of winter customers were scarce, and all he had made the previous week he had spent on food. He started violently as a hand reached suddenly through the broken window and pulled the curtain aside.

"Open the door. I know you're there."

Jacob straightened up. He wiped his sweating palms on his breeches and went to the door, turned the key and pulled it open.

It wasn't the rent collector, at least not the one Jacob knew, but the man carried the same black pocketbook and pencil. It was a rent collector all right, just not the usual one.

The stranger smiled tightly from a sensual mouth. "Jacob Doran?" He was a tall man, dressed impeccably in black frockcoat and stiff, starched shirt, a burgundy waistcoat beneath and a black cravat pinned with a red stone. He wore a top hat.

"Yes," Jacob said reluctantly.

The man removed his hat and inclined his head gracefully so Jacob got a better look at his face. He was about thirty-five years of age, uncommonly attractive and fine-featured, his pale eyes silvery in colour, his dark blond hair cropped short. "My name is William Brock. I work for Mr Figgis."

Mr Figgis was Jacob's landlord, a reclusive man whom Jacob had never yet set eyes on. He owned every miserable house on this row and he threw out tenants who were three months' behind.

Jacob nodded. What had happened to the other man? Had he got so downhearted at kicking these miserable souls down further that he'd thrown himself in the Thames?

"So, Mr Doran." The man looked down at his book, tapping his pencil against it. "Do I serve you with an eviction notice today?"

Jacob bit his lip. "I don't have the money," he blurted out, twisting his hands together. "But I can get it. Please."

William regarded him sceptically. "And how are you going to procure three months' rent? Are you a magician, Jacob, or do you charge more than the going rate?" A smirk curled his mouth, and Jacob's cheeks heated with humiliation.

He scowled at the rent collector. The man watched him silently, perhaps enjoying this torture. "Well?" he asked at length.

"If you would just give me another month..."

The man laughed shortly. "Another month! Mr

Figgis has a business to run. He gives tenants three months."

"I know that."

"Then why should you be any different? It's not like you haven't been in arrears in the past. You have. Plenty of times."

"Please," Jacob beseeched him. "I have nowhere to go."

The man regarded him stonily. Then he wrote something in his book and closed it, putting it and the pencil inside his breast pocket. He stepped forward onto the doorstep so he towered over Jacob by some inches.

"I would have to cover some of your debt myself to appease Mr Figgis," he said, eyes never leaving Jacob's. "How exactly are you going to make that worth my while?"

In the heavy silence which followed, Jacob understood with a sinking sensation what William wanted. It was bad enough earning so little doing this job, but to have to give it away for free was a fresh degradation to a man who had seen degradation in all its forms.

"What do you want?"

"Perhaps you should invite me in rather than we discuss this on the doorstep."

It was like a fly inviting a spider into his home, but Jacob stepped back anyway, letting the man enter. He closed the door and waited as William looked around the room. He tried not to see it from the rent collector's eyes.

Jacob lived in one room, a bed in one corner, a table and two chairs in the other. A narrow counter ran along one wall where Jacob prepared food, a cupboard above it, usually empty. With the broken window it was freezing, and Jacob never had enough logs for the fire. Never had he felt his poverty more acutely than standing and watching this man appraise his hovel.

William finally turned to face him. "Lock the door."

Jacob didn't want to lock the door. Not when this man might be the Ripper, graduating to men from women, killing them in their own home just like he had Mary Kelly, but he did as he was told, cursing his cowardice.

William stepped forward. He put his hat on the table, then he unfastened his coat and threw it over the back of a chair. "Undress and lie down on the bed," he told Jacob.

This was not a room for getting undressed in. Jacob usually slept in his clothes to avoid dying of hypothermia in his sleep. He would have much preferred to stay partly dressed for this.

He shed his gloves and scarf and his thick coat, laying them on the other chair. He removed his boots and socks, wincing at the icy floor. He discarded his waistcoat and unfastened his shirt, already shivering at the cold. His thick undershirt followed and then he was down to his breeches.

"You're thin," William said in distaste as Jacob unfastened his breeches. "Don't you eat?"

Jacob turned his back, pushing his breeches down and stepping out of them. Clearly this was all about control because William obviously could not have felt desire for him. He'd had men in the past who'd shown desire for him, who had told him he was beautiful and treated him well, but those men had been few and far between, especially this winter when his weight had plummeted.

"Can I get under the covers?" he asked over his shoulder. "It's very cold."

"As you will, but don't forget your undergarments."

Jacob pushed them off his hips and tossed them on the chair. He climbed into the bed and pulled the covers up to his neck, shivering violently.

William regarded him. He pulled his boots and socks off. He unfastened his shirt to expose a hard, muscular torso. If the situation had been different and Jacob wasn't so cold and hungry, the man's body might have incited a response in him. As it was, it did nothing for him. William stripped and Jacob turned over onto his front, hiding his face. He laid waiting, legs parted.

Soon enough the covers were pulled back. Rough hands gripped his hips and pulled him up onto hands and knees. William spat on his hand. He slicked up his cock before he guided himself inside.

"You're tight boy. Relax for me," he grunted.

"I can't, you're hurting me."

William growled in frustration. He pulled Jacob hard against him, forcing his way deep inside.

Jacob held his cries in. He knelt motionless on the bed, head hanging down. William gave a few thrusts, groaning before he finished. Jacob took both their weights as William fell onto him, crushing him to the bed, gasping for breath.

"It's a wonder you make any money. You're like a fucking corpse," he said, pulling himself free. A rough hand groped Jacob's groin. "You're not even hard."

Jacob's smart mouth always got him into trouble. "Was there something to be aroused about?" he asked over his shoulder.

William cuffed him hard over the back of the head. "Whore." He climbed from the bed and walked across to the chair for his clothes. "You'd better have the money next month or I might not be in the mood to let you off so lightly."

Jacob pressed his face into the pillow. He didn't lift it until he heard the door close.

Jacob trembled as he answered the door on that Tuesday morning a month later. He prayed his old collector was back, a man who would have never dreamed of asking for payment in kind. But no, it was the smirking William Brock.

"Hello, Jacob, how are you this fine morning?"

"I don't have it," Jacob said without preamble.

William's face darkened. "That's a shame. You'd better let me in."

Jacob stood back. He locked the door once William had entered.

"Do you have anything at all to give me, or do I evict you this time?" William took his hat off.

"I've got two weeks."

"Well that's better than nothing but obviously it leaves me out of pocket again. You'll have to appease me a bit better than you did last time. You almost froze my dick with your coldness."

Jacob eyed him stonily. Turning away, he started to undress. He climbed beneath the covers and waited. He turned his head just as William lifted a knee to climb into the bed, and he saw the rent collector naked. His body was beautiful. In other places and other times this would have been a pleasure. Jacob felt the smallest twinge of desire push at him, despite himself.

He got up onto his knees without being pulled and

shivered as a hand stroked his bare backside. Before William could get down to it, he said quickly, "If it pleases you, I'd be grateful for lubrication this time. I lost two nights' work last month."

William was obviously taken aback. "And where would I get that?"

"I don't know. Look in my cupboards."

William huffed. He climbed from the bed, and Jacob's gaze followed his naked form to the kitchen cupboard. Jacob knew there was only one suitable thing in there and sure enough, William located the slab of butter wrapped in greaseproof paper and brought it back to the bed. "We'll have a job," he complained. "It's rock hard."

Jacob took it from him. He lay on his back and pushed the butter between his thighs, holding it tight. "A few moments to soften it."

William looked amused. He drew a finger down Jacob's sternum all the way to his groin before he fondled his limp cock a little roughly. "I expect more from you this time," he said in stern warning.

Jacob looked up into the grey-silver eyes. He doubted William would get more. He put a hand down to check on the progress of the butter which was chilling his skin through and through.

"Come on," William said impatiently, snatching it from him. "Turn over."

Jacob braced himself on hands and knees. The greaseproof paper crinkled behind him and then the butter thudded onto the pillow by his head, minus a chunk. Hands rubbed together behind him and slicked up flesh. Jacob flinched when fingers probed between his legs. "There," William said, rubbing around his entrance and then insinuating one then two fingers. "Maybe this will be better."

William had used plenty, and the heat of Jacob's body melted the butter to rivulets which ran down his inner thighs. Hardness pressed against him, and William slid slickly inside. Jacob stifled a gasp.

William held onto his hips and withdrew, spearing him again. "Oh, that's better." His voice was a soft moan. "I bow to your wisdom on these matters, Jacob. Thank you for pointing out the error of my ways."

Jacob didn't reply. His head hung down, and with eyes tightly closed, he kept quiet. William kept up a slow, steady pace. He didn't seem in a rush this time, and the easy strokes threatened to arouse Jacob. This was not what he wanted. Showing any pleasure might make the rent collector keen to come back.

But William sealed his dilemma. He sat back and pulled Jacob onto his lap, arms around him, holding him firmly. His mouth found his neck and Jacob moaned uncontrollably. Caresses and kisses were few and far between in this job and something which Jacob craved. He was soft of heart and dreamed of tenderness.

William laughed softly against his skin. "Mmm," he murmured, "you feel good." He rocked slowly into Jacob, hands stroking his torso. "Do you like that?" His mouth sought Jacob's ear and temple.

"Yes..." Jacob moaned helplessly.

"Good boy." A hand slid down his body. "You're hard too. That's good." Jacob gasped at the fingers around him, but they soon moved away, much to his frustration. The mouth continued against his neck though. Jacob's head fell back against William's shoulder. The mouth devoured his throat. The torso against his back was damp with sweat. Jacob was cold no longer. He was desperate to put his own hand around himself and move against the cock inside him but he refrained with an effort. No. He wouldn't give this man the satisfaction.

William groaned. "Oh yes, my sweet little whore." Jacob tensed angrily at the words even though he'd been called worse. "Yes. Oh, God." He gave another couple of jerky thrusts and then stopped, moaning softly in ecstasy.

Jacob opened his eyes, nowhere near climax and disappointed. But he knew by now that most clients didn't see it as part of their job to get the whore off too. Why should they? He rarely came during his work unless he struck lucky with a customer who liked to go down on his knees for as long as it took. It didn't matter. His own hand was much better.

William eased himself free. Jacob lay down on his face and waited for him to leave. His erection pulsed with need. He pulled the covers up around him and curled up into a ball. A hand stroked his buttocks. "Very good. I'll see you next month."

Jacob didn't reply. He didn't need to speak to this man now that they'd finished. In a few minutes the door closed. Jacob put a hand between his legs but the desire had left him now, and he had withered just fine.

When he woke from his customary nap before going out to work, someone had reached through the broken window and left a fresh slab of butter on the sill. Rich, salted butter too, not the cheap stuff Jacob bought.

Jacob had given himself a set of instructions next

month. No noise, no signs of arousal, no masturbating while he's doing it to you. Coldness and indifference were paramount or this man would be getting it free the rest of his life.

But William had a new opening gambit. He stood on the doorstep holding a dish covered with a cloth. "My wife bakes regularly for the people on the row," he explained, looking almost sheepish. "This week it's your turn." He thrust the dish at Jacob and Jacob, stomach rumbling from dinner time last night without abatement, stepped back and allowed the rent collector in.

He'd seen the wedding ring, of course he had, but he had hardly expected William to mention his wife this way. He put the dish down on the table as William locked the door behind him. "I have a month's rent."

William nodded approvingly. "Good."

Jacob looked at him for another moment and then started to undress. Snow lay on the ground outside and he'd had no logs for the fire for two weeks, desperately trying to save the money for the rent.

"It's colder than a witch's tit in here," William said helpfully, blowing on his hands.

Jacob climbed naked into the bed and sat up, covers pulled up, shivering.

William withdrew a small, dark glass bottle from his coat. "I have some oil. A little more refined than butter."

Jacob didn't say anything. He sat and watched while William undressed and the beautiful body was revealed. As he walked towards the bed, already half hard, Jacob felt the sudden stab of arousal in his groin. He shuffled over for William, and their eyes remained locked. Jacob didn't turn over and present himself willingly; he stayed still and he felt the tension thrum through the air as William almost pinned him to the bed, mouth seeking his.

Jacob turned his head away with a soft moan.

"Kiss me," William insisted.

"No, I can't. I don't kiss."

William growled in frustration. "You'll kiss me one day, boy, I promise you that." He pressed down against Jacob's stiffening cock, and Jacob whimpered, spreading his legs, face turned away.

"Do you want it?"

"Yes," Jacob said shamelessly.

"Good."

William sat back on his heels and reached for the oil. He pushed Jacob's knees up. One finger ran lightly around Jacob's entrance, teasing with feather-light strokes before he pushed it inside. Jacob's hands gripped William's thighs.

"Mmm, you're so much more relaxed than you were that first horrid time. Come here, I want you to suck me."

Jacob did as he was told, bending over William, taking him in his mouth. William groaned, and he sought Jacob again, putting two fingers inside while Jacob sucked him. Jacob almost yelped as William pressed against just the right place.

William laughed softly. "How hard you are for me today. I want you to sit on me and ride me where I can see your hard cock."

Jacob scrambled to obey. He was so aroused he could barely think straight. He couldn't remember the last time he had felt this way. William lay down, and Jacob straddled him, gripping his shaft at the bottom as he impaled himself slowly.

William's hands held his hips. He threw his head back, groaning as Jacob engulfed him. Jacob sat still a moment, gasping before he started to move. His cock twitched with every slide of William against his insides, the head leaking pearl drops. It was good, it was so good. If it was like this every time, he would gladly give it away free from now till doomsday.

"That's good, boy, that's so good," William groaned, thrusting up hard into him. "I love seeing you hard like this. Love watching your hard cock bouncing on me." His hand fondled Jacob's balls, squeezing, before stroking his cock.

Jacob moaned, head thrown back. He had to come this time. He had to. To his shame, as William went to pull his hand away, Jacob pushed it back, gripping it tight, forcing it around his arousal. "Please," he begged. "Make me spend."

William laughed in delight. "What a whore you are once you get going. I love it." He slid Jacob slowly and teasingly through his fingers. "Like this?"

"Yes." Jacob bounced harder and faster on him, grinding William into his prostate, stabs of electricity shaking him with every movement. He listened to his own panting and gasps with amazement. He couldn't remember the last time he had been fucked so gloriously and lost all his control this way. He never wanted it to end.

"God, you're wonderful." William's hands gripped his buttocks hard. "I love your sweet little arse. I want to put my tongue in it and eat it until you spend all over me."

Jacob shrieked. He bucked his hips hard and spurted violently over William's chest. William growled in excitement. He filled Jacob full with a shout, then fell back exhausted and quivering. Jacob fell forward onto his chest motionless, almost comatose.

William laughed softly beneath him, his chest vibrating against Jacob. One hand gripped his buttock possessively then slapped it. "I knew I'd warm you up in time. My God, how frigid you were that first time."

Jacob didn't say anything. He crawled slowly off William and lay on his back, turning his head to look longingly at the table. William laughed almost fondly. "Go and eat your pie, boy, you deserve it tonight."

Jacob slid from the bed and pulled on his threadbare robe. He located a spoon and sat down at the table, throwing the cloth from the dish and digging in. It was still warm, amazingly, the pastry rich and melting, the filling fish and vegetables in a creamy sauce. He ate it like a starving man which was what he was. Then he checked himself when he saw William watching him from the bed. He swallowed, sitting back. "Do you want some?" he offered politely even though he'd rather die than give some of the wonderful pie away.

William shook his head. "No, I'll have lunch when I get home. It's good, isn't it?"

Jacob shovelled another mouthful in, nodding his head vigorously. William continued to watch him, a slight smile on his face.

"What?" Jacob finally asked, uncomfortable.

"Nothing." William climbed from the bed, still half hard. He reached for his underwear, and Jacob averted his gaze while he dressed, concentrating on his pie. He had sat back for a rest when William finished and came over to him. He bent over him, hand on the back of his chair, and Jacob froze, looking up at him.

"Can I ask you for one thing more before I leave?" his voice was a murmur, grey eyes fixed on Jacob's.

"What?" Jacob asked warily, heart almost in his mouth.

"A kiss."

"I told you, I don't kiss."

"In exchange for the pie. And I'll make sure to bring you another one."

Jacob hesitated. The pie was probably worth a kiss but if he kissed this man then he broke his number one rule. Actually, his only rule. But he had no money for food and who knew if he would earn any tonight?

"When will you bring me the next one?" he tried to bargain.

William smiled and his eyes seemed softer. Perhaps he felt sorry for Jacob, which made him bristle. "Tomorrow."

"Really?" Jacob hardly dared hope. "Do you promise?"

"Yes."

Jacob was a fool, he knew that, trading kisses for pies when kisses were all that he kept back of himself. Now there was nothing left to give. He tilted his head back and closed his eyes.

William took him by the back of the neck. His mouth closed over Jacob's, soft, warm, pliable. His kiss was agreeable. The most agreeable Jacob had had in a long while. He was almost gasping in surprised pleasure when William drew back.

William smiled again. His fingertips stroked Jacob's cheek. "I like you, Jacob," he said. "I hope you can find it in your heart to not think too badly of me for doing this to you."

Jacob closed his mouth before he caught flies. He didn't know what to say.

"And I *will* bring you the pie. Tomorrow, before you go out to work." He put his hat on. "Good day."

Jacob didn't speak. He sat there with spoon still held in his hand as William let himself out.

When he had gone, Jacob ate the full pie. He rolled into the still warm bed and fell instantly asleep, dreaming of pie and sex and succulent kisses.

William didn't come next day until it was dark and Jacob was dressed and almost ready to go out. He had had nothing but an apple to eat all day, one he found rolling in the gutter by the market, and he was lightheaded with hunger. William wasn't going to come, he told himself a hundred times, that much was obvious. He had bargained a kiss for a pie and lost. And then there was a knock on the door.

Jacob opened it to see William standing in the gloom outside holding a dish. His stomach leapt with excitement, and his mouth filled with saliva. Right then he would have pounced upon William and given him a dozen kisses if he so wished.

"Can I come in?"

"Yes." Jacob stepped back, still eyeing the dish.

"There you are."

The dish was hot. Not hot enough to burn but more or less fresh from the oven. Jacob held it greedily against his body, willing the heat to radiate into him.

"Are you on your way out?"

"Yes."

"But you can spare a few minutes to eat, can't you? You look like you're going to faint."

Jacob nodded. He put the pie on the table. William moved past him, procuring Jacob's one and only spoon. "Here. Sit down." He pulled Jacob's chair out for him as though he were an obsequious waiter and then he retreated to sit on Jacob's bed, watching him by the light of the one candle.

Jacob wished he would leave. Which was ungrateful of him considering William had kept his promise and brought the pie.

He watched Jacob eat half the pie, and then he said, "Tell me, how much do you earn on a good night, Jacob?"

Jacob bristled. "That's none of your business."

William bit his lip. He took his hat off. "Forgive me. Let me rephrase the question. If I gave you twenty shillings, would you stay here with me tonight instead of going to work?"

Jacob stared. *Twenty shillings?* "You want to stay here in my bed with me?" he asked carefully.

"Yes. Until dawn."

"And how many times would you want to...?"

"As many times as I can."

Jacob regarded him a while longer. "Why?"

"Why?" William echoed. "When a customer approaches you in the street, do you ask him why he wants to lie with you?"

"No."

"Then why are you asking me?"

"Because... you were getting it free and now you want to pay for it."

William sighed. "I'm sure I could blackmail you

into lying with me every day of the week Jacob, considering all the money you owe, but something about that wouldn't be quite right. I'd be a man of the lowest kind. The arrangement is once a month. For extras, I should pay."

Jacob didn't know what to say.

"I dare say you already think of me as a man of the lowest kind?"

Jacob looked at his pie. He didn't reply. He had, of course he had. And then William had nearly blown his head off last time. Something about getting paid to experience the same kind of pleasure again was very attractive.

"I'll take that as a yes then."

"Won't your wife wonder where you are all night?"

"She and I... we have an understanding."

Jacob took another spoonful of the pie and then put the cloth back over it. "There's the other dish," he motioned to the side. "Take it with you when you go."

William nodded. He stood. "Do you and I have an arrangement?"

Jacob hesitated. "I don't usually have customers here."

"I understand."

"I would want something else apart from the twenty shillings."

William arched a brow, looking amused.

"A pie every day for two weeks."

William laughed. "You drive a hard bargain, young sir. My wife doesn't cook for the same person for so long, but spreads out her charity among the row. I would have to give you someone else's pies."

Jacob shook his head. "No, I won't take anyone else's. There are families with children."

William walked over to him. He smiled gently, leaning over him, fingertips brushing his cheek. "You have a good heart, Jacob Doran," he murmured.

Jacob turned his head away, a sudden lump in his throat.

"You've had it hard, haven't you?" William turned Jacob's face back so he could look into his eyes.

Jacob closed them. They burned with sudden tears.

William drew closer. He stroked Jacob's neck. "I'll take a month's rent off your debt."

Jacob's eyes flicked open, staring. "You don't... I wouldn't expect you to... I owe you, sir."

William shook his head. He unfastened his frockcoat and threw it on the chair. "No matter. You're a good man. I hate to see you like this."

Jacob swallowed. He stood, moved to the bed and turned his back, undressing. He was unsettled and upset. He didn't dare ask if now he was getting a month knocked off the debt, it would mean William wouldn't pay him the twenty shillings for tonight. It seemed churlish of him.

He slid between his cold sheets and pulled the thin blanket over him. William walked towards him naked, his skin almost glowing in the candlelight. He put the bottle of oil on the bedside table before he pulled the covers back and climbed in, pressing close to Jacob and putting his arms around him. The feel of his warm skin made Jacob shiver. "How do you want me?" he asked.

"Not yet," William responded. "Lie with me a while. I want to hold you. I can't remember the last time I held anyone. Do people hold you, Jacob?"

Jacob shook his head. Stiffly, he nestled closer to William, hands on his back. Of course no one held him.

They usually fucked him half dressed in an alleyway or doss house then threw some coins at him.

"Relax, you're tense." With his hand, William smoothed the knots from his shoulders and spine.

Jacob willed his body to uncoil. He laid his face against William's neck and inhaled the delicate scent of his cologne, his lips pressing gently.

William shuddered unmistakably, and his arms tightened around Jacob. "I hope you can forgive me for treating you badly," he murmured. "This is wrong of me. I told myself that if I behaved like a beast, I could keep you at arm's length, not feel sorry for you, not get attached. But I *am* attached. I've seen you in the market place. I've watched you and I've longed to be close to you."

Jacob lifted his head in astonishment. He stared into William's silvery eyes. He was shocked to the core to find there was more to this than William blackmailing him over the rent. Had William planned this? Had he watched Jacob for a while, contemplating his move? Was this the only way he thought he could win Jacob?

Jacob hid his face against William's neck. He pulsed with arousal and shifted against William. William pushed one thigh between Jacob's, pressing against his hard cock, and Jacob caught his breath on a moan. God, he wanted this.

"Tell me what you want me to do to you," William breathed in his ear.

"You know."

"I want to hear you say it. Tell me what you want."

Jacob clutched at him. He ground himself against William's thigh. "I want you to fuck me."

William pushed him onto his back, pressing down

on him. "How?"

"Hard."

William growled. His hand found Jacob's cock and stroked. "I want to fuck you so hard that you scream for more," he whispered. "I want to suck you into my mouth until you cry out. I want you to sit on my face and beg me to lick your sweet arse."

Jacob shuddered, bucking into William's hand. "Please... do whatever you want to me."

William slid abruptly from the bed. He took his cravat from the chair, and then he came back to Jacob, stretching it slowly, meaningfully between his hands, eyes fixed on Jacob's.

A shudder of desperate excitement went through Jacob. He was not fond of being tied up by clients when there was no guarantee it wouldn't lead to sadism and violence, but this was different. He was William's slave at that moment.

William straddled his body. He took Jacob's wrists, stretched them above his head and tied them together firmly. Then he tied them to the bed head, leaving Jacob exposed and helpless. He pulled the covers back, and his hot eyes perused Jacob's body. Jacob shifted on the sheets, cock twitching and leaking against his belly, almost at the point of begging for it again.

William cupped his balls and lightly squeezed. Sliding his fingers around Jacob's cock, he tugged slowly. Jacob bucked up into his hand, gasping.

"You like that?"

"Yes."

"What do you want me to do?"

"Suck it."

William smiled. "You're the one tied up here and you're making demands?"

Jacob tried to backtrack. "No... I... you asked me."

William grinned impishly. "I'm teasing you, Jacob." He bowed his head and sucked Jacob all the way into his mouth.

Jacob cursed and blasphemed. He writhed on the bed, straining at his bonds, lifting his pelvis, rocking himself into the sucking mouth which went faster and faster the more excited Jacob got.

For sure he was a lucky man, but he was afraid of the control William so clearly had over him. He opened his eyes to see William looking up through his lashes, watching him closely as he sucked.

"Please..."

William drew back. "Please what?"

"Please, don't stop. I like it so much."

"Good boy. It pleases me that you do. Do you want me to swallow your spendings?"

"Yes." It was a gasp of excitement. This was the stuff of fantasies.

William smiled. He licked wetly over the head of Jacob's cock before he dragged his tongue down the shaft.

Jacob groaned. He couldn't remember the last time anyone had done such a thing to him. To actually put his mouth around him and stay there until Jacob's end. He was the luckiest man in the world.

He bucked up, almost yelling, his bonds straining and cutting into his wrists. "Oh God, oh God..."

He spilled into William's mouth helplessly, and his lover sucked it all down, keeping his mouth there until Jacob fell back exhausted, whimpering.

"Mmm." William drew his mouth slowly off Jacob. "How beautiful you are."

Jacob regarded him from under his lashes. "Thank you for pleasing me."

William smiled. "That was only the hors d'oeuvres. I haven't even started yet."

The blood rushed back to Jacob's cock. William leaned down over him and unfastened his bonds and Jacob stared at William's hard cock. The rent collector turned him briskly onto all fours.

Jacob swayed, legs spread, backside presented.

"Wider." William slapped him on one buttock.

Jacob did as he was told, shifting his legs, dipping his head.

"Nice, very nice." William reached for the oil. A finger rubbed his entrance slickly. Large hands pushed him apart, and a wet tongue circled him, causing Jacob to shudder and cry out.

"You like that?"

"Yes."

"I knew you would, you dirty little boy. I always know the boys who like a tongue in their arse."

"Do it again."

William squeezed his balls. "Who's in charge here?"

"You are!"

"That's right. I'll lick you if I want to lick you. If it pleases me."

Jacob grunted and shifted, trying to rub his erection against the bed.

"Whore. Whose whore are you?"

"I'm your whore, William. I'll do whatever you want me to do. If it pleases you, please lick me. *Please*."

William laughed. Then he spread Jacob apart again and set about him with a tongue to rival all tongues.

Jacob was noisy in his pleasure, and he had never had pleasure like this before. Each wet flick and stroke sent him senseless. Saliva ran down his inner thighs and onto his balls and he pushed back, trying to take William's tongue inside him, begging for more with every lick.

William gripped his cock and pulled it back between Jacob's legs. He sucked at it and fucked Jacob with one finger while he did.

"You're so open and wet, boy. Ready to pull me inside."

Jacob gasped, cheek resting against the pillow with exhaustion. "Take me."

"Oh, I'll take you. I'll take you until you forget your own name."

A strong arm gripped him around the waist. Hard flesh jabbed into him, filling him full. Jacob whimpered, arms shaking as he supported himself on the bed.

William growled. He planted kisses on Jacob's back. "How different you are from that first time, Jacob."

Jacob didn't reply. He didn't know what had changed. Had he some finer feelings towards William now, or was it just he had found a body that suited his own? Either way, he didn't want to let him go.

Each long stroke into him gave him such pleasure he couldn't think properly. He cried out William's name hopelessly, and William responded by holding him ever tighter, driving into him ever more quickly and pulling that second orgasm from him.

"Oh God, oh God."

William had to hold him there as Jacob spent on the

sheets, trembling violently with release.

He was just about aware of William finishing too, before he collapsed face first on the bed.

Jacob came around slowly to find himself on his side, William lying behind him, a strong arm around his middle. He felt warm for the first time in a long while with the heat radiating from William's body.

A wan sun filtered behind the thin curtain, illuminating the room with grey light.

William kissed his ears and his throat and murmured to him. "For sure, I never had such a lover as you before, Jacob. Consider your debt cancelled."

"What?"

Jacob turned over in his arms to look at him.

William sighed. "Oh Jacob, I was never your rent collector, just a man who liked the look of you in the marketplace."

"I don't... understand," Jacob stammered.

"I paid your rent collector a fee amounting to your rent every month to come here and masquerade as him."

Jacob stared.

"So you don't owe him, only me, and I consider that debt settled."

Jacob slid from the bed, pulling on underwear. He began shivering immediately in the frigid air. "Why would you..."

"I only wanted to be close to you, that's all." William got out too and pulled on Jacob's robe, which barely closed over his muscular chest.

"You deceived me!"

"Now don't excite yourself." William reached a

purse from the inside pocket of his coat. "Here's the twenty shillings for last night and here's another five to buy some damn logs for the fire and whatever else you need. If it's agreeable to you, I'll come back next month and pay you twenty shillings then too."

"You can't just..." Jacob was speechless with outrage at the trickery William had employed. "My rent collector would never have asked for sexual favours the way you did!"

"I know that. Because he's a better man than I'll ever be." William dropped Jacob's robe and started to dress, and Jacob took note of every muscle, every inch of hard flesh. "So forgive me."

Jacob folded his arms. "I'll have to think about that."

"Of course you will. Think about it until next month."

"I shall." Jacob pouted.

William smiled. "You're adorable. I can't wait until the next time I'm inside you."

Jacob flushed. He pulled on his breeches and shirt.

William caught his cheek in one hand. Lips hovered near his. "A kiss, Jacob?"

"No." Jacob turned his face away.

William turned it back. One arm encircled Jacob's waist firmly. "I said, a kiss, Jacob." And he claimed Jacob's mouth.

So fiery, so passionate was the kiss that Jacob might have fallen down if William hadn't have been holding him. It heated Jacob inside and out, left his lips scorching and his head spinning. He clutched at William, mouth open and presented, tongue dancing with his.

William swung him up into his arms and carried him to the bed, lying him down. "I'm not quite ready to leave yet, Jacob, if that's all right."

Jacob looked up at him dazedly as William unfastened his breeches and revealed hard flesh. "That's fine. Stay as long as you want."

William grinned. His hand massaged Jacob's crotch through his breeches, coaxing him into erection. "That's what I like to hear, my sweet Jacob. Now why don't you tell me what you want me to do to you?"

Jacob writhed on the bed, pushing against William's hand. He pulled William down by the shoulder, before gripping his head in both hands and bringing his ear to his mouth. He whispered urgently.

William drew back, beaming. "Why Jacob, you dirty, dirty boy. You're a man after my own heart. I think I might have to start coming more than once a month seeing as you're someone who needs satisfying on a regular basis. Have you any objections to that?"

Jacob shook his head mutely, eyes wide as he watched William's fingers nimbly unfasten his breeches.

William's hand slid inside. He massaged Jacob's hard cock. "That's good. That's very good."

He leaned down and kissed Jacob again and, lost once more to pleasure, Jacob sank away.

HOMELESS

It all started after the fight with Melinda. Michael had been seeing her three months when it all came to a head. He was tired of being used and abused. Tired of the other men and being her plaything when she wanted him. He could do better, and he told her so. A vicious and public fight followed. He was ejected from the bar, thrown out onto the street by doormen who put the boot in a couple of times while he was down on the sidewalk.

Seething, Michael walked across town, taking a shortcut through an alley which led to home. He weaved on his feet, drunk and cursing. He stopped half down the alley, leaned against a dumpster ready to vomit. Instead, he yelled and shouted and pounded his fist against the plastic beside him.

"Who's made you so mad?"

Michael whirled around, startled. Behind him, huddled on the ground against the opposite wall was a young, fresh-faced homeless man with short dark hair, jagged and uneven as though he'd done it himself. He wore a thick jacket, a blanket pulled around his knees. He had to be about twenty-four or younger.

"A chick, it's got to be a chick, right?" The man answered his own question when Michael didn't reply.

Michael leaned against the wall, regarding him, ready for the pearls of wisdom these guys always delivered to anyone who'd listen. "Yeah, it's a chick."

"What did she do? Break it off?"

"No, I did."

The guy nodded sagely as though he were an advice

columnist who heard this sorry tale on a regular basis. "Yeah. That's why you know where you are with guys."

"What?" Michael frowned, then laughed. "No man, you've got it wrong…"

"So you wouldn't, if I asked?"

"What?" Flustered, Michael couldn't believe his ears.

"I'm offering." The man stood up and let the blanket drop, stretching his lean frame provocatively so his jacket and shirt rode up to reveal several inches of pale flesh. "How about it?"

Michael shook his head in disgust. "I don't think so."

"Why not? My rates are reasonable. I don't ask you to take me out for dinner first or cuddle me after. And I've got my own protection." The man held out a foil square.

"You're fucking crazy. Be thankful I don't punch your lights out." Michael pushed himself off the wall as the guy's hands went to his belt buckle. Releasing it quickly, he unfastened his pants.

"Try me once. If you don't like it, you get it free. I don't make offers like that to anyone, you know. But you look to me like you need it." The guy turned around and dropped his pants and boxers.

He leaned against the wall, with his pert, rounded backside jutting out towards Michael, and grinned over his shoulder.

Michael stood staring.

"You're the hottest guy I've seen all month. Wouldn't you like a guilt-free fuck with no strings?" The man took something else out of his jeans pocket. It was a tube of lubricant that he opened to squirt a few drops onto his fingers. Then, as Michael watched, the man trailed his fingers lazily down his own ass crack, seeking and stroking.

Michael's brain told him to move, to leave this sordid freak show behind. His body told him something different. His cock was standing at attention watching this stranger lube himself up.

"Okay," the man said, taking glistening fingers away. "I'm ready for you. All you have to do is stick it in and go." He leaned against the wall, his pants sliding to his ankles, bent at the waist with legs spread obscenely, so Michael saw exactly what he was offering.

His cock twitched. When he had come out to meet Melinda tonight, he had been in a frenzy of need after she had denied him all week. He had intended to fuck her senseless and some of his anger at her had been lust not sated. Here was a hole being offered. Never mind it belonged to a man.

Michael moved forward. He snatched the condom from the man and tore it open. He opened his pants and rolled it on. He guided his cock between the ripe cheeks and rubbed it back and forth, greasing his way.

The man moaned theatrically. He pushed back against Michael and Michael, with his cock pressed tight between those cheeks, gripped his slender hips and pushed forward. He hissed as he was engulfed in tight heat. His partner shuddered, gasping loudly. Michael caught his breath a moment, and then he held onto the stranger and rode him for all he was worth, spilling his anger, his need, his frustration.

It was going to be quick. He felt himself on the edge within a couple of minutes. He held his partner's hips harder, pressing his torso against his, crushing him to the wall. With his face against the man's neck, Michael mouthed soft skin, finding it smooth and pleasantly scented. He kissed and bit lightly.

His partner cursed and bucked back against him. His elbow moved swiftly as he jerked himself off.

"Fuck." Michael groaned as the orgasm rolled over him. He gave into it, grasping his partner hard around the torso, face buried against his neck.

He came to a panting halt, leaning against the stranger. The man moaned softly. He moved back against Michael's softening cock. His elbow worked quickly.

He stiffened suddenly, gasped and his thighs shook so hard that Michael held him tighter, afraid he was going to fall down. He clenched in delicious waves around Michael, milking his cock still further before he slumped against the wall.

Michael pulled free with difficulty. His heart raced, and he felt dizzy. He stumbled back, discarded his condom and fastened himself up, trying to process what had just happened.

His partner turned around, smiling like the cat that got the cream, and Michael felt endless shame and disgust. "Nice, very nice. I know you enjoyed it so I'm going to ask that you pay. Fifty bucks, please."

Michael stared at him. He could be an asshole about it. This guy was smaller than him and not as well-built, what could he do? But these guys usually had a weapon tucked away. He would probably knife Michael as he tried to walk away. And besides, the guy was homeless. Selling his ass to men probably hadn't been his career choice in high school. It would be cruel to take the goods for free, even if this guy had clearly enjoyed it.

Michael reached into his back pocket for his wallet. "You got change?" he asked pointlessly, holding out a hundred.

The guy raised one sarcastic eyebrow. "What do you think?"

Michael shrugged. He held out the bill.

The man hesitated before he took it. "Fine, but I owe you round two. Come back for it whenever you want. I'll be ready." He smiled, his teeth pearly white.

Michael flushed. "I don't think so."

The stranger laughed as he walked away. "Yeah, that's what they all say."

Michael woke up in his four poster bed in his penthouse at seven the next morning with a terrible headache. He blinked a few times before he remembered. No. Surely it had been a dream. He wasn't in the habit of picking up random men—random male prostitutes—and fucking them in alleyways. He was straight for God's sake, and he'd never looked towards the dark side. He couldn't believe he'd done it and paid a hundred bucks for the pleasure. *And hadn't it been a pleasure?* A sly little voice whispered. *The best sex you've had in ages.*

Michael worked as assistant director to a large multinational company. He drove a Porsche and dined out five nights a week. He wasn't short of female company, so he asked himself that morning why he'd tolerated Melinda as long as he had. Had he even really liked her? Hadn't she just been arm candy when he attended work functions?

No matter, it was done now, and he was happily single again. He didn't need to think about what the break up with Melinda had driven him to. An unfortunate blip. And didn't all men experiment with the same sex at one time in their lives? Perhaps not with a homeless hooker ten years younger than him though.

Michael avoided like the plague walking through the alleyway even though it was a convenient shortcut from work at lunch time to the sandwich shops and restaurants he frequented. At the end of the week though, due to meet up with friends in town, he chose to walk rather than get a cab and forced himself to cut through the alleyway to save time. The guy wouldn't be there, he was sure of it. Homeless people didn't stay so long in one place, he told himself, like he was an expert on the habits of those with no fixed abode. And even if he did see the guy, he only had to walk past and ignore him. It had been dark, and he probably wouldn't even recognise Michael among the many men he slept with.

Twilight was falling as he entered the alleyway, walking briskly, head up, looking neither left nor right.

He had made it past the dumpster where he had stopped five nights ago and was half way down the alley when a voice shouted. "Hey, gorgeous."

Michael stopped, frozen, the voice instantly familiar. He turned around slowly to see a shape unravelling itself from a blanket, the figure lean.

His hooker of Sunday night smiled at him, teeth as perfect as Michael remembered, rather at odds with his lifestyle. "Why are you walking past? Don't you want what I owe you?"

Michael shook his head. "Keep the money. That night… it was a mistake."

The man stepped forward, still smiling. "Come on now, I've heard that before. You were drunk but not that drunk. You had a great time and so did I. Now let me give you the other half." He started to unfasten Michael's belt.

"I said no," Michael said loudly.

"I understand." The man's voice had dropped. It was soft and cajoling. "You're shy."

If there was one thing Michael was not, it was shy.

The guy took hold of Michael's belt and pulled Michael towards him, to the wall behind the shadow of the dumpster. Then he put a hand between his legs.

"Hey." Michael gripped his wrist hard.

The guy looked up at him, and moonlight illuminated jade green eyes and perfect, milk-white skin. Christ, he was beautiful. A sudden shudder went through Michael, and he started to stiffen.

"Let me," the man said in a seductive whisper, and then he unfastened Michael's pants and drew him out, half hard.

Michael, blushing in shame, had no power to stop him. He didn't *want* to stop him. He watched as the man sank to his knees and put his mouth around Michael. Oh God, it was perfect. It was like Michael had given him precise instructions on how he liked lips and tongue to be used, and he was following them to the letter. If he'd ever had a better blowjob in his life, he couldn't remember.

The stranger drew him steadily to the end, swallowing when Michael exploded with a gasp, gripping his partner's hair. He looked down into the man's face, and the man looked up, licking some white from his top lip.

"What's your name?"

"Michael."

"Well Michael, I'm Poe."

"Poe? Is that your first name or last?"

"First. What can I say? My mother was a reader. My sister's called Brontë."

Michael found himself wanting to smile at the man's easy charm. He fastened himself away as Poe stood up.

"So, a blowjob's only forty so I still owe you ten. Come back again, and I'll give you a handjob."

"I don't think…"

"That's what you said last time, and here you are."

"Hey, I was on my way into town. This is a shortcut."

Poe smirked. He sat down in his nest of blankets and pulled them up around his knees. "I'm a shortcut? I don't know if I should be offended or not."

"You know what I mean. I won't be back."

"Sure, Michael, but think of me when you ask yourself why you're feeling so good tonight, okay? I sure won't forget you in a hurry." He smiled, and his eyes glittered with something resembling fondness.

Michael turned and marched out of the alley.

The question was, did he walk home or get a cab? Two of the guys had already bailed to their wives, which left Michael with his best friend, Simon, drunk and thinking about earlier. It was nearly time to leave. It was a nice night to walk, and Michael took exercise whenever he could get it. But what if Poe still lurked in the alleyway? What if he offered Michael that ten dollar handjob? He'd refuse, just like he'd refused the previous two times they'd met, and then he'd let Poe do it anyway and love it.

He sighed, tipping back his glass of JD and Coke.

"What's up man? You've been distracted all night."

"You wouldn't believe me if I told you."

"Sure I would."

"You'd be disgusted. You'd never want to speak to me again."

"Hey." Simon was suddenly all seriousness. "You're my best friend and a good guy even if you're terminally vain. I love you. There's nothing you could tell me which would disgust me."

Michael scowled. "Are you sure?"

"Sure I'm sure. Now what've you done? Embezzling from work again?"

"If only. Okay then, but you asked for this. Remember I finished with Melinda last Sunday? On the way home I got propositioned by a prostitute, and I took up the offer. Since then, I've been back again. Tonight."

Simon shrugged. "That it? You're not the first, you won't be the last. I did it once upon a time. Just don't start relying on it okay?"

Michael cast a sideways glance at him. "He."

"What?"

"It was a he."

"Ah." Simon still remained calm. "Always knew you would one day."

"What?" Michael's gaze whipped to his, startled.

"If I had to say which one of our group would be interested in experimenting, you'd fit the bill."

"Why?" Since when had Michael ever given that impression?

"I don't know. Perhaps it's the clothes or the hairstyle. You're too gay, dude."

Michael's face heated. "You think I'm gay?"

"I'm joking. Look, you've done it, it's done. Get over it. Just don't go back."

Michael lowered his head. "I feel so bad. Not just because he's a guy but because... he's younger than me and he's... homeless. I took advantage of him."

Simon sighed. "Listen to me. You didn't take advantage of him, you paid him his going rate, right? Did he indicate to you that he was unhappy with the arrangement?"

"No."

"Right then. But listen, why did you go back tonight?"

"I was walking through the alley where he sleeps. He came onto me again. I couldn't..."

"You're weak as fuck." Simon was exasperated. "Don't do it again, or you'll have to admit that you're really, *really* gay." He smirked.

Michael didn't reply. He didn't want to catch a cab home. He wanted to walk.

The alleyway was in darkness but there was enough light to see the heap of blankets and the human-shaped form beneath. Michael approached quietly. Poe didn't move. Michael bent down to look at him a moment. As he did, the moon came out from behind the clouds and illuminated Poe's face.

He was battered black and blue, a half inch wide cut above his eyebrow dribbling blood steadily, so it coated and clumped his long lashes. His left cheek was grotesquely swollen, and his lips were cut.

Michael drew in his breath. "Poe."

One pale green eye flickered open, the left one swollen half shut.

"Oh my God, who did this to you?"

Poe actually smiled. "Hey, Michael. How nice to see you again. I'm sorry but I'm not sure I'm going to be up to giving that handjob. Mainly because I think my hand's broken. However, I could try with my left even though it's not as dexterous."

"Oh Jesus Christ, I don't want anything from you. Tell me who did this." Michael was surprisingly distraught.

"No one, man. Just a misunderstanding. I deserved it."

It was pointless; Poe wasn't going to say anything even if Michael would have readily played the avenging angel at that moment in time. "You need to go to the hospital."

"Nah, I'm good."

"Listen to me. You need sutures. You need X-rays." Michael pulled his wallet from his back pocket and pulled out all he had, plus a business card. "Take this. If it's any more, you give them my card and ask them to bill me."

"No way, man. No way." Poe struggled to sit up. "I'm okay."

"All right, let's go." Michael manhandled him to his feet, Poe protesting all the way. He folded up Poe's blankets and swung a backpack over his shoulder—which seemed to be all Poe's possessions—and then he took Poe's arm and pulled him from the alleyway.

Outside on the street, he flagged down a cab. He pushed Poe into the back seat, thrusting his backpack and blankets at him. Then he passed the driver a twenty and directed him to take Poe to the hospital.

Poe stared up at him wordlessly as Michael pressed the money into his hand.

Michael closed the door. The cab drew away.

"You've seen him again, haven't you? I know you have."

Michael sighed. It was two days later at lunch with Simon, and he had done nothing but think of Poe and whether he had made it as far as the ER or not.

"I saw him briefly. Nothing happened."

"Why?"

"Because someone had beaten the crap out of him. I put him in a cab to the ER."

"Jesus. Did you give him some cash?"

"Yeah."

"Oh, he'll feel indebted to you now."

"That's not why I gave it him."

"Sorry, I didn't mean it like that. But seriously, how attached is he going to get if you start acting like his knight in shining armour?"

"He's not going to get attached. He sleeps with men for money to feed himself Simon, why the hell should he get attached to me?"

"Hello? Because you're a perfect catch. Tell me you're not going to see him again."

Michael paused. He spoke in a low voice. "I just need to make sure he's okay. I'm not going to do anything with him."

Michael couldn't stop thinking about the battered and bruised Poe. The ER hadn't called him with a bill. There was a free clinic in town though; Michael wouldn't even have minded if Poe had gone there and kept Michael's money. Just as long as he got treatment.

Michael couldn't see him going under his own steam though. He should have gone with him in the cab to make sure Poe had actually gone to the ER and booked in and not spent his money on drugs and booze.

He ventured back down the alleyway after three days and found Poe in the same spot as always. Poe sat with his back against the wall and blanket around his knees. On his lap was a paper bag which he ate hungrily out of with his fingers.

He glanced up, and an almost shy smile crossed his face. A smile of pleasure and fondness. Something tugged at Michael's heartstrings. It looked like Simon had been right.

"Hey," he greeted Poe.

"Hey, you."

"Did you make it to the ER?" He already knew the answer because Poe had a neat line of stitches above his eyebrow.

"Yeah. I owe you twenty bucks. I kind of spent it." Poe looked sheepish. "I'll give you a handjob."

"Forget it. I don't want anything from you."

Poe studied him with those clear green eyes. "Then why do you keep coming back?"

He put his dinner to one side.

Michael swallowed. "I wanted to make sure you were okay."

"I am. Thanks to you."

"No problem."

"Listen." Poe uncurled himself from his blanket and

got to his feet. He came and stood right in Michael's personal space. "You gave me a shit load of cash. That means I owe you whatever you want to do to me. Times ten."

Michael stepped back. "Look, I didn't give you money to rack up sexual favours with you." His heart was beating hard.

Poe came closer. He put an arm around Michael's neck, going onto tiptoes so they were eye to eye. "And if I want to give them to you?" he asked in a whisper. "The way I'm feeling now, I could go plenty of times in a row quite easy."

Michael thought he would groan. A hand groped his groin, and he was powerless to pull away. The green eyes held him entranced with promises of pleasure beyond his wildest dreams.

He took Poe by the back of the neck and leaned down to him. Poe turned his head away.

Of course.

"How much do you charge for a kiss?"

Poe turned his gaze back to his. His pale eyes were a little defiant. "I don't know. I never got asked before."

"Well, I'm asking now. How much?"

Poe held his gaze for the longest while. "I guess… five hundred." He looked unsure and embarrassed.

"Fine." Michael opened his wallet while a voice inside his head screamed that he couldn't possibly kiss the prostitute, the most intimate contact of all. He withdrew five hundred-dollar bills, leaving his wallet empty. He pushed them into Poe's jeans pocket, the hard-on he felt there unmistakable. "Don't spend it all at once."

Poe shook his head. "Wait, I can't… You gave me

all that money already."

"That was different. That wasn't for a service. This is."

Their gazes met for the longest time. Poe looked like he was going to cry. Michael's fingertips grazed Poe's cheek, finding the pale skin soft as silk. He traced the light pattern of faded freckles which could only be seen when standing this close to Poe.

He lowered his lips, seeking Poe's, letting his mouth rest against them like a butterfly against the sweetest flower for only a moment. He heard and felt Poe draw his breath in. One hand clutched the front of Michael's jacket.

Michael drew away. It was enough. One kiss told him Poe was going to drive him out of his mind. He turned and walked away as quickly as he could, vowing never to step foot in the alley again.

Michael lasted two days this time before he went home from work, changed into jeans, ate, drank a glass of wine for fortitude and then went back to the alleyway. The wine was a mistake. It merely made him want Poe even more.

But the nest of blankets lay empty, the rucksack gone. A note was propped up, scrawled on torn cardboard. *Gone to the soup run under the bridge.*

Michael stared a moment. Was this note for him? Why should it be? Surely Poe had other men on the go, not just him? Other men he held on a string so they gave him five hundred fucking dollars for one tiny kiss. He clenched his fist, angry at himself and angry at Poe. Then the anger was gone just as soon as it had come, replaced by guilt as he read the note again. Michael had just cooked himself dinner in his penthouse. He could have brought some of the leftovers down here to Poe. Instead, Poe had gone to the soup kitchen for dinner.

Michael shook his head. He left the alley.

Michael had no idea what went on under the bridge in his own home town at night and had his eyes opened as he walked down the cobbled lane to the square under the arch of the bridge. Two cars were parked there, trunks open, cooking pots inside. At a long table, a woman ladled soup into polystyrene bowls. A queue of people waited. Farther along were chunks of buttered bread on plates and at the end a man poured coffee and tea.

Michael scanned the faces of those waiting, coming up empty. He turned around to the benches behind him overlooking the river and stopped short when he saw a familiar face grinning at him.

"Hey, gorgeous."

Michael blushed furiously and took a seat next to Poe who ate his soup delicately with a spoon, blowing on each mouthful.

"Good?"

"Yeah. Tomato tonight. I love tomato."

"Was that note for me?"

"Sure it was." Poe turned his head, smiling. "How many other people do you think I leave notes for?"

Michael fell silent. Poe had expected him back. He was confident he had hooked Michael like a helpless fish. Staring ahead, he saw a man on the opposite bench watching Poe.

The man, in his thirties with dirty hair and a few days' beard growth, grinned while slurping his soup straight from the bowl. "Hey, slut," he addressed Poe. "You opening your legs for me tonight?"

Michael stiffened. "What did you say?"

"Was I talking to you, punk?" The man shot back. "I was talking to my little whore, the guy with the tightest ass in town."

"Leave it, Michael," Poe said urgently as Michael shot to his feet.

Michael ignored him. He stalked across to the other bench and yanked the man out of his seat, soup splattering the pair of them. "You apologise to him right now or I beat your head against these cobbles until your brain leaks out of your ears. Your choice."

"Michael..." Poe said helplessly, on his feet behind him.

The man was drunk and stank of cheap cider, but he recognised the intent in Michael's eyes regardless. "Yeah, whatever," he mumbled, looking afraid.

Michael shook him hard. "I didn't fucking hear you." He yanked the man forward, pushing him almost into Poe's face. "*He* didn't hear you."

"I'm sorry," the man said quickly to Poe. "Okay? I'm sorry. I didn't mean to call you names."

Michael shoved him back onto the bench ferociously. When he turned around, Poe was running away. Michael chased him under the arch of the bridge, into the dark, mazy backstreets.

He caught up with Poe and grabbed him hard by the arm. "What are you doing? You left your dinner."

Poe pushed him back, chest heaving, his face ghostly white in the dim streetlights. "You scare me."

Michael shook his head in disbelief. "Come on."

"Go away."

"No." He caught Poe's arm again, and Poe tussled with him, pushing and shoving.

Michael threw him against the wall. He caught Poe's head in one hand and kissed him hard.

Poe stopped struggling. He put his arms around Michael's neck and kissed back greedily.

Michael swore. He turned Poe roughly to face the wall, and Poe was already unfastening his pants without prompting while Michael unfastened his own and found a condom in his wallet.

He pushed into Poe, one arm around his torso, holding him hard and Poe gasped and rocked back against him, groaning loudly.

It was even better than that first drunken time. Michael was close to exploding within seconds. Poe craned his head around and their lips met, clinging together as Michael thrust into him.

His hand felt in Poe's groin, closed around his erection and jerked him off. Poe moaned, whimpered and slid sensuously against him so they moved perfectly in tandem. Michael wished for more. He wished for Poe beneath him on his silk sheets in his four poster bed. He wished to see the man's beautiful face as he came. He held Poe hard as his orgasm tore into him, leaving him weak. He pressed Poe into the wall, leaning on him for support.

He felt fluid on his hand and Poe bucked back against him, crying out. He turned his head once more and caught Michael's mouth again, kissing fiercely.

"Oh God," Michael moaned. "I don't want anyone else to have you. Do you understand?"

Poe turned his face to the wall. He was silent.

Michael drew himself free. He knotted the condom and tossed it away. He pulled a tissue from his pocket to wipe his hand off, then watched as Poe fastened himself up and walked away without a word.

Michael didn't follow him back to the alley. He slunk home, stewing in shame over the words which had fallen unbidden from his lips. What the hell was going on? Where had the words come from? He was afraid. Afraid of the feelings in his breast, his own lack of control. He had to stay away. He couldn't let Poe do this to him.

He lasted until the early hours of the morning and then he got out of bed and dressed. The air was frigid, passers-by scarce. As Michael entered the alleyway, he heard sounds.

He strained his ears, slowed his footsteps, almost crept on tiptoes. It was sounds of a struggle he could hear, muffled shouting and crying, sounds of fists against flesh. Michael rounded the dumpster with his heart in his mouth.

The man from the bridge had Poe face down on the ground in his nest of blankets, pants around his knees. He held his neck with one hand while his other hand guided himself forward as he thrust repeatedly between Poe's buttocks trying to penetrate him.

Poe shouted and cried, no match for the bulk and strength of his attacker.

Michael saw red. He charged forward and dragged the man off Poe like he was a rag doll, blind with fury. He threw him clean across the alley and against the dumpster, following the man's body to grab him up again and punch him in the face. The man fell against the wall with a grunt, nose and lip split open. Michael caught him before he fell and hit him again. He grabbed him by the hair and pounded his head against the wall until the man became limp in his arms and slithered to the ground.

Breathing heavily, knuckles bleeding, Michael turned around to look at Poe.

He had picked himself up off the floor and was fastening his jeans. Fresh bruising warred with those fading from his earlier beatings. His lip was bleeding. He looked across at Michael.

"Here he is again." His voice was low and sardonic. "My knight in shining armour."

Michael didn't like his tone. "Fuck off," he told him. "You'd rather I let this asshole rape you?"

Poe shrugged. He sniffed and wiped his nose on the back of his hand. "Don't really care anymore."

Michael stared at him. "Jesus, what the fuck is wrong with you? You don't care that some filthy tramp just tried to fucking violate you? Are you so far gone that nothing means anything to you?"

Poe lifted his head and fixed Michael with a hard glare. "*You* mean something to me," he said. "And that confuses me, so you should stop coming around."

Michael swallowed. "I don't want to."

Poe turned away abruptly. He bent down and started to gather his blankets together, throwing his rucksack over his shoulder. Without a glance at Michael, he walked away.

"Come back here." Michael ran after him, furiously grabbing his arm.

"I won't do this again with you!" Poe cried, shoving him back. "Leave me the hell alone." He reached the road and coming up behind him, Michael pointed the remote at his car, which was parked directly in front of Poe.

The doors unlocked and Michael pulled one open and bundled a furiously fighting Poe inside.

"What the hell are you doing?" Poe demanded as Michael got behind the wheel and locked the doors behind him.

"Taking you home."

"What?"

Michael started the engine. "You heard me. I want to be alone with you. Somewhere we can talk."

Poe sank back against the seat. He said nothing further.

At Michael's home, Poe kicked off his shoes, put his bag and blankets down in the hall and followed Michael into the kitchen. Michael took two beers from the fridge. He opened them both, put one on the table and took a long swallow of the other.

Poe approached the table carefully. He picked the beer up and took a drink, watching Michael all the while. For a long moment there was silence.

Poe looked around the kitchen. Michael was almost embarrassed by the gleaming fixtures, the glittering granite and marble, the huge fridge.

"Want something to eat?"

Poe shook his head. "Can I shower?"

"Sure. Back down the hall. If you leave your clothes outside, I'll wash them."

Poe looked dubious a moment. Then he took his beer and left the kitchen. Michael watched him grab his bag again and disappear into the bathroom. He sighed, went into the living room and sank onto the couch. It was almost light. It was a good thing he wasn't at work in the morning.

He heard the shower start, and against his will he imagined Poe's lean body under the spray, droplets of water on his eyelashes, his mouth open in pleasure as the hot water pelted him.

Michael stiffened. He passed a hand over himself. He got up and went into the hall. There were no clothes outside the bathroom door, and as Michael stood there debating what to do, the door opened.

Poe stood there with a towel around his waist. What interested Michael most about the state of his undress was the fact that the towel had a neat tent in the centre.

Pushing his clothes at Michael, Poe flushed. Michael took them and then just as soon let them fall to the floor. He reached out and pulled Poe's towel free.

Poe gasped as Michael pushed him back, kicking the door shut behind him and started to strip, eyes on Poe's erection.

It was the first time he had seen Poe naked and the first time he had seen, rather than felt, his cock. It made Michael so hard he could barely speak.

He pushed Poe into the running shower, followed him in and closed the glass door.

"Don't," Poe said half-heartedly, turning his face away. Michael merely held his head firmly in place and kissed him. He took Poe's cock in his hand and slid it through his wet fist.

Poe groaned. He tried to squeeze away in the enclosed space and Michael pinned him to the wall effortlessly. "I want you. Don't make me beg."

Poe's hands gripped his shoulders. "You don't know what you're saying. Please, we have to stop this."

"I don't *want* to stop it. Jesus, I can't stop thinking

about you. I don't know what you've done to me."

Poe let out a sound like a whimper. He pulled Michael close and kissed him hard. Michael growled, held both their cocks in one hand, jerked them off together so Poe squirmed and panted.

Poe sank abruptly to his knees. He sucked Michael's cock into his eager mouth and Michael held him by the hair, staring down at him, thinking that all his Christmases had come at once. What was he going to do? This was never going to go anywhere. Poe was homeless and he was a *man*. But this darkness consumed Michael whole. He wanted only this. He would never be able to get enough of Poe.

He yanked him to his feet, thrust him against the wall and spat on his hand, slicking up before he buried himself in Poe's tight ass.

Poe cried out. He bucked back wantonly against Michael, hands scrabbling at the wall and started to beg for more in the filthiest terms a sexual partner had ever used on him before. It turned Michael on to no end. He fucked Poe harder and harder until his cock was squeezed by convulsions and Poe shot his load into Michael's hand. Michael came in a rush, gasping, groaning and sagged against Poe, holding onto him with one arm.

There was silence apart from pants for breath, and then Michael took a net ball and the shower gel and washed Poe all over. Poe seemed nervous at the attention but the pleasure he felt at the touch of Michael's hands was obvious. He almost purred like a satisfied cat.

Once Michael was done, Poe climbed swiftly out of the shower. Michael washed, watching Poe dry himself. Poe had his back turned, lifting each foot in turn so Michael saw the heavy swing of balls between his legs and more; a dribble of semen on his inner thigh.

Michael stared. Jesus Christ, why hadn't he used a condom? But his cock was still firmly in charge. He pushed the shower door open, grabbed a towel and tied it around his waist. Then he gripped one of Poe's hips, fingers of his other hand feeling between his buttocks. Poe clung onto the edge of the sink, looking back in surprise.

Michael's fingers delved into wetness. He pressed himself close, hard again. "You're still wet and open," he said into Poe's ear.

"So I am." Poe used the coy voice which had seduced him on that first drunken night in the alleyway. "What are you going to do about it?"

Michael pulled his towel free. He rubbed his cock against Poe's pert backside. "What do you *want* me to do about it?"

"I want you to eat me out."

Michael stilled in shock. "Excuse me?"

"You heard me. What's the matter, straight boy? Too kinky for you?"

Michael only hesitated a moment, then he shoved Poe face first over the sink, spread him open and put his tongue to him.

He soon realised he'd discovered Poe's kink.

They were quiet in the aftermath, sitting side by side on the couch in robes, drinking beer. Poe seemed embarrassed, and Michael marvelled at how this self-acknowledged prostitute swung between sluttiness and shyness. Was he always so coy after he'd blatantly asked a man to put a tongue in his ass and that man had agreed to his demands? He was a contrary one, that was for sure, and it only intrigued Michael more.

"Hey," he said quietly.

Poe turned his head to look at him.

"Are you going to tell me about yourself, Poe?"

Poe looked instantly wary, his eyes shuttered. "I don't think so."

"Come on, I don't bring strange guys back to my place and give them a rimjob without getting at least a brief biography."

Poe didn't look amused. He bit his lip and looked away.

"Hey, listen to me. What I said, about not being able to stop thinking about you. That was all true. I want to know you. I want to know how you came to be in such desperate circumstances and how I can help you."

Poe lurched off the couch. Michael grabbed his wrist and dragged him back down onto his lap. "Look, I only want to talk."

"If you want to fuck me, let's fuck. I don't do talking," Poe said angrily, his pale skin flushed.

"Don't be an asshole."

"I don't know what you want from me. You're some straight boy who gets off fucking a cheap whore in a dirty alley. That's fine, but don't think that bringing me back here means you don't have to pay."

Michael sat back, lips pursed. "Do I have to pay you for putting my tongue in your ass too, Poe?"

Poe reddened further. He mumbled something inaudible and hung his head.

"Poe." Michael stroked the pink cheek. "I don't think of you as a cheap whore. I don't like it when you say that. I just... wish you didn't have to do it."

"Well, I do," Poe said sullenly. "I'm homeless. I have to eat."

"Tell me how you became homeless."

Poe heaved a heavy sigh as though Michael was tiresome. "My dad threw me out when he caught me fucking my boyfriend in my room."

"How old were you?"

"Seventeen."

"How long have you been out on the streets?"

"Five years."

Poe was only twenty-two. He had spent a quarter of his life homeless. Michael stroked his hand. "What about your mom?"

"She backed up my dad."

"Have you tried to get in contact?"

"No."

"Poe..."

"Don't. I'm not interested in ever seeing them again. I hope they burn in hell."

"Don't you think they might be out of their minds with worry?"

"No."

Michael sighed. "Are you from here?"

"No. I'm from Iowa."

"Jesus, Poe, you go to California and don't speak to your folks for five years, don't you think they had the police looking for you?"

"I don't care."

"You should."

Poe turned furiously to face him. "Listen to me, when my dad caught me, he hit my boyfriend. He threw his clothes at him and told him to get out of his house. Then he caught hold of me and threw me against the wall. He broke my nose and he slammed my head against the wall until I almost passed out. My mother cried and begged him to stop, but he didn't. He told me I was a filthy little fag, and I was no longer his son. He told me I had ten minutes to pack up everything I owned and to get out. When I came to the living room carrying my bags, I tried to say sorry. I told him I loved him and that I wouldn't ever touch a man again if that was what he wanted. He turned his face away and told me to get out. My mother sat crying on the stairs as I left." Poe's voice broke, and his face was streaked with tears. "So please don't tell me I should care because my love for them died long ago."

Michael pulled Poe into his arms and held him, stroking his hair and listening to the soft sobs which wracked Poe's body. "It's okay," he murmured. "I promise it's going to be okay." And he meant it because from now on, Poe had Michael to look out for him.

Their lovemaking started on the couch and ended up on Egyptian cotton sheets in Michael's bed, when Michael carried Poe up in his arms. Poe dozed, drowsy and satiated beside Michael, their fingers entwined.

"Your bed's so comfy." It was a sleepy murmur.

"Get used to it."

"What?" Poe was suddenly wide awake. "Oh no, Michael. I won't be coming back here again."

"We'll see about that. You're not going back to that alleyway."

Poe turned onto his front, leaning down over Michael. "Oh really? You're going to keep me here as my sugar daddy, are you?"

Michael glowered. "I'm not old enough to be your sugar daddy."

"Whatever. It's not going to happen."

"Why not?"

"Because I'm not going to be your kept man."

"Who says I'd be keeping you? You'll be finding a job."

Poe stared at him. "I can't."

"Why not?"

"I…" Poe stammered, blushing. He threw himself down on his back with a sigh. "You're crazy. You want a whore under your roof? Who says I won't steal the silver and run off?"

"You're welcome to steal whatever you want. What's mine is yours."

Poe glanced at him. Tears stood starkly in his eyes. "You're absolutely out of your mind. Why would you do this for me?"

"Because I see plenty in you worth saving. Don't cry again." Michael pulled the suddenly weeping Poe into his arms. At that moment nothing had ever felt so right to him. Poe seemed to be the piece missing from his life, and he was determined not to let him go.

He held Poe in his arms until he finally fell asleep.

Michael woke alone at one in the afternoon. He reached for Poe and found the other side of the bed empty and cold. He sighed, got up and pulled on a robe. He checked to see if Poe's rucksack was gone along with his clothes from the tumble dryer. Everything was gone, including Michael's wallet and watch from the bedside table. He sat thinking a moment. Sure he'd told Poe to steal whatever he wanted, but he hadn't expected him to follow his instructions to the letter.

Little bastard.

His anger overwhelmed his memories of the evening they had shared. He showered and shaved before dressing, drinking a cup of coffee and taking the keys to his Porsche.

He found Poe in his customary place.

"All right, give them back, you thieving little twat."

Poe looked calm. He opened his rucksack and produced Michael's wallet and watch. "I took them to see if you'd be mad, that's all. After you said I could steal what I want. I didn't spend a penny, you can count it."

Michael snatched the two items with his anger rapidly deflating.

"And I was right, you *are* mad. You said what's mine is yours."

Michael sighed. He knelt down before Poe. "I was just surprised, that's all."

"You thought you could trust me? Now you know better."

Michael shook his head. "I still trust you, Poe."

"Then you're stupid."

"Maybe. What say I buy you some lunch?"

Poe stared at him. "That's all you can say? I steal your wallet and watch and you ask to buy me lunch?"

"Yes. Then how about I take you home and make love to you?"

Poe's pale eyes darkened as his pupils grew large. "That sounds like a plan." He got to his feet, gathered up his blankets and rucksack.

Michael slung his arm around Poe's shoulders as they walked from the alley. "Have you ever seen *Casablanca*, Poe?"

"Sure. It's my mom's favourite film."

"Then you'll know what I mean when I say this is the start of a beautiful friendship."

Poe leaned into his body. "I won't let you down Michael, I promise." His voice was a whisper.

"I know you won't, because I'll kick your ass right back to this alley if you do."

Michael opened the door to his Porsche and ushered Poe inside. He took his things and put them in the trunk. As he went to close Poe's door, Poe caught him by the shirt and pulled him down into a kiss.

The passers-by on the street receded into the distance. There was only this. Poe, his homeless whore. The man he adored.

He drew back, looking into the pale green eyes, stroking the perfect peachy skin of Poe's cheek.

He smiled, and it was mirrored on Poe's face.

REMATCH

Luke Adams surveyed the eleven men standing in a row before him, trying not to linger too much on the figure at the end. Truth be told, all he'd done was look at other men since he'd slept with Dieter Müller, darling of English football, three months ago. Over the long summer break he'd had plenty of time to think, plenty of time to analyse every moment of that quick, desperate fuck in the away team's dressing room on the last day of the season. Luke had lost his head and been sent off, and while his team lost the championship, he had fucked the opposition's star striker into oblivion.

Regrets were swift and plenty. A celebrated womaniser, Luke numbered more notches on his bed post than he'd had hot dinners. Never once had he considered the idea that another man could give him what he needed. But God, Dieter had. His body pressed against Luke's had pleasured him effortlessly. Luke hadn't stopped reliving it since. And now he was about to come face to face with Dieter in the ultimate grudge match. England v Germany in Berlin, in a World Cup qualifier.

He was filled with shame at what he had done with the enemy. He glanced down to the end of the line and dark eyes locked with his. A smirk curved Dieter's sensual mouth and Luke flushed, averted his gaze, clenched his fists. He had to get a grip. He couldn't allow his lust for Dieter to lose England this match. Over his dead body. He set his jaw as the German team filed down the England line, shaking hands with every man. Dieter loomed up, a grin still on his plump mouth, pearly teeth gleaming. He gripped Luke's hand.

Luke almost shuddered at the contact. He squeezed Dieter's hand hard, glared with his most intimidating stare. Dieter seemed oblivious. He walked away, the swing of his hips drawing Luke's gaze to his pert little backside.

Damn him.

Luke still wanted him. He couldn't *not* want him. Dieter excited him beyond belief.

Luke got into position. The whistle blew, and the German team kicked off. Luke didn't expect to win this match, realistically. There was too much water under the bridge and too many thrashings at the Germans' hands for there to be too much confidence on the English side. But Luke had heart and soul enough for all of them. He had enough courage and enough belief and if his teammates had enough too, they could do it. If Dieter didn't take Luke to pieces before they could.

The Germans had the ball. They launched an early attack, and Luke went back defending, put an elbow in Dieter's side as he tackled the ball away from him. Dieter growled in anger. He chased Luke, pulling at his shirt, but Luke was away, off into the German half, passing across the pitch to his midfielder on the edge of the area.

Luke raced into the penalty box. As his colleague swung the cross in, Luke rose and met the ball with his head. Two defenders fell in front of him as he pushed them. The net bulged, and an almost stunned roar went up behind it.

Luke turned, raced away, arms aloft, such joy pumping through his veins he thought he would cry. Less than two minutes in and England had scored. Someone jumped on his back and flattened him. He disappeared beneath a sea of bodies.

Things didn't get any better than scoring for your country. This maybe was the only thing which could beat the thrill of fucking Dieter.

When Luke was finally allowed up and had finished posturing arrogantly at the antagonised German crowd, he allowed his gaze to wander across the field to Dieter.

Dieter scowled. Luke smiled serenely. The only thing which could make this rematch sweeter than an England win was if he ended up balls-deep in Dieter for dessert. Just thinking about it stirred him inappropriately.

The Germans were fired up. They took immediate possession and mounted an attack. Luke loitered lazily at the back because he had done his job, and now it was time for his defenders to earn their money. He watched Dieter with the ball. The man was sheer poetry, twisting and turning, beating every man effortlessly, his body beautiful, all graceful, fluid lines and flowing limbs. God, Luke wanted him so much it hurt. The game receded into the background. There was only this need. This need for more of the same bliss Dieter had provided him with three months ago.

He stood staring as Dieter beat five men and scored from thirty-five yards. *Jesus Christ.* The stadium erupted, the England fans drowned out, and the England team trudged back dejected to the halfway line. Dieter was mobbed by his teammates, and Luke was jealous of every man who touched him. The equaliser just made him more determined. If Germany won this match, Dieter would pay in kind. He wouldn't be able to walk by the time Luke finished with him.

Dieter came strolling nonchalantly back down the

pitch. He flashed his pearly grin at Luke and winked.

Luke fell into step behind him. With mouth close to his ear, he whispered. "I'm going to fuck you senseless after this match. You've been warned."

Dieter's body stiffened. He turned his head over his shoulder so he and Luke were intimately close. "I can't wait, Luke. You've no idea."

Luke drew back. He walked away with flushing cheeks. Nobody would have heard the words, but commentators all over the world were probably speculating on what the two opposing star strikers had just said to each other. Luke could relax. He doubted anybody would make such a leap as to presume the conversation had been sexual, even if Dieter was out and proud.

He had less than ninety minutes left before Dieter was his.

The match went on, end to end with near misses from both teams. Dieter was on fire, and Luke couldn't help feeling hopelessly in his shadow. Thoughts like this just made him want Dieter more though, made him want to show the German who was boss off the pitch even if he couldn't show him on it.

The time drifted towards ninety minutes. Someone needed to pull something spectacular out of the bag. In times of crisis, any self-respecting footballer resorted to cheating. Just ask Diego Maradona.

An opposition defender gripped Luke's shirt with the lightest of touches as Luke entered the penalty area. Luke responded as though he had been hit by a bulldozer. He lurched full length into the box, a spectacular dive Jürgen Klinsmann would have been proud of in his heyday. These Germans knew a thing or two about diving. Let the boot be on the other foot for a change.

The home crowd howled their disgust, and the German team spat vitriol as Luke climbed to his feet and looked innocently across at the ref. It was not his style to demand the penalty, that was too obvious. Let his gymnastics do the talking. That one had been worth a nine at least.

The ref had been right behind him. He blew his whistle and pointed to the spot, waving away irate Germans. Luke took the ball calmly, his face carefully expressionless. This had to be the last kick of the game and this had to be the one which won England the match. An historic victory over the old enemy.

He caught Dieter's eye. The object of his lust stood with arms folded, glaring coldly at Luke. Luke smirked. Oh, the sex was going to be even sweeter with the beaten, humbled Dieter taking it from him with reluctant pleasure.

He placed the ball on the spot and faced the goalie down for a moment before he stepped back a good few paces, taking his time, judging his run.

Luke had never missed a penalty in open competition. He had only ever missed them in training. This was the most important penalty of his life so far, and he didn't intend to screw up. He believed in the power of positive thinking. If he wanted that ball to go into the net, it would do.

He ran up and powered the ball right at the goalie. The goalkeeper, who had clearly watched videos of Luke and knew he favoured his right, dived that way.

The ball slammed into the back of the net, and Luke wheeled away, yelling. He charged towards the England fans who leaned over the barrier in front of him, mobbing him, gripping his hands and pulling his hair, screaming their adoration.

Luke turned around. He stood with arms aloft for the photographers to get their nice shots for the back pages the next day and waited for his teammates' congratulations. Back near the goal, a lone figure with dark hair turned his back and walked away. Never mind. Luke would soon put a smile on his face.

The German team went through the motions, kicking off again, but the ref blew the whistle as soon as they did. The stadium exploded. The England bench spilled onto the pitch, and the manager congratulated Luke. His teammates held him aloft and carried him from the pitch as though England had won the goddamn World Cup, and Luke gloated down at Dieter as he was borne aloft. The German *wunderkind* had a smudge of mud on his cheek and his hair was all wet. He looked adorable. He would look even better beneath Luke moaning for more.

Champagne flowed in the dressing room, and Luke drank a glass before he plunged into a hot shower, thoughts of Dieter consuming him whole. The team spoke of the celebration dinner they were going to have, but Luke began to worry. Dieter was going to slip away unnoticed, and Luke wouldn't be able to find him. How did he know which hotel the German team was staying at? He didn't much fancy searching Berlin all night until he found him.

He got out of the shower, dried himself and dressed in his suit. Sidling up to the kit manager, he asked, "Any idea where the German team's staying?"

"Yeah, The Adlon. Not thinking of causing trouble are you, Luke?"

"Me?" Luke asked innocently.

The cab dropped him off outside the hotel, and he made his way through the sumptuous lobby and enquired at the desk for Dieter Müller's room number.

The receptionist had a face like a slapped arse and clearly knew this man had just been responsible for Germany's humiliation.

"I can't give you that."

"Then ring his room and ask him if I can come up." Luke was unruffled.

The receptionist glared some more and then finally dialled three numbers stiffly, before firing off a rapid stream of German.

He put the phone down and looked at Luke like he'd stepped in something. "You may go up."

"The room number?"

"One one two."

"Thank you." Luke smiled sweetly and trusted the man wouldn't go to the papers.

He got in the lift with damp palms and his heart beating hard. In his pocket he carried condoms and lube.

He knocked on the door of one one two and stood nervously outside, waiting. The door swung open. His dream come true stood there. Dieter, in a bath robe, with hair all wet looking like some sort of sex nymph.

Luke shoved him backwards. He stepped inside, slammed the door and gripped Dieter in his arms.

Dieter pushed him away roughly. "Oh, no you don't. You're not coming anywhere near me until you admit you're a cheating English bastard."

Luke lifted an eyebrow. He threw his jacket over a nearby chair and tossed the condoms and lube on the bed.

"I don't know how you dare. You lot wrote the book on cheating."

Dieter pretended not to hear. "I mean it."

Luke stalked forward.

"Get the hell off me."

"Listen to me, Dieter. I promised I'd see you for the replay and here I am. You and I have got unfinished business." Dieter, playing hard to get, was undeniably hot. Luke was hard as hard could be.

Dieter continued to dance away every time Luke reached for him. Luke sighed. He unfastened his tie and draped it over the end of the bed. He started on the buttons on his shirt, watching Dieter's expression as he revealed his rippling torso.

"Fuck," Dieter whimpered. "Either put it away or tell me what a cheating English bastard you are."

Luke ignored him. He tossed his shirt away and kicked off his shoes. He peeled off his socks and undid his belt. Then, standing close in front of Dieter, he slowly popped his button and unzipped his fly, revealing the hard bulge in his boxers.

He pushed his pants down and stepped out of them. "Tell me you don't want it." He thrust his groin forward so Dieter's eyes were riveted.

"I'm not your fucking toy," Dieter growled.

"Aren't you? That's exactly what you are. You're going to be my toy and you're going to love it." Luke lunged at Dieter and threw him on the bed where he wrestled him into submission, holding his hands down by his head.

Dieter fought him fiercely, dark eyes flashing, cheeks flushed, until Luke kissed him and it was game over.

Dieter's mouth opened beneath his. He pushed his pelvis up, writhing sensually beneath Luke. The kiss was furious with passion.

Luke broke away, leaving Dieter gasping for more. He sat back on his heels and wrenched Dieter's robe open, exposing his glorious body and hard cock.

"I'm going to fuck you until you scream my name," he told Dieter. "Understand?"

Dieter nodded, eyes wide, hand stroking his own cock.

Luke could barely tear his eyes away from this delicious sight. "Turn over."

Dieter did so, presenting that ass Luke had fantasised about for three months. He reached for the lube, squirted it between Dieter's cheeks and pushed his fingers between his buttocks to rub it in.

Dieter's breath caught. He moaned when Luke pushed a wet finger inside him. "Please... give it to me."

Luke rolled the latex onto his cock. He rubbed himself tantalisingly down Dieter's arse crack, watching the little hole flutter beneath his attentions before it grasped him inside. Luke slid all the way in to an accompanying yell of delight.

"Mmm," he said in appreciation, one hand sliding around Dieter's torso. "You know how to have a good time."

Dieter groaned and pushed back, taking every inch greedily, panting for breath. "I've been waiting for this for three months."

Luke held him tighter. "Me too."

Dieter grabbed hold of his hand and guided it down

into his groin. Luke's fingers closed around his hard shaft and stroked.

"Fuck. Don't stop."

Luke bowed his head. He licked the sweat from the perfect curve of Dieter's spine. Dieter arched and shivered. He bucked into Luke's rapidly moving hand.

"Oh God, oh God."

"Come on. I want to feel you come around me."

Dieter gave a cry. "Luke, oh God, Luke..." Luke went harder, faster. Dieter trembled below him. This was something else. This was like the first time. And then some. If Luke had thought his memories were rose-tinted, he was wrong. His memories didn't even do the act of fucking Dieter justice.

He growled, spilling himself in endless waves, holding onto Dieter hard, hand still automatically jerking so hot fluid coated his fingers as Dieter clenched around him.

They slid moaning and cursing to the bed, Luke smothering Dieter beneath him. Dieter offered no complaint.

After several minutes, Luke managed to collect his senses enough to pull free. He discarded his condom onto the floor and lay on his back with his eyes closing rapidly.

"You're still a cheating English bastard."

Luke opened one eye to glare. He had hoped he had fucked the smart-mouthed German into silence. No such luck.

"How many times have you taken a dive in the penalty box, Dieter?"

"Not telling." Dieter's plump mouth was drawn into a pout.

"That's because you'd run out of fingers and toes to

count them on."

"Shut it."

"Make me."

Dieter was on him in an instant, knees over Luke's shoulders, thrusting his still half-hard cock into his mouth.

In shock, Luke opened up and sucked him down. His hands gripped Dieter's firm buttocks, rocking him forward, encouraging Dieter to fuck his mouth. He was astonished at how much having Dieter on his face aroused him. Dieter thrust until he almost choked Luke but Luke stuck to his task doggedly, looking up at the German's flushed, beautiful face as he sucked.

Dieter moaned and groaned. Swiftly he changed position, straddling Luke's head backwards, bowing his head to Luke's groin and taking him in his mouth. Luke swore. Confronted with muscular arse and dangling balls, he reached his hands up to touch. Spreading his partner open, he looked at the still wet entrance he had been buried in a few minutes ago. He pulled Dieter back onto his face and put his tongue out, licking swiftly.

Dieter went crazy. He squirmed and ground himself down. Luke put a hand around his hip, feeling for his cock and jerked him off. He swelled to rock hard in Dieter's mouth. Luke was a stallion but it was unheard of, even for him, to be ready to go again within minutes. He even felt like he was going to come within moments, rather than going all night as he tended to do with a second erection.

He doubted Dieter would mind. Luke could barely keep him from falling off, such were Dieter's frenzied movements, almost smothering Luke beneath him. With Dieter on his face and around his cock? What a way to go.

Dieter cried out around Luke's cock. He pulled his

mouth away as he shot his load onto Luke's neck and chest. Luke carried on, thrusting his tongue into the tight little hole and Dieter went back to sucking him off with even more enthusiasm. Luke's balls tightened. He felt the rush to orgasm and came right down Dieter's throat.

Dieter didn't complain. He swallowed it all before lifting his head and licking gently at Luke's cock.

Luke felt beneath him again. Dieter was still hard and still pushing against his tongue. "My God, are you insatiable, man?" Luke asked in admiration.

"Make me come again, Luke," was Dieter's almost whimpered reply. "Please."

Luke growled. He pulled Dieter back so his cock was in Luke's mouth again, sucking the cum from it, while fingers probed inside his wet entrance.

"Fuck. Oh God..."

Luke lay there while Dieter fucked his mouth. His cock started to stiffen again, incredibly, for the third time. He thought of Dieter sliding onto his cock, riding him bareback, the cum running from his arse afterwards.

But this was reality. He fumbled for a condom and rolled it onto his cock. "Sit on my cock, Dieter. I need to fuck you again."

Dieter slid down his body without turning around and impaled himself. Luke arched back and gripped his partner's hips, groaning deliriously. Jesus, three times. Three fucking times! Luke was the luckiest man in the world tonight. He didn't know where he got his stamina from. All he knew was he wanted to come and come and come until Dieter killed him.

Luke pushed himself up against the headboard, dragging Dieter with him, holding his back firmly to his torso, mouth against his shoulder. While Dieter rode him, Luke could jerk him off smoothly and fondle his balls.

Panting hard, Dieter rested his head against Luke's shoulder and Luke kissed his throat. "Let me feel you come, Dieter."

Dieter wailed and shivered. "Fuck, Luke. *Fuck.*"

"Come on."

Luke was right on the edge again, ready to explode. He held himself back until he felt Dieter tighten around him, thighs tense and gripping him hard.

"Luke... Luke..." Dieter came, shaking violently, hand over Luke's so the two of them milked his cock of every drop.

Luke held him firmly, thrusting up over and over again until his climax hit and he almost passed out. He fell back on the bed, semi-conscious.

"You've got cum all over you. You should get in the shower."

Luke opened one eye to see Dieter lying beside him. "I'm not sure I can move."

Dieter laughed musically. He pressed a kiss to one of Luke's nipples, tongue darting out to lap. "We should do this again."

"I might not survive round four with you, Dieter."

"Come on. You English. No fucking stamina."

His lips closed deliberately around Luke's nipple now and sucked slowly.

"Don't."

"Why not?"

"Because I'm not sure I can get it up a fourth time."

"I bet you can." Dieter fondled his cock and balls.

"Turn over."

With a reluctant moan, Luke did so. Dieter pushed his legs apart. His hands spread Luke's buttocks.

"Don't."

"Don't what?" Dieter lapped over Luke's entrance with a hot, wet tongue.

"Fuck. Do that."

"Do that? Okay, I will."

"No, I mean..." But it was too late. Dieter rimmed him with gusto and Luke, who had never explored this in his life thought he might pass out in pleasure. Dieter felt below him, pushing Luke's hard cock down between his spread legs so he could suckle at the head.

"Oh, my God. Dieter, really... I can't..."

"Of course you can, Luke. Just lie back and think of England. And what a cheating bastard you are."

"Fucker."

"That's me. I'm going to loosen you up just nicely, Luke. Then I'm going to stick my cock in you and fuck you until you beg me for more. By the end of tonight, you're going to be a slave to German *bratwurst*. You're going to beg me for my phone number, and when we get back to England, you're going to come to my house twice a week and beg me to fuck you. Do you understand?"

"Yes..." Luke moaned helplessly.

"Good boy." Dieter slid a finger inside him, touched a spot which made Luke yelp. "Now pass me the lube."

You haven't won this round, Luke thought fiercely. *Just you wait until we get back to England. I'll show you just who's boss here.*

Dieter Müller, I'm going to fuck you and fuck you until you're mine and mine alone.

CHARLIE

It all started because Jude wanted a costume for his Halloween party. Determined to go as something different from the usual witches and vampires, he chose his theme and set off to the thrift stores in town for an outfit.

Four down and six to go, he entered the local animal shelter shop. It was empty except for one lady browsing the books at the back. The man behind the counter looked up and smiled as Jude entered, and Jude almost did a double take.

God was smiling down on him that day. The shop assistant had a lean, toned body and stood about six feet tall. He looked to be in his twenties, with chestnut hair, cropped short and a boyish, clean-shaven face. Stunning was an inadequate word. Jude almost forgot his mission. He pushed his hair back, straightened his jacket and strode forward.

"Hi, there. I'm looking for a costume like this."

He held a photo up of the man he wanted to dress like.

"Charlie!" exclaimed the shop assistant in delight with a grin which showed white teeth. "Oh, my God, I love him! My favourite bit is when he eats the streamers in the restaurant, thinking it's spaghetti. Or when he wants to dance with everyone so he dances with the waiter." He hummed a song loudly, the theme tune to *City Lights.*

Jude smiled, but it was fixed frozen on his face now. Something was off here.

"Come on, let me help you." The man came out from behind the counter. To Jude's shock and discomfort, he took Jude by the hand and pulled him across the shop. Jude trailed behind with flushed cheeks, his heart sinking. It wasn't just the way the stranger held his hand like Jude was an old friend but also the way he walked with a slightly hesitant gait, the way he enunciated his words slowly and carefully.

He had learning disabilities.

Jude disentangled his hand as gently as he could and came back to his senses. *Not appropriate Jude, not appropriate at all.*

"You need some big baggy pants. Look at these." The man held a pair against Jude. "You're tiny just like him."

It was hardly a compliment, but then one of the reasons Jude had decided on this get up was his physical resemblance to Chaplin. He would hardly have gotten away with the tight jacket if he'd had broad shoulders and huge pecs to strain it or the baggy pants if he actually had an ass to put in them. With his slight build, his black hair and his big blue eyes, he'd pull it off just fine.

He took the pants from his helpful assistant and tried to move away to another rack.

"Here's a shirt." The assistant held up a white formal shirt.

Jude took it gratefully. He had a waistcoat at home, some battered shoes and a cane. All he needed now was the jacket and the hat. He drifted towards the children's section. How had Chaplin found a man's jacket that was too small for his delicate frame anyway? Had he had them specially made or had he chosen a child's?

He plucked an old-fashioned, black velvet jacket from the rail. Just perfect.

His assistant bustled across the room in high excitement. "Your hat! Your hat!" He forced a bowler hat onto Jude's head and then shoved him towards a curtained off area. "Get changed!"

Jude shook his head in disbelief as he closed the curtain and stripped off his coat. The trouble with the hot men these days was they were all either straight or they had... issues. He felt guilty for his thoughts. Disability shouldn't preclude this man from Jude's attentions, he knew that, but one of the main issues had to be whether this man was attracted to either sex at all, never mind men. Perhaps he was too childlike to understand. In which case, Jude couldn't be the big, bad wolf who introduced him to the real world.

He sighed, pulling off his top, and then buttoning the formal shirt. It was too big around the neck, but he could probably pin it and the bow tie he had at home might cinch it in a bit.

The jacket had two buttons at the chest, but only one would fasten. It was tight and perfect. He pulled the pants on and laughed as they drowned him. He would have to take them up or he'd be falling over them all night. He'd borrow some of his granddad's braces to stop them sliding down.

He put the hat on and looked at himself in the mirror. Wow. Chaplin was reincarnated, minus the joke-shop moustache which sat at home.

He stepped out for the praise of his admiring audience. The shop assistant jumped up and down clapping his hands. "Oh my God, oh my God, it's Charlie!"

Jude smiled bashfully as the woman at the back looked over curiously. "You like it then?"

"Yes! Now walk like him!"

Jude took a few steps out of the cubicle, feet out turned, waddling, pretending he held a cane, preening at the pretty assistant's gaze on him.

"Charlie! Charlie! Charlie!" the assistant chanted like he was cheerleading.

His exuberance started to wear thin. "I'll take them," Jude muttered and closed the curtain quickly.

When he came out, his friendly assistant was sitting behind the counter, reading a comic. He smiled and put it aside, reaching a plastic bag out to put Jude's purchases in. Then he racked them up slowly and methodically on the till before he folded them neatly and precisely into the bag with almost loving care. Did he have OCD, too?

Jude stared at him. He was beautiful, that was for sure. His eyes were the darkest brown, almost black, his lashes lush and long. Perfectly clear, his skin looked soft as a peach.

If he had been any other man, Jude would have asked for his phone number by now.

"Twenty dollars please, sir."

Jude handed the cash over.

"What's your name?"

Taken aback, Jude told him.

The assistant pushed his bag towards him with a shy smile. "My name's Charlie."

Jude burst out laughing.

The man's face fell slightly, and he looked confused. "No really. Charlie Chapman."

Jude regarded him, trying to decide if the man was yanking his chain. The assistant pulled a wallet from his pocket and showed Jude a library card.

Charlie Chapman.

Jude smiled slowly. "Nice to meet you, Charlie Chapman." He held a hand out.

Grinning, Charlie squeezed it in his bigger one. "I'll be seeing you."

"Bye, Charlie."

Jude went to his party and his outfit caused quite a stir, even if his moustache kept falling off and he tripped over his pants and lost his hat. When he got home and lay drunk in bed looking at the framed Chaplin print on the opposite wall, he thought of simple-minded, beautiful Charlie Chapman and wished things were different.

Out shopping in town the following week, he walked past the thrift store. In the window, lovingly decorating a mannequin with a garish orange shirt and hounds tooth pants, stood Charlie.

Jude stood drinking in the view for several seconds. Charlie was bent over, pert, rounded ass outlined nicely in his tight jeans, shirt pulled over rippling shoulders. Had nature given him this lovely body or did he work out? Jude doubted he would have sufficient ego to work out. Did he realise then how beautiful he was? Jude sighed in pleasure as he stood watching.

Charlie turned around, saw him and waved then gestured him over, grinning from ear to ear. Jude only hesitated a moment before he entered the shop.

"Jude," said Charlie, clearly delighted, dark eyes dancing. "How was your party?"

"It was great thanks," Jude replied. "How are you doing, Charlie?"

"I'm okay. *The Gold Rush* was on TV last night." Charlie's white teeth blinded him.

"That's great. Well, I'd better be on my way..."

"Don't you want to buy anything?"

"No, I don't really need anything."

Charlie looked crestfallen. "Oh, okay then. Bye, Jude."

Jude hesitated. "What time do you get off?"

Charlie glanced at the clock. He seemed to do a calculation in his head. "In half an hour."

"Do you want to... get some coffee?"

"Umm, I don't really drink coffee, Jude. What about a chocolate milkshake?"

Jude smiled. "Sure. Do you know the Sunset café? Down the block?"

"Yeah. Shall I come there?"

"Yeah, see you in half an hour."

"Okay, Jude, see you." Charlie looked beyond ecstatic.

Jude backed out of the shop. He hurried down the street, castigating himself. He was a pervert trying to seduce a handicapped man, he told himself. Charlie didn't know why Jude wanted to have coffee with him. If Jude started making eyes at him over the table, would Charlie even notice or would he just think Jude was being funny? He chastised the voice in his head. He wasn't trying to seduce Charlie, not all. He wouldn't take advantage of someone that way. He wouldn't.

He was on his second coffee when Charlie arrived, looking around and then greeting Jude with a huge wave from the door which caused Jude to sink down into his seat with embarrassment.

"Hi, Jude."

"Hi, Charlie. Here's the menu. What are you having?"

"Just a minute." Charlie took a wallet out of his pocket, opened the coin section and started laboriously counting change onto the table.

"What are you doing?"

"Seeing how much money I've got."

"You don't have to do that. I'm paying." Jude didn't doubt the thrift store was Charlie's only job and probably unpaid at that.

Charlie stared at him a moment. "Oh, okay." He looked doubtful.

"So look at the menu."

"Yes, sir." Charlie stared down for a few seconds before he lifted his head, sensual mouth drawn into a pout. "They don't do chocolate milkshakes."

"Are you sure?" Jude pretended to look but he'd already noticed that before Charlie came in.

"I'm sure."

"Well I'll ask them to make you one."

"Really?"

"Really. Now, do you want anything to eat?"

Charlie bit his lip in concentration as he studied the menu. "I like carrot cake," he said shyly.

"Then I'll get you some."

"Okay." Charlie put the menu down and leaned back in satisfaction.

A waitress hovered. Jude got her attention. "Hi, there. Can you make my friend a chocolate milkshake?"

She looked down at Charlie, and Jude saw her

interest fade rapidly as he looked back at her, all big-eyed like a loyal puppy. "I guess," she told Jude reluctantly. "And for you?"

"Another latte. And two pieces of carrot cake."

"Okay." She went away. Jude stared after her in irritation. He wondered if Charlie got this all the time, this judgment by strangers as soon as they figured out he was different. And Jude hadn't judged him any differently either had he? He'd written Charlie off as a prospective partner the moment Charlie had spoken.

He felt ashamed.

"What's the matter, Jude? You look sad."

"Nothing, Charlie."

"It's nice here. I've never been before." He pointed to a black and white photo on the far wall. "Buster Keaton!"

"You know your silent movie stars, don't you?" Jude smiled.

"Yes. My mom made me watch all their films when I was a little boy."

"Do you live with your mom?"

"Yes."

"And your dad?"

Charlie frowned. "No, not my dad."

Jude regarded him. Charlie sat with head bowed, playing with a coaster, folding its edge up. "What time do you have to be home, Charlie?"

Charlie lifted his head. "I don't know. For supper I guess. I usually go straight home after work. My mom'll be wondering."

Jude rather hoped Mrs Chapman didn't call the police. "What time's supper?"

"Seven."

Jude glanced at his watch. It was only six. "We've got an hour," he said.

Charlie's smile was shy and happy. "Good."

Jude relaxed back in his seat. Strangely content, he could have sat here with Charlie for much more than an hour. "How old are you, Charlie?"

"Twenty-seven. How old are you, Jude?"

"Thirty."

Charlie gasped. "You're old, Jude!" He grinned, putting a hand mockingly to his mouth.

"Cheeky bastard."

"You swore!"

"Sorry, Charlie. I'm a grown-up, I'm allowed to swear. You are, too."

Charlie dipped his head and mumbled. "My mom doesn't like it when I swear."

"Well, you can swear when you're with me, I won't tell her that you do."

"Okay then. *Asshole*."

Jude laughed.

"Fuck face."

"Why, Charlie Chapman, what a foul mouth you've got."

"It's your fault. You're making me do it."

"Am I really?"

"Yes."

The waitress arrived with a tray and dished out two plates, a steaming mug and a tall glass with a bendy straw. Charlie took his milkshake eagerly. "Thank you, miss."

She smiled hesitantly at his politeness. "You enjoy now, sir."

"Oh, I shall. Chocolate milkshakes are the best, don't you think?"

"They're pretty good." She went away.

Jude watched him drink.

"Mmm, it's good Jude. Want to try?" He held the straw out.

"I don't think…"

"Go on. Please."

Like anyone could resist a request from Charlie when he looked at you with those big dark eyes and flashed those pearly teeth.

Jude leaned over the table. He felt the wetness of saliva on the end of the straw as he sucked. He sat back. "It's good," he agreed.

Charlie put the glass aside, then took a spoon and started on his cake. "If they can make chocolate milkshakes, why don't they say so on the menu?" he asked with his mouth full.

"Good question," Jude said.

Charlie looked at him blankly. "I know it was. What's the answer?"

Jude started to laugh. This was the best and strangest date he'd ever been on.

"What are you laughing at?"

"You, you're very funny."

"Am I? Like Charlie?"

"Yes, like Charlie." Jude dug out his phone and pressed a couple of buttons. He showed it to Charlie. "Here's a picture of me at my party last week."

"You look just like him, Jude. I love your moustache."

"Thank you. It wouldn't stay on. It kept falling off

all night." He started on his cake. He remembered kissing in a corner of the room with a man who told him the moustache was annoying and eventually wrenched it off him.

Charlie giggled. "You should have grown a real one."

"I'm not very hairy. It might have taken me a month."

"That's a shame. I wonder how long it took Charlie."

"It wasn't real. He stuck it on."
"Really?"
"Really."
"Oh." Charlie looked thoughtful. He took another slurp of his milkshake. "What do you do, Jude?"
"I work in an office."
"What do you do in the office?"
"I sell books."
"That sounds fun. I like books."
"It's boring."
"Oh, dear. Do you want to come work with me?"
Jude smiled. "Is there an opening?"
"I don't know. I could ask my boss."
"It's okay."
"Don't you want to work with me?"
"I… you shouldn't work with your… friends."
Charlie smiled self-consciously. "Am I your friend, Jude?"
"If you want to be."
"I do." Charlie held eye contact steadily.
Jude stared into his mesmerising eyes. What was he doing? Where exactly was this going?

When they had finished and Jude had paid, he ushered Charlie out of the shop and they stood outside a moment.

"I have to catch my bus," Charlie said.

"Do you want me to give you a ride?"

"Do you have a car?" Charlie looked thrilled.

"Yes. Come on."

Charlie hung back. "I don't know. My mom told me not to get into cars with strange men."

"Am I strange, Charlie? I thought I was your friend."

"You are."

"Come on, then."

Charlie's probably right to be unsure about getting in the car with me.

He pulled up outside the quaint white house near the beach. Charlie carefully unbuckled his seatbelt. "Thank you, Jude."

Jude glanced towards the house. A woman stood in the front window. He sighed inwardly, wondering what Charlie would say to his mom and what his mother would make of Jude's motives.

"You're very welcome."

"Will you come and see me again at the shop? We could go for another milkshake and I'll pay."

"Sure." Jude smiled.

Charlie leaned over the seat and before Jude could expect it, he was pecked on the cheek. "Bye, Jude." Charlie got out and closed the door before he hurried up the path, gait both awkward and yet somehow graceful, waving at his mother through the window.

Jude pulled away from the kerb. Did Charlie kiss all his friends this way?

Jude couldn't stop thinking about the beautiful man with the childlike mind and mesmerising eyes. Reading the paper at his desk during lunch five days later, he noticed a Chaplin retrospective on at the new cinema on the outskirts of town. Could he? Did he dare? Sitting in the dark with Charlie would likely lead to him making an idiot out of himself. He couldn't afford to be inappropriate. He either accepted friendship or he didn't see Charlie again.

He had a half day on Friday and went to the shop. Charlie was busy. He was serving customers while a young blond woman folded their purchases into bags. The woman seemed pleased to be working with Charlie. She smiled at him a lot and stood very close to him. It was such a sweet image it made Jude scowl. He browsed at some rails until the queue had gone and Charlie came out from behind the desk.

"Jude!"

"Hi, Charlie. You're busy today."

"Yes."

"I just wondered if… you might want to come see a movie, when you finish?"

Charlie smiled shyly. "I love the movies. What's on?"

"*City Lights*."

Charlie gasped. "Oh my God, yes."

"What time do you finish?"

"Five thirty."

"I'll be outside waiting then. It starts at eight I think,

so we could get dinner..." He trailed off at the look on Charlie's face.

"That's late. I don't know if my mom'll let me go."

Jude stifled his frustration. "Why don't you call and ask her?"

"I will. Stay here." Charlie disappeared into the back.

Jude looked at some books, pretending to be engrossed reading the blurbs as he waited.

When Charlie came back, he was grinning. "She said it was okay, but I have to be back by ten-thirty, and she wants to meet you when you take me home."

Shit. This was not something he was interested in. Jude could count on the fingers of one hand the number of times he'd met the prospective in-laws. And never after the second date. Perhaps his mother was wily. Perhaps she knew too well this was a date, and Jude had nefarious designs on her innocent son.

But Charlie looked so hopeful, he couldn't pull out now.

"So, see you at five-thirty?"

"Yes. See you later."

Jude left the shop. He started to walk down the street towards his car, telling himself he would stand Charlie up tonight.

Showered, shaved and scented, Jude stood on the sidewalk like some misguided Romeo, looking at Charlie through the window. When Charlie finally appeared, locking the door behind him, he was grinning. "That was like the end of *City Lights*," Charlie said, "where Charlie is looking at the flower girl through the window and she comes out and gives him a flower." He produced a red, plastic rose with a flourish and presented it to Jude.

"Why thank you, Charlie." Jude took it. He didn't know quite what to make of it, and his treacherous heart beat a little faster. As they got in his car, he said casually, "Who's the girl you work with?"

"Oh, that's Virginia. Like Virginia Cherrill who was in *City Lights* with Charlie." His grin was dazzling.

"And I can just bet you've reminded her of that one or two times."

"Maybe."

Jude laughed. "Is she your girlfriend?"

"No!"

"Why not? Don't you like her?"

"She's okay but…"

"But what?"

"I don't like girls."

Jude raised an eyebrow. "Don't you? Do you like boys then?" That was too far. He regretted the words as soon as they came out of his mouth.

Charlie stared at him. He stumbled over his words. "I… don't… know. Isn't it wrong to like boys?"

So Charlie wasn't quite as innocent as Jude feared.

"Some people might say it is. You can't help who you like though, can you, Charlie?"

Charlie looked dubious. "I guess not."

Jude started the engine. He had said more than enough.

They got dinner at a pizza place near the cinema. Of course, Charlie adored pizza, but his mother rationed it. Jude was getting tired of hearing about mother. Was he out with Norman Bates here or what? He began to regret the offer of tonight. He should have gone out drinking, picked himself up a nice little something in one of the clubs and spent the evening lying on his back. When Charlie looked up and caught his gaze, smiling sweetly, Jude took it all back. He didn't want to be anywhere but here.

He ordered beer with their pizza and Charlie put it away with gusto—"*Don't tell mother I've been drinking.*"—followed by a chocolate sundae which Jude shared.

Jude paid despite protests from Charlie, and they walked over to the cinema, where Jude purchased the tickets.

"Are you going to let me buy anything tonight?" Charlie asked as Jude bought popcorn and Cokes.

"That depends. What do you earn at the shop?"

"My bus fare."

"Then no, I'm not."

"You're very generous, Jude."

"Am I?"

"Yes. Jude rhymes with dude. Jude, the dude."

Jude reached up and squeezed his neck. "Ouch, Jude, stop beating me up." Charlie grinned down at him from his several inches advantage.

"Come on, the film's starting."

Jude had never seen *City Lights* at the cinema. He had never watched the film with anyone who appreciated Chaplin the way he himself did. Charlie appreciated Chaplin all right. And then some.

He cooed, fawned and guffawed his way through the film, his head falling on Jude's shoulder half way through. Jude glanced at him. Charlie wasn't asleep though;

he still stuffed popcorn in his mouth.

Play this carefully, Jude. Do not act like a lecherous old perv.

He touched his fingertips lightly to Charlie's hand, stroking the knuckles. For a moment Charlie didn't move. Then he entwined his fingers slowly with Jude's and held his hand.

Jude sat there with breath stuck in his throat. Charlie lifted his head, his face close to Jude's. In the darkness, his eyes were black, the whites startling.

"I like you, Jude," he whispered.

"I like you too, Charlie."

"I thought you wouldn't like me because I'm... different."

Jude swallowed a sudden lump in his throat. "I don't care about that."

"Don't you?"

"No."

"That's good. Charlie was different, too, though. He was a genius. Not like other people."

Jude smiled.

Charlie turned his head back to the screen. He continued to hold Jude's hand.

When they reached Charlie's house and Jude nervously noticed all the lights were on, he thought about bolting. "Come on," Charlie said as Jude sat there. "You have to meet my mom, remember."

"Sure." Jude got out, slammed the door and locked it once Charlie was out. He followed Charlie up to the door and waited while he fished his key out of his pocket. He let Jude into a neat, somewhat old-fashioned house. As he stepped into the living room, Jude couldn't help but think he had walked into a museum. Or a mausoleum.

Mother sat waiting.

White-haired and wearing pearls and a cardigan, her red lipsticked mouth set in a thin line of displeasure, she was older than Jude expected.

"You're late, Charlie."

Charlie looked at his watch. They were all of four minutes late. "Sorry, Mom. This is Jude."

"Go upstairs and put your pyjamas on."

"Yes, Mom." Charlie scampered up the stairs leaving Jude alone to face mother's wrath.

She stood and faced him. "What are you doing with my boy?"

"I took him to a movie."

"I know that. Why?"

"Because... I... like him."

"Why? People don't just take Charlie to the movies." Her eyes narrowed in displeasure. "Do you have unnatural designs on him?"

"What?" Jude didn't like the way this conversation was going at all.

"You heard me."

"Mrs Chapman..."

"Don't Mrs Chapman me. Are you gay?"

Jude lifted his chin defiantly. "Yes."

"Then do you have unnatural designs on my son or not? Yes or no."

"No."

"You're lying. What are you taking him out for then? His conversation?"

"I like being with him, Mrs Chapman. I don't think

that's a crime."

"Charlie's a very attractive boy. Are you denying that?"

"That's just it, Mrs Chapman. He's not a boy, he's a man. You treat him like a child. Having him come home at ten-thirty! He could have stayed out all night if he'd wanted to. And telling him to put his pjs on like he's ten years old. Jesus!" Jude shook his head in disgust.

"He *is* ten years old. Do you really think he knows what you want from him?"

"He knows more than you think. He doesn't like girls, he told me that."

"Oh please, which ten year old boy *doesn't* say he doesn't like girls?"

"He said he likes boys."

Mrs Chapman paled. "Not in the way *you* like boys," she said scornfully.

"I wouldn't bet on that. He told me he liked them, but people had told him it was wrong."

Mrs Chapman was stunned into silence. She sank back onto the sofa. "You've corrupted him already," she muttered. "If you so much as touch him, I'll have you arrested."

Jude shook his head. "You're ridiculous."

"And you're a pervert, preying on the innocent. Get out of my house and never set foot in here again, do you understand?"

Jude was about to throw back a reply when Charlie appeared in the doorway, dressed for bed, looking from one to the other. How much had he heard? Jude had expected him to be wearing Spiderman or Batman pyjamas but no, he was soberly dressed in black pjs with a dark blue dressing gown over the top.

"What's wrong?" He looked fearful.

"Nothing, Charlie. I've just been talking to your mom. I'm going to go now."

"Oh, don't you want to stay for milk and cookies?"

"Your friend has to get up for work in the morning," Mother said firmly.

"But it's Saturday tomorrow."

"I work on Saturdays, Charlie," Jude said, edging to the door. "I'll see you."

"I'll see you soon, Jude." Charlie lunged forward as though he would kiss Jude goodbye, but Jude shrank away, opened the door and hurried out.

"I'll get your milk and cookies," Mrs Chapman said in the silence that followed.

Charlie went after her into the kitchen. "Why don't you like Jude? I heard you shouting at him."

His mother sighed, back turned. "I do like him, I just… don't want you to see him again."

"Why not?"

"Because he's too old for you."

"He's only thirty!"

"That's not what I mean. He's too…"

"You mean he's too smart for me, don't you, Mom? That I should be friends with Virginia because she's like me."

"No, I don't mean that. But Virginia is a lovely girl. Why don't you take her out some time?"

"I don't want to take her out. I like Jude." Charlie folded his arms, pouting.

"Here, eat your supper and then go on up to bed. It's

late." Mrs Chapman put milk and cookies on the table.

"I don't want them." Charlie turned and left the room, taking the stairs quickly. He locked himself in the bathroom where he brushed his teeth and washed his face. Then he stared at himself in the mirror. He had held Jude's hand. In the dark of the cinema the only people who had existed were him, Jude and his hero, Charlie.

Charlie Chapman dominated Jude's every waking thought. Being told he couldn't have something usually had the effect on him to make him want it more. Maybe that was all it was. But no. He wanted to see Charlie's big brown eyes once more and his beautiful smile. He wanted to sit in a darkened cinema once more holding hands and feeling like the luckiest man alive.

He went back to the thrift store a week later, standing in the rain and looking through the window.

Charlie was unaware of his presence. He sat behind the counter reading a book and eating an apple. The shop was empty. Jude couldn't bring himself to go inside. Charlie's mother had told him to stay away. No good could come of this.

He slunk away into the rain.

He lasted another week before he was back. He stood looking through the window until this time, Charlie saw him. He stared at Jude for the longest time, frozen in place, an undeterminable expression on his face, before he turned and walked away, disappearing into the back.

Jude's heart sank. That wasn't good. He hovered outside the shop. He should leave now. Go away and never come back.

He pushed the door open.

A few customers browsed in the shop. Virginia stood with back turned, so Jude pushed the curtain aside and entered the back room. Charlie turned around from where he stood stirring a spoon in a mug at the counter.

His eyes wide, his face quickly settled into hard displeasure. "You can't come back here, Jude, it's private."

"I want to speak to you."

"I don't want to speak to you." Charlie pouted rather adorably.

"I guess you're mad at me for not coming around…"

"I thought we were *friends*, Jude."

"We are."

Charlie shook his head. "You're not my friend. You haven't come to see me in two weeks."

Jude sighed. He hung his head. "Charlie. It's not… it's difficult."

"My mom didn't want you to see me again, did she?"

Jude looked up. Whoever underestimated Charlie was a fool. When he didn't reply, Charlie folded his arms, glaring.

"My mom isn't the boss of me."

Jude almost smiled.

"You know that, right, Jude? I know you think she is, but she isn't. I see who I want to see, and if I want to see you, I'll see you. Got it?"

"Yes, Charlie," Jude said softly.

"Good. So are you taking me out for a milkshake or what?"

"Yes. Five thirty at the café."

"I'll see you then. Now get out of here, Jude, you're

not allowed."

Jude backed out of the curtains almost shaking his head in admiration.

Jude was waiting in the café at five forty with a piece of carrot cake and a chocolate milkshake on the table in front of him. The same waitress had asked him if his friend was expected, and Jude answered in the affirmative.

Charlie burst through the door, a little pink-cheeked from the cold, his scarf flying out behind him. He grinned at Jude, hurried over, threw his coat over the back of his chair and sat down. "Thanks, Jude." He guzzled a quarter of his milkshake and sat back with foam on his top lip.

"You've got a moustache."

"I don't. I shaved this morning."

Jude smiled. He leaned across the table and gently wiped the smudge off with his thumb. Charlie sat perfectly still, staring.

Jude looked at the milk on his thumb, debating with himself before giving into his urge. It was hardly the dirtiest of the things he wanted to do to Charlie. He sucked his thumb.

Charlie watched, gaze on the thumb in Jude's mouth and then on Jude's eyes. "Jude." His voice was low and he stared at his glass now.

"Yes, Charlie?"

"I want to kiss you."

Jude almost spat his coffee out.

"Can I?"

"You can't do it here." His voice was unsteady.

"Why not?"

"People wouldn't like it."

"Then they shouldn't look."

"I know that, but they will. We're in a public place."

Charlie sighed. "Can I kiss you when we leave?"

"If you want to." Jude's blood boiled.

"I do want to."

They held eye contact steadily. Charlie started to eat his cake. Nothing else was said.

Jude paid the bill. He got up and put his coat on, watching Charlie do the same from the corner of his eye. Charlie wrapped his scarf tightly around his throat, glancing once at Jude before he led the way out of the café.

They stood on the sidewalk in the drizzle. "Do you want to see a movie?" Jude asked.

"No, I want to kiss you." Charlie put a hand on Jude's shoulder and backed him into the window, then leaned down towards him.

"Not here." It was almost a whimper.

Charlie backed away. "Then let's go to your place."

Jude regarded him a moment. Jesus, did Charlie know what he was getting into here? Charlie's mom was going to kill him. He led the way to his car wordlessly.

Charlie grinned when he saw the framed Chaplin photos in Jude's hall. He kicked off his shoes and unfastened his coat as he followed Jude into the living room, staring at the pictures all the way. The *pièce de résistance* was an art canvas of Chaplin above the fireplace. A photo of him with eyes turned skywards, the words *City Lights* in gold above him.

Charlie stood beneath it, staring. "I need to ask my mom for this for Christmas."

"Do you want a drink?"

"Do you have any orange juice?"

"Yes."

"Then I'll have that please, Jude."

Jude went into the kitchen. His face felt uncomfortably hot and when he opened the fridge door, he stuck his head in it for a moment. He poured the orange juice, reached down and adjusted his half hard cock in his pants. He stood at the work surface. This couldn't get out of control. Charlie wanted to kiss him. Jude hadn't done anything wrong. He'd accept the kiss and then he'd drive Charlie home. He wouldn't take advantage or lure Charlie into something he didn't want.

He took the glasses back into the living room.

Charlie slouched on the couch, knees open, eyes still riveted to the Chaplin canvas. He accepted his drink with thanks, taking a sip before leaning forward and putting it on the coffee table, using a coaster.

Jude put his own glass down. He hovered a moment, looking down at Charlie before sitting beside him. Charlie leaned towards him.

There was nothing childish or clumsy about Charlie's kiss. He pressed his lips softly to Jude's with care and tenderness. He held them there, pressing softly and sweetly, until Jude took him by the back of the neck, opened his mouth slightly and invited Charlie to take.

And Charlie did. In style.

His plump, velvet soft mouth moulded to Jude's like it was made to fit. He kissed with passion, with sensuality, with honest emotion. He told Jude everything he needed to know and when he drew back, Jude was breathless, trembling and desperate.

"Charlie," he gasped. "How many people have you kissed before?"

"None." Charlie looked him earnestly in the eye. "I guess I saved it all for you."

It was all Jude could do not to groan. "You're very good."

Charlie beamed. "Thank you, Jude." His lips were dark with colour. He ran his tongue nervously over the top one. He reached out, touching the curve of Jude's cheek with hesitant fingertips. Jude pressed his lips to Charlie's palm.

Charlie's pupils were large. His fingers moved to the top button of Jude's shirt, played with it a moment while he looked into Jude's eyes.

Jude could barely breathe.

"Can I...?" Charlie's fingers slid the button open before Jude could speak.

He sat still while Charlie, with utmost concentration and nimble fingers, unfastened all his buttons and drew his shirt open. He looked for a moment, while Jude waited nervously, and then he lifted his hands, placed them on Jude's chest and squeezed his pectorals, stroking thumbs slowly over both nipples.

Jude gripped his wrists. "Listen to me before we go any further."

"What's the matter?"

"Do you... do you know about sex, Charlie?"

Charlie blushed. "Of course, I do."

"Do you know how two men make love?"

"Yes. One man puts his cock in the other's bum." Charlie slid his hands free, looking down, face flaming.

"How do you know that?"

"I've seen it on the Internet."

Of course. "Did you like what you saw?"

"Yes. It made me hard."

Jude swallowed. "It might not be as sexy as you saw. It can hurt."

"Not if *I* put it in *you*." Charlie grinned cheekily.

Jude thought he would explode. "And that's what you want do you?"

"Oh, yes."

Jude let his gaze slide downwards. The bulge in Charlie's pants promised great things. He tried to clear his head of its lust before it was too late. "Listen... do you understand what I mean by consent? If I... did something with you and you didn't like it, you could tell your mom and I'd get in terrible trouble. Do you get that?"

Charlie frowned. "I wouldn't tell my mom. It would be our secret. And haven't I already consented? I told you I wanted to put my cock in your bum."

Jude was all out of resistance. Let Charlie have his wicked way with him. He'd tried his best. He was only a man after all.

He kicked his shoes off and removed his socks. "Come on." Standing, he pulled Charlie up by the hand and led him into the bedroom.

As soon as they got there, he went to the drawer for a condom and lube. Behind him, Charlie started stripping hurriedly. When Jude turned around, he was dressed in tight, white boxers which were filled to eye-popping status.

Jesus Christ, if Jude wasn't the luckiest man in the world right at that moment, then he didn't know who was.

He unfastened his pants and pulled them off hurriedly. Stripping off his boxers and climbing onto the bed, Jude lay on his back. Charlie stood there a moment with eyes riveted to Jude's groin, then he peeled his boxers off. He crawled onto the bed with cock and balls swinging free.

"You're smaller than me, Jude." Charlie fondled his own cock absently.

"That's not something you need to point out."

"Sorry." Charlie put his hand down. He let his fingers play over Jude's cock. "Do you like to touch yourself, Jude?"

"Yes." Jude shifted beneath Charlie's touch.

"So do I. My mom caught me once." Charlie's fingers tightened around Jude's shaft. He slid Jude through his hand.

"That must have been very embarrassing."

"It was. She told me I'd go blind. And I haven't yet, so I don't think it's true."

"It's not."

"That's good."

Jude shivered and writhed under Charlie's caress. "Have you ever had a blowjob, Charlie?"

"No."

"Would you like one?"

"Yes!"

"Come up here, then."

Charlie crawled up Jude's body. He put his knees over Jude's shoulders at his prompting before delicately guiding his cock into Jude's mouth.

Charlie gasped as Jude swallowed him down. Smiling around his cock, Jude looked up at the pleasure on Charlie's face.

"Oh my God, Jude," Charlie moaned. He held onto

the headboard, pushing himself lightly into Jude's mouth.

Jude held him by firm buttocks. Charlie's balls rested against his chin. Jude was so turned on by having Charlie in his mouth this way, he was sure he was going to blow his load without being touched.

Charlie looked down at him. "I saw this one video where the guy on top, he turned around so he could suck the other guy's cock too. Do you want me to do that, Jude?"

Jude nodded eagerly with his mouth full.

Charlie drew back. He turned around and Jude came face to face with plump, peach-like cheeks. Charlie was a work of art.

A hesitant mouth slid down his shaft, engulfing him. Jude hissed his appreciation. He sucked one of Charlie's balls into his mouth.

Charlie drew back, his wet tongue lapping at the head of Jude's cock. "Am I doing this right, Jude?"

"You're doing just fine."

"I like this. I like it a lot. I like your cock in my mouth."

Jude shuddered. *And I like it when you talk dirty to me.* He guided Charlie's cock into his mouth.

Charlie groaned around Jude's cock. His mouth slid wetly up and down, sucking Jude with gusto.

Charlie's cock leaked into Jude's mouth. Jude ran his fingers lightly down Charlie's ass crack. His buttocks were spread and he could see the tiny hole between his cheeks. He rubbed it with one finger.

Charlie flinched a little.

Jude drew his mouth back. "Is that okay?"

Charlie came up for air. "Yes. I want you to touch me there."

Jude sucked on his finger. He touched it to Charlie's entrance, rubbing the saliva in, pressing lightly.

Charlie caught his breath. Putting his mouth back around Jude's cock, he sucked with ever increasing enthusiasm.

Jude pushed his finger inside, fucking Charlie with it gently as he listened to the groans Charlie made around his cock. When he stopped for a moment, Charlie pushed backwards on his finger and fucked himself, groaning.

Jude withdrew the digit. He grasped Charlie by the buttocks and pulled him down. Lightly, he rimmed him with a stiff tongue.

Charlie's mouth slid off his cock. "Oh, my God."

"Do you like that?"

"Yes. You're a dirty boy, Jude."

"I know I am. Are you going to fuck me now, Charlie?"

"Yes."

"Good boy."

Charlie climbed off him and turned around. Jude spread his legs invitingly, lewdly. Charlie knelt there, wet, erect cock curving up to his belly, eyes black with lust. Jude reached for the foil square on the next pillow, tearing it open.

"Do you know how to put a condom on, Charlie?"

"No."

"I'll show you." Jude sat up. "You must never let anyone fuck you without a condom," he said as he rolled the latex onto Charlie's shaft. "And you must never fuck anyone without a condom."

Charlie frowned, looking confused. "But I'll only be fucking you, Jude. No one else."

Something lodged in Jude's throat. "I know, but I mean... after me."

"There won't be anyone after you. There'll only be you."

Jude swallowed. "Come here." He pulled Charlie close and kissed him. "Listen to me. Nothing lasts forever. When you don't want me anymore, there'll be someone else. And after that, there'll be someone else. I don't want you to do this if you think..."

"If I think it's going to last forever?" Charlie's eyes brimmed with tears. He pulled away, unrolling and yanking off the condom, scooping up his clothes before leaving the bedroom.

"Charlie." Jude stopped to pull on his boxers. He followed miserably into the living room. "Look..."

Charlie pulled away as Jude tried to grab his arm. "I have to go." He pulled his pants on quickly, fastening up. "I don't want my mom to shout."

"Don't go like this. Let's just talk about it."

Charlie shook his head. He swiped fiercely at his eyes and crammed his feet into his shoes. Without tying the laces he made for the door.

"Charlie."

Jude caught him by the wrist as he stepped through the door.

Charlie turned back. "You said we were over before we even started."

Jude stared at him a moment before Charlie pulled away and disappeared. Jude swore. He rushed to the bedroom to pull on a robe before hurrying out of the apartment. Taking the stairs, he caught Charlie at the front door.

"Wait."

Charlie let the door swing shut behind him. Jude chased him outside, bare foot. "Charlie, do you know how to get home?"

Charlie stopped and turned, his face pale and pinched. "I'll take the bus. I know where I am. I'm not as stupid as you think I am." He walked away.

Jude stood miserably in the cold watching him go.

Charlie let himself into the house and ran straight upstairs. He closed his bedroom door and threw himself on the bed.

"Charlie? Charlie?" His mother's footsteps sounded on the stairs. "Where have you been? It's almost eight o'clock." The door opened.

"Go away."

"I beg your pardon?"

"I said go away and leave me alone."

"Are you crying? What's going on? Please do not tell me you've been with that man again."

Charlie turned over and sat up. "I said go away, Mom!"

His mother blanched. "Don't you shout at me, young man. Have some respect for your mother."

"All I've ever done is have respect for you, Mom. I've come home when you've told me to, I've worked where you've told me to and I've seen who you've told me to. You told Jude not to see me again, didn't you? Well I *have* seen him!"

His mother folded her arms, her mouth a thin, pinched line. "Then why are you so upset?"

"Because he threw me away. He doesn't want me. I

hope you're happy." Charlie threw himself back down on the bed and wept.

The memory of that night tortured Jude. Over the coming days he couldn't sleep for thinking about it. How had the passion curdled so swiftly? When Charlie had obviously learned everything he knew from porn films, who had put these romantic notions into his head? Had he really thought that sleeping with Jude signalled the start of a once in a lifetime romance? Jude was fickle. He convinced himself he was deeply in love with whatever man he was currently infatuated with, only to blow cold just as quickly. He didn't want this to happen with Charlie. He wanted Charlie to understand that sex didn't mean love, but obviously Charlie didn't.

And yet... Charlie had a point. It had been poor protocol for Jude to talk about the men who would come after him before they'd even had sex. He'd said they were going to end before they even started. He owed Charlie a big apology for that. But he couldn't go back. Not now. He'd had a narrow escape from a clingy, needy albatross. Whatever fun Jude had been looking for, Charlie was not the one to have it with.

It was over before it had even begun and try as he might to be glad about that, Jude ached for what he had thrown away.

Two weeks later he had his nose pressed against the glass of the thrift store, watching an oblivious Charlie serving a customer at the counter.

"What are you doing here? Haven't you hurt him enough?"

Jude turned around with heart sinking. "Hello, Mrs Chapman." What exactly had Charlie told her about that night? Had he told her about how Jude had taken advantage of Charlie in the most terrible of ways and would have done a whole lot worse if Charlie's heart hadn't got involved?

"He's cried over you every day for two weeks and you *dare* to stand outside watching him like some peeping tom?"

Jude regarded her. He didn't doubt that she saw the same misery as Charlie's etched across his own face. "We had a little misunderstanding. I can make it up to him…"

"Don't even think about it. What exactly did you do to him?"

Jude swallowed. So Charlie hadn't gone into too much detail. "I like him, Mrs Chapman, but I was worried that Charlie… liked me too much. I tried to explain to him that…" Jude lowered his gaze to his feet, shuffling them awkwardly.

"That you're just out for what you can get and once you've seduced my son, you'll be away? Is that it?"

Jude's face flamed.

"*Did* you seduce my son?"

"No."

"I don't believe you."

"Mrs Chapman, I'm not about to discuss details with you. Charlie's twenty-seven years old and has the right not to have his sex life dissected."

"His sex life! He didn't *have* a sex life before he met you. Mother of God! What have you done?" Mrs Chapman actually crossed herself like Jude was all sorts of vampire, ghoul, and monster rolled into one.

As Jude prayed to let the ground just open up and swallow him, the door to the shop opened.

"Mom, what are you doing?"

Jude looked up, locking gazes with Charlie.

"Trying to keep this pervert away from you, son. Go back inside."

Charlie shook his head stubbornly. "Leave him alone."

"Charles Chapman," his mother said furiously, wagging her finger.

"It's all right." Jude held his hands up. "I'm going." He walked away, resisting the urge to look back.

Jude wasn't short of male admirers. When he wanted someone to warm his sheets he could usually find a volunteer in the clubs without too much of an effort. So why did he insist on going over and over that night with Charlie again like it was the hottest thing which had ever happened to him? And why would his mind and his heart not leave Charlie alone? There were better catches than a disabled boy with a Norman Bates complex who would never be able to aspire to anything. There was better conversation to be had and better no-strings sex to be had. But nobody had captured Jude's attention the way Charlie had in years. No one had left such a lasting impression long after he had gone, so that Jude still tasted his mouth and still felt velvet skin pressed against his own. He thought he would go crazy with longing and he prayed to a God he didn't believe in to be put out of his misery.

It was another month before Charlie turned up at his door. Jude had just got out of the shower and was drying himself when the bell sounded. He hurriedly pulled on a robe and walked down the hall, his hair wet.

Charlie leaned against the doorjamb, a rucksack over his shoulder, his eyes red and swollen, an expression of anguish on his face.

Jude sighed, even as his heart leapt up and demanded attention. "What are you doing here?"

"I've run away."

"What?"

"I don't have any place to go. Can I come in?"

Jude reluctantly stepped back and allowed him admittance. As much as he felt relief that Charlie was here, he didn't want to become embroiled in the war between him and his mother.

Charlie went into the living room and sank down on the couch. He pressed his knuckles into his eyes. "I hate her. I hate her. I wish she were dead."

"Don't say that. She's your mother."

"And she's controlled me all my life. I can't go on. I..." His voice trembled and broke suddenly. "I took some tablets."

"What?" Jude stared, unable to believe his ears.

"I didn't want to live anymore, Jude. Not when I can't see you and she..."

"What did you take, Charlie?" Jude shook him furiously by the shoulders, until Charlie's jaw dropped open at being handled so roughly, his eyes welling with aggrieved tears.

"Some Advil. Here." Charlie took a blister-pack from his pocket.

Jude sighed. He let go of Charlie and ran a hand through his hair. "How many?"

"I don't know. Five or six."

"Idiot. All you'll have from that is a stomach ache. Advil's never going to kill you, Charlie."

Charlie jumped up, fists clenched, eyes glittering. "Don't call me an idiot, Jude, just because I'm not smart like you and I don't know how to kill myself! Maybe I'll jump in front of a train next time or hang myself. That'll work won't it?"

"Don't you fucking dare."

"Are you going to stop me?" Tears spilled down Charlie's cheeks. He grabbed at Jude's robe.

Angrily, Jude pushed him back. They struggled, Charlie shoving him, Jude getting madder and madder until finally, he snapped. He pushed Charlie back down on the couch, straddled his lap and kissed him furiously.

Charlie gave a soft gasp. He gripped Jude around the waist, pulling him closer, returning the kiss with desperate passion.

Jude was sucked beneath waves of desire which obliterated all rational thought. They kissed and kissed until Charlie pulled his robe open and stroked Jude's hard cock firmly. Jude arched back as Charlie planted kisses on his throat, lifting his pelvis so he felt Charlie's erection pressing against his bare backside through denim.

He couldn't do this. He couldn't hurt Charlie again by doing this act which would not be forever, no matter how much Charlie wanted it.

He climbed off Charlie's lap, pulling his robe closed. "You can stay tonight because it's late, but you'll have to have the spare room. And tomorrow, you go back to your mother."

Charlie stared up at him as though he didn't

understand, eyes glazed, luscious lips all kiss swollen, his pants tented.

A noise in the dark awoke Jude. A silhouette at his bedside, scrabbling in the drawer.

"Charlie, what are you doing?"

"Looking for a condom and that liquid stuff."

"What? Look, we can't..."

Charlie withdrew his hand and closed the drawer. He pulled the covers back and slid in beside Jude, pressing hot, naked skin to his.

"Don't."

"Why not?"

"Because we can't."

"Why?"

Charlie pressed Jude face down. Lips touched his neck; Charlie ground his erection against Jude's buttocks.

Jude smothered a moan into the pillow. "Stop."

"No."

Charlie sat back. Jude looked over his shoulder to see Charlie fumbling with the condom, laboriously rolling it on. "There, I did it. I know how to put a condom on."

"You might as well take it off because you're not doing it to me."

"Yes, I am."

"Jesus, take no for an answer."

Charlie crushed him to the bed. Lube landed in his ass crack so Jude almost yelped. Fingers rubbed it in.

"I said stop, Charlie. Do you know what rape is?"

Charlie's mouth stopped pressing kisses to his neck. "It's where a man does things to a woman she doesn't want him to do," he said confusedly.

"Or a man does it to another man. I said 'no' and I meant 'no', which means you have to stop."

Charlie's hand slid under him. "But you're hard, Jude. That means you want me."

Jude groaned helplessly as hot fingers jerked him nimbly. "It doesn't. It just means…"

"What?" Large hands pushed his legs apart. "What does it mean?"

"That… that…"

Hardness pressed against his slick entrance. "That?"

"Oh fuck, fuck…"

Charlie penetrated him.

Jude cried out.

"Oh God, that's good, Jude. You feel so good. I know this won't be forever anymore. I'll take what I can get." Charlie gripped his hips. He buried himself all the way in, lying full length on Jude's prone body.

Jude gasped, nearly smothered by the hot, heavy body above him, the feeling glorious.

Charlie thrust into him gently, rhythmically, taking his time. "Am I doing it right, Jude? Is it okay?"

Jude groaned something incomprehensible into the pillow. Hadn't he told Charlie, no? The fact that Charlie had carried on anyway felt like the hottest thing to ever happen to Jude in his life.

"I hope I am. I want to make you come, Jude."

Jude shivered at the words. His protests were lost to desperate desire. "Let me up."

Charlie rose with him so they were both on all fours. Jude guided Charlie's hand to his groin. "Make me come like this."

Charlie's fingers closed around him. As he thrust

into Jude, he jerked him off swiftly while his mouth pressed hot kisses to Jude's back.

"Jesus," Jude hissed. He was going to explode. He was going to scream the place down when he came, and Charlie would be so scared he would be put off sex for life. He almost grinned to himself.

Charlie pushed harder into him. His cock stretched Jude to painful proportions but the pain was edged with a pleasure so intense he could barely control himself.

"Please, Charlie..." he moaned helplessly.

"Please what?" Charlie held him tightly with one strong arm.

"Please, don't stop."

"Okay, I won't. But I think I might come soon, and then I might have to stop."

"Shut up."

"What?"

"Stop talking. You don't talk during sex."

"Don't you?"

"No, unless it's to say dirty things."

"Do you want me to say dirty things?"

Jude panted and gasped. "Yes."

"Okay. Er... your bum feels so tight around me. I love it."

Jude grabbed at the pillow, buried his face into it, groaning.

"I love touching your cock. It's so hard. I can't wait until you come all over my hand."

"Fuck, Charlie, fuck me harder, *harder*."

Charlie growled and redoubled his pace. "I've been thinking about you using your tongue on me for the last six weeks, and it makes me so hard that I have to touch myself.

Nearly every day, Jude. Nearly every day."

"Fuck, *fuck*! I want to see you do that, Charlie."

"You can. I'll show you. After this."

Jude wailed, dancing on the line of orgasm. To think this was Charlie giving him so much pleasure. Sweet, innocent Charlie whose mother had said he didn't have a sex life. He cursed again, and his ass clenched hard around Charlie as Jude spurted over his hand.

"Oh Jude… Jude…" moaned Charlie. "I love you." He stiffened, his thrusts becoming jerky, shuddering as one hand clenched Jude's hip hard, nails digging in.

The two of them fell together on the bed in a sweaty heap.

"What is it you don't understand about 'no'?" Jude had wriggled out from under an almost comatose Charlie and lay on his side next to him.

"What?" Charlie lifted his head, hair tousled.

"I said 'no'. You said you knew what rape was."

Charlie frowned. "But you were hard, Jude."

"That doesn't matter. If someone says 'no', they mean 'no', hard or not. You need to remember that in future before you end up in jail."

Charlie's mouth drew into a pout. His bottom lip trembled. "But… but… you liked it. I made you come."

Jude sighed. He drew his fingers down Charlie's cheek. He was a hypocrite for giving this lecture. He'd *wanted* it. And Charlie had given it to him.

Charlie shrugged away. He climbed out of bed, pulling his condom off. "I'm going back to my bed."

"You can stay in here."

"I don't want to. You think I'm a rapist." Charlie

went out of the room and shut the door.

Jude lay back, sighing. *What a mess, what a fucking mess.* And the worst thing about it? What Charlie had said to him.

"I know this won't be forever anymore. I'll take what I can get."

Even though he had then told Jude he loved him.

That broke Jude's heart.

Some time before dawn, Jude crept into Charlie's bed. He lay behind him, with an arm over him, holding him close, breathing in the scent of his hair. Charlie's fingers found his. He brought Jude's knuckles to his mouth and kissed them.

Jude fell asleep with Charlie breathing softly beside him.

Jude was up and drinking coffee at the kitchen table, debating whether to take a cup into Charlie when last night's lover walked into the kitchen, fully dressed and carrying his rucksack.

"I'm going back to my mom."

"Good." Was it good? Jude felt miserable.

Charlie hovered, shuffling his feet. "I'm sorry for being a rapist, Jude."

Jude got up. "Oh look…"

But Charlie had turned to go.

Jude caught him by the arm as he opened the door. "I don't think that, Charlie. I just…"

"It doesn't matter." Charlie shook his head. "I know I was wrong, and I'm sorry. I won't come back again." He shrugged away and disappeared down the stairs.

Jude went slowly back inside and closed the door, leaning against it. He put a hand over his face, lip trembling with the need to spill emotion. No. This couldn't be all he would ever get of Charlie. It could never be enough.

"Where have you been all night young man? Get back here!"

Charlie's mother followed him up the stairs, pushing open his bedroom door when he closed it in her face.

"Well?" Hands on hips, her usual stance. Face like thunder. "You've been with him again, haven't you, when you told me it was over!"

Charlie sat down on the bed. He nodded mutely, eyes downcast.

"And he's made you miserable. Again."

Charlie didn't respond. Had Jude made him miserable or had his own actions done it? Sure, the sex had been spectacular, but not Jude's words after it. He thought badly of Charlie. He thought he was a rapist. Had he really done it against Jude's will? He didn't remember anymore. Things were hazy and confused, the memory of the pleasure overwhelming everything else. All he knew was he was sorry, and he loved Jude to distraction. Was love always like this? Did it always make you feel like killing yourself? Charlie hoped he would never be in love again in his life. But then again, he didn't expect to be. Not when he had once thought he and Jude were forever.

Jude suffered and knew it served him right. It had been laughable that he had even mentioned the word rape to Charlie and put the idea in his head when Jude wanted it as much as he had. Charlie had gone away thinking the wrong thing and his first taste of sex had ended in misery.

And Charlie loved him. He loved Jude unquestioningly, purely, passionately. It was more than Jude deserved, to have such a man in love with him. More than he could have ever hoped for.

This time he lasted five days before he took his Halloween costume from his closet and dressed in it, carefully adjusting his collar and sticking the moustache to his upper lip.

He went into town carrying his cane and sat on the bench outside the thrift store. Passers-by believed him to a street entertainer and he collected twenty dollars in his bowler hat much to his bemusement.

He sat there until five-thirty, until the lights went out and the door of the thrift store opened.

Charlie's jaw dropped as he saw Jude waiting. "Charlie," he said in an awed whisper.

Jude doffed his hat. "At your service. I come to beg your forgiveness."

Charlie waited, saying nothing.

"I wanted that, you know I did, and you didn't do anything wrong. You only pleased me like I'd never been pleased before in my life, and if you'd agree, I'd like more of the same."

A shy smile spread across Charlie's face. He blushed.

"I'm sorry I hurt you." Jude took a breath. "I love you, Charlie Chapman."

Charlie beamed with tears in his eyes. "I love you, too, Charlie Chaplin."

Jude put his arms around Charlie's neck and kissed

him.

"Your moustache tickles, Jude."

"Want a chocolate milkshake?"

"Yes."

They set off walking down the street hand in hand, Jude obliged to do the waddling Little Tramp walk.

"Remember the dance Charlie does with the bread rolls in *The Gold Rush*?"

"Of course, I do."

"Want me to do that for you at the café?"

"Yes please, Jude."

"Here, take this." Jude gave Charlie the handful of change he'd earned.

"What's this?"

"Money I earned impersonating Charlie while I waited for you. It's yours."

Charlie laughed. "This is like the final scene in *Modern Times*. Where Charlie and his girl walk off into the sunset."

"If I'm Charlie, you must be my girl."

"Oh no," Charlie said superciliously. "I'm Charlie, *you're* my girl."

"Whatever you say, boss."

"That's more like it."

MY LOVE IS ME, AND I AM HIM

My love is me, and I am him. Sometimes I feel he's the only thing which keeps me anchored to the world. I am one of his flock, his lost souls.

My lover is in bed already, worn out by the demands of others. He never complains. He is sweet and pure as the driven snow, and his love for me is as deep and true as everything else about him. I come and go under cover of darkness with a key to his house.

He cannot reconcile his love for me with the needs of his life, and I have long accepted this even though he hasn't. I am his secret. Sometimes this is exciting to me. Other times it's a strain. It has become commonplace, something I no longer question.

My lover is curled beneath the covers of his bed on his side. He breathes softly, the sound I hear in my dreams. I can't spend every night here, much as I would like, so the times I do are like a special treat, like it's my birthday.

I fold my clothes on the chair in the corner, then walk naked from the bedroom to the shower. My lover hasn't moved when I return, hair damp and teeth brushed. Now I have almost ten hours of luxury by his side ahead of me, holding him to me as though he were mine and I didn't share him.

I crawl into bed behind him and slide a hand over his hip and around onto his lean stomach. I just want to hold him; I don't want to disturb his sleep, but selfishly as always, I half hope he will awake.

Sometime he does; sometimes he is too deeply asleep.

I press lightly against him, my face resting on the back of his neck, breathing in the scent of his hair. He stirs, stretches, one foot colliding with mine. "Hello," he whispers through the dark, and even that one word is loaded with affection and welcome. I'm the luckiest man in the world, because while I share him, at times like these I know he is mine alone.

"Sorry I woke you," I say automatically.

"It's all right. I wanted to stay awake for you. I missed you."

I cuddle closer. With one hand, I stroke his hair, my lips tracing his delicate ear. "I missed you, too."

"How was work?"

"The usual. How was your day?"

"Just fine." As I said, he never complains, no matter what his work throws at him.

When I met him, I was desperate and needed a friend. He was there. He talked me down from the edge physically and metaphorically. I owe him everything.

He turns over into my arms. He kisses me, his lips soft and warm. I know he kisses no one but me and never has. I know no one else shares this bed but me. I can't say the same about his heart. He presses his head against my chest, arms around me.

"Goodnight, my love."

"Goodnight."

My lover is a priest. Still, he can't reconcile his love for me with his love for God. I tell him this is not wrong, and I hope one day he will believe it.

My love is me, and I am him. He is all that keeps me anchored to the world.

The End

ALSO BY SCARLET BLACKWELL:

Available at **Silver Publishing**:

Rescue Me
Anthology, Volume 1
Sanctuary (July 9)
Snowbound (Aug 6)
Half a Man (Sept 10)

CLEAR WATER CREEK CHRONICLES
Into the Light
Smashed into Pieces

Available at **All Romance Ebooks**:

Captive
Stand and Deliver
Life Class
Just Desserts
Second Helpings
Beached Hearts
The Vampire's Prisoner
And So Is Love
Love Bites
Of Genies and Sea Monsters in *Myths and Magic: Legends of Love*
The Unlikely Vampire in *Just One Bite, Volume 1*
Secondhand Heart
The Last Supper
The Golden Haired Boy

Available at **Dreamspinner Press**:

Apathy
The King's Man

CPSIA information can be obtained at www.ICGtesting.com
Printed in the USA
LVOW130845160613

338678LV00001B/26/P